THE ART OF BEING DEAD

THE ART
OF BEING DEAD

Stephen Clayton

Bluemoose

Copyright © Stephen Clayton 2008

First published in 2008 by
Bluemoose Books Ltd
25 Sackville Street
Hebden Bridge
West Yorkshire
HX7 7DJ

www.bluemoosebooks.com

Reprinted 2008

British Library Cataloguing-in-Publication data
A catalogue record for this book is available from the-British-Library

Hardback   ISBN 10: 0-9553367-3-2
ISBN 13: 978-0-9553367-3-7

Paperback ISBN 10: 0-9553367-4-0
ISBN 13: 978-0-9553367-4-4

Printed and bound in the UK by Cromwell Press, Trowbridge, Wiltshire

To Judith

"I think I've killed somebody."

I was so taken aback that I had no idea how to react. I don't think I understood his statement as having any basis in reality. It meant nothing to me. In a confused haze of remembrance I quickly went over the events of that evening. There had been a violent and bloody encounter, certainly, but nobody, to my knowledge, had died.

I watched him drink. I watched the pressure of his lips, the suction of his mouth and the regular beat of his Adam's apple. His head was thrown back, his hair hung over his shoulders and his skin gleamed pale and damp in the glow from the single lamp positioned by the side of my mattress – and suddenly I knew that he was telling me the truth.

"Who have you killed?" I said. "I don't understand."

He lowered the bottle.

"You believe me then?"

"Of course," I said, "why should you lie?"

Slowly he wiped his mouth with the back of his hand, but made no reply. He took another mouthful of whisky and began idly to wander about the room, stopping every now and then to investigate some object or other, or to flick disinterestedly through the pages of some book whose title or cover had caught his eye. He returned nothing to its rightful place.

I was eager to know everything, but I knew better than to push him for an explanation. This was *his* show. "You look terrible," I said. "You ought to go to hospital."

"Right," he said disdainfully, "and why don't I go to the police as well? I'm sure they'd be glad to see me."

In truth, I cared nothing for his health and perhaps I was even a little bit thrilled to be in the presence of someone who had obviously suffered so much physical damage. I was waiting only for him to tell me everything and, by implication, to bring me into his story.

"I might have to stay here for a few days," he said casually, adding, in a tone of voice that immediately removed any possibility of disagreement, "that is, of course, if you don't mind."

"No, of course not," I said, "you're very welcome."

The politeness of my response seemed to amuse him. "Oh good," he said, "how kind."

ONE

My first attempted act of creation was, not surprisingly, a failure. I was young, only eleven or twelve years old. I had read practically everything that a boy of my age and class was supposed to have read: Defoe, Melville, Scott, Jules Verne, Lewis Carroll, Dumas, Stevenson and Swift, and some that were thought beyond me: Poe, Wilde, Camus, D. H. Lawrence, Woolf and Baudelaire.

If I had failed to understand much of the actual content of some of these more esoteric works, then just the mere presence of such works in my life had still managed, somehow, to have a profound effect upon my imagination and the way that I perceived myself existing in the world. My role was not to be the hero, the villain or any of the minor characters, not even the mysterious creator of such sublime works of fiction, but the actual work itself. I was the island, the town, the storm at sea, the horse galloping across the countryside, the sound of the blind man's stick tapping along the cobbled street, the birds that hurled themselves into a tumbling sky, the sky itself and the blood needlessly spilt in defense of a doomed cause.

At that age I still played, alone and in silence, as rapt in concentration as if I were reading. I arranged my hundreds of soldiers in a long line, two by two, so that when I wished them to advance I had to take up the last two soldiers from the rear of the column and, scurrying forward, place them at the head of my army. Back to front; again and again; pick up, shuffle forward, position them with care and then repeat. This technique was not entirely perfect, for my leading troops, the most attractive and efficient of my army, were soon lost in the general chaos of movement. This, for me, was the most painful part of the exercise, but the ecstasy and the feeling of satisfaction when at last they were returned to their rightful place at the head of my army was beyond compare; with their power eventually restored I had no doubt that they thanked me profusely and would go on to gain even greater glory. But no battles were ever fought. Their journey, it seemed, was enough, or perhaps in my world death, as yet, had no part to play. Such was my sensitivity that I could hardly bear the sight of a horse and rider toppled over in the bottom of my toy box. It seemed to me, even at that early age, that everything had been born or created with a specific form and purpose in mind, and that any deviation from that original construct was simply unacceptable, an aberration, an insult not to be tolerated.

Did I think that such play was an actual act of creation? No, certainly not, for I was only too aware that these objects, these tiny toy soldiers that gave me so much pleasure, were the physical manifestation of another's time, energy and effort, and that I was merely the recipient of such marvels. But books were different. Although I understood, vaguely, that there must be a creator, it seemed to me that the product of their imagination seemed to exist solely in my head. Writers did not exist, I assured myself, only their work.

And then I ran out of stories. My world had become prescribed by another's imagination. It was not that there was any shortage of character, vision or incident, only that the conceit that was offered to me now no longer seemed to satisfy. Things were never quite as they should be: the landscape was inappropriate – too rich or lush or barren; the interior of buildings took on an aspect that meant nothing to me, and the characters began to behave in an oddly erratic and unconvincing manner. I had become separated from my own imagination.

Something had to be done.

By this time I had been forced, by necessity, to confront more directly the world into which I had been born. My mother and father had, to their credit, understood that certain things were required of them if they were to fulfill even adequately their role as parents. Consequently, I was born into a warm and safe environment, if somewhat lacking in affection. I was given a room of my own which, later, I was allowed to decorate in any way that I saw fit. Toys were provided, some of an improving nature and some not. Food was plentiful and, I believe, of the recommended type and quality to provide all the minerals and nutrients necessary to guarantee healthy growth. My mother taught me to read long before I attended my first school at the age of five; in consequence, I was considered by the staff and my fellow students alike to be rather well advanced for my age. Despite my somewhat precocious behavior, my sense of the ridiculous and my refusal to take myself too seriously ensured my popularity.

It was only later that I realised that my parents, far from being motivated by any sense of love or even affection for me, were acting purely out of the need to be seen to be doing the right thing and to be behaving responsibly. That my parents loved each other passionately was never in any doubt, but it was a love of such an all-consuming intensity that it left very little room for anything or anybody else, not even their only son.

They shouldn't, of course, have had any children at all. Perhaps, in a more indifferent age, or at a time when the pressures to conform to the *mores* of a society striving to reclaim its identity after six years of war were less intense, they would have had the courage to live their lives in splendid and selfish isolation. But the Second World War had ended only five years earlier, and my parents were as enthusiastic as the rest of Britain to move towards a new future.

My father, a short, rotund man with a jolly face and a mop of black hair, owned a small engineering firm in the North of England. He drank whisky at all times of the day and was considered to be a 'good sport'; while my mother, a gentle creature with pale blue eyes and an unnatural amount of pale blonde hair, played the part of wife and housekeeper to perfection: not in frustration or with resentment, but with a true belief in her role as a devoted helpmate to her husband.

Like many other species of animal, their concern for my future and my well-being waned once they were convinced that I could survive independently to a certain extent. Far from resenting them for this lack of concern, I learnt very quickly to appreciate the freedom that such neglect bestowed on me. If, at times, I was lonely, I always had my imagination and my play to entertain and comfort me. Looking back I can only marvel at just how well I survived. But then I ran out of stories.

I prepared myself to write, to create a world purely of my imagination: one over which I would have total control; one in which only I could truly exist.

I began confidently and with no fear of failure:

Long after he had gone his voice remained, quivering against the side of my head like a knife stuck in a tree.

And then I stopped. The image I had conjured up overwhelmed me, frightened me, almost took my breath away. I placed my pen by the side of my notebook and looked once again at the words I had written. What, in my head, had seemed so perfect, so innocuous, now, in the cold, impersonal black and white of ink and paper seemed to shout out at me, to condemn me as if I were being accused of some dark and frightful crime. I had been found out and I knew that I was guilty.

I understood instantly the texture of the bark of the tree, could feel its roughness beneath my hands; and the colour and the shape of the knife with its ivory handle; and the noise it made as it quivered, its blade embedded in the trunk of the tree. There, in that one sentence was all the power, love, hate and insanity of the world. And I was responsible.

Yet I had, rightly or wrongly and in complete ignorance of the consequences, made a start. I had begun and whatever happened next, whatever decision I made, whether to continue or not, that one sentence would exist forever.

Who was the man that had spoken so violently? What were his final words and were they directed at me? And if so, who was the 'me', the twelve-year-old boy staring in stupefaction at the words spelt out before him, or the 'me' in the guise of another; and if so, whom? I began to cry, such childish tears of frustration and despair. It seemed to me that in trying to create my own world from my imagination not only had I failed, but that I had even lost that which I had held so dear. The mere act of putting pen to paper had destroyed forever the illusion that such works of creation came fully formed into the world. Now it was me who was the writer and the mystery and the magic had been obliterated for all time.

I closed my notebook, placed my newly acquired fountain pen back in its case and continued to live my life.

At the age of fifteen I fell in love. She was a year older than me, small and pretty with a mass of auburn hair, blue eyes and a pale, oval face. Her mouth was exquisite: small but of a perfect shape with full red lips. The difference in our ages, although negligible, seemed much greater when one took into consideration my relative naivety and her apparent unquestioning belief in herself and the world around her. She appeared at all times to be totally aware of the person she was and the effect that she had on those closest to her. If I conjure up an image of those times it is of me as the devoted acolyte (if not actually kneeling at her feet) and her as the adept whose life and behaviour I wished to adopt and emulate. At the height of my passion I could hardly differentiate between my love of her and my longing, almost painful in its intensity, to be her. When, eventually, she left me it was not just her that I missed and longed to regain, but everything that I had come to associate with her life: the clothes that she wore; the pale blue ribbon that she sometimes fastened round her neck; the way that she held her knife and fork; the inflection of her voice when she laughed; the house where she lived and her tiny bedroom, so exotic and alien. It seemed to me, at that moment of separation, that I had been cut off from the most important part of me. What else was left?

If there is one event in my life that I can identify as the point at which I began to understand just how I was to behave if I wished simply to survive in the world then it was that one, painful act of betrayal. If, I reasoned, I was, despite my honesty and devotion, incapable of influencing even to the smallest degree the events and behaviour of the people around me, then not only would I accept whatever fate had in store for me but I would also use such random events to give meaning and direction to my life. I, myself, would become the work of art I so desperately wished to create; no creator except life itself.

I am fifteen years of age. Susan and I are sitting in the small living room of her parent's house. She has just returned after a three-week student exchange trip to France. I can hardly recognize her. I am more aware than ever of the difference between us. In the time that she has been away I have become static, almost atrophied. Without her presence I am too solid, too lumpen, too rooted to the earth. I look at her in amazement, mesmerized by her beauty, her life and her energy.

She reaches into her bag and produces a small, brightly coloured packet of photographs. She is so happy. "This is the central square in Tourcoing, and this is the Hotel de Ville, and this is the canal that runs right through the centre of the town, and this is the flower market." She holds each photograph out towards me for my inspection. "And this is looking out towards Lille – we went there three or four times. It was amazing. I really loved it. And this is the bar in Tourcoing where we spent most of our time. And this is the family I stayed with, Monsieur and Madame Dupont, and their son Marcel."

Just something in the way that she says Marcel, the slight hesitation before pronouncing his name, tells me everything that I wish to know. I look closely at the photograph, the only one that interests me. Monsieur and Madame Dupont, Marcel and Susan are standing in front of what appears to be an old farmhouse: a long, low building of pale yellow stone with a blue painted door and faded blue shutters over the windows. Marcel and Susan have their arms around each other and are smiling for the camera. I wonder, just for a second, who took the picture. Susan continues to hold the photograph in front of me, her hand resting lightly on my knee.

I turn my head away and let my gaze wander idly around the room, this room that I know so well: the floral wallpaper; the heavily patterned carpet; the hearth-rug and the three-bar electric fire. The Beatles are playing on the record player. It hardly seems possible that a moment of such high drama could take place in such mundane surroundings.

"Did you sleep with him?"

I have asked the question almost careless of the answer. I already know it is too late. She stands up, leaving me with the photograph, and crosses the room to switch on the fire. She turns and smiles at me: a wonderful, open and confident smile. "It's just a photograph, Jonathan," she says. "That's all."

I watch her carefully. "You've changed," I say. "You're not the same."

"Do you really think so?" she says, brushing the hair from her face. "Perhaps you are right."

She has taken my comment as praise and begins to wander around the room, drawing the curtains, running her hands over the furniture and rearranging the ornaments on the mantelpiece. She is showing herself off to her best advantage; posing for me in a dress that I don't recognize.

"Is that new?"

"This?" she says, looking down and smoothing away the material from her waist. "Marcel bought it for me. You should see some of the fashions in France, Jonathan, they're wonderful. We even had a day out in Paris."

She is so obviously happy, so confident in the person that she is becoming that I hardly know how to behave. I have no rights over her, I know that, and any relationship that we might have had was by mutual consent, but I find it almost impossible to believe that she no longer cares for me. And yet, I doubt if I have even the strength or the courage to hate her.

"Will he be coming to visit?"

"Who?"

"Marcel."

She shrugs her shoulders nonchalantly.

"Oh, I suppose so. We talked about some time next month."

"So soon?"

"Well, he hasn't much time left before he has to go back to school."

I am trying so hard to be polite and understanding, but all I can think of is the two of them together, of Susan's body, the body I know so well, being given to somebody else.

"I want to touch you."

She laughs out loud. "Don't be silly."

"I'm not being silly. I want to touch you."

"My parents are just in the next room."

"It's never stopped you before."

"It's too dangerous, and anyway, I'm not in the mood." She is no longer laughing.

This I have great trouble in understanding. I could, with a good deal of effort just about convince myself that we are no longer together, but why should that change the way that she acts towards me physically? Have I suddenly become so repulsive to her that she can no longer even bear the thought of me touching her? After all, surely she allowed Marcel to touch her when she was supposedly still involved with me. I am confused and can feel myself growing angry.

"I'm only asking to touch you," I say. "It doesn't matter whether you enjoy it or not. Just think of it as doing me a favour, and if that's too difficult for you, you can always close your eyes and pretend I'm Marcel. I'm sure that won't be too unpleasant for you." I know I have gone too far, but there is a small part of me that is almost proud at the thought that I might have hurt her.

Her expression is one of pure disdain. "If you are going to say things like that," she says, "then I think you'd better leave." She moves towards the door, but as she passes by I stretch out my arm and thrust my hand up her dress and in between her legs. Immediately she jumps away, pushing me from her. I expect her to say something, I want her to say something, anything to prolong our time together, but she leaves the room in silence, slamming the door behind her.

As the door closes, the Beatles music comes to an end with the stylus lodging itself in the final groove of the record, giving rise to an endless series of repetitive clicks; perhaps the only incident of pure, natural drama of the whole evening. I wait a few moments and then put on my jacket and leave.

I decide to walk home. It is a distance of some five or six miles, late at night and, I am pleased to discover, raining very heavily; I have a desire to feel myself suffering. Despite the pain and the shock of the evening, however, I feel unnaturally calm, almost light-headed. I begin, without intention, to relive the events of the past few hours, starting with my excitement at the thought of seeing Susan again, and ending with the final slam of the door. How else could I have behaved? What other choice had she left me? Perhaps, even now, she is regretting the way that she treated me and is slowly becoming aware that it has all been some sort of terrible misunderstanding. Perhaps tomorrow she will ring me up and apologize. But I remember every word of our conversation, and the way she smiled when she spoke of Marcel and the look of horror on her face when I thrust my hand in between her legs. (I raise my hand to my nose to see if I can smell her on my fingers.) Why had I done such a thing? What had I hoped to achieve? And yet, I had felt it necessary to respond in some way, to impose my presence on the situation; and that, obviously, was my mistake. Now it was to be me who would suffer the most and to experience the full horrors of guilt and remorse. Up until then I had done nothing. I was totally innocent. It is me who is the wronged party, but now I feel nothing but shame. It soon becomes obvious to me that in any situation, whatever action I take, whether for ill or good, I will be the one to suffer.

Keep walking, that's the only answer; remember, Jonathan, the journey is everything; the endless going forward; no battles, no unnecessary acts of bravery; just movement. Bring the last two soldiers up to the front of the column and soon everything will be as it was before. But with every step I take the desolation and the loneliness of my journey home only increases. Suddenly I wish to stop altogether, to sit down here by the side of the road in the dark and the rain and to fall quietly asleep.

Cars speed by, their headlights throwing distorted shadows into the night, the regular swish of their tyres on the wet tarmac echoing the run-out track on the Beatles record. People are in their homes watching television and drinking tea. How can I possibly indulge in any grand gesture when surrounded by such indifference? I continue on my way home, the outsider and the hero.

It is only much later that I find stuffed in the pocket of my jacket the photograph of Susan and Marcel standing close together in front of the blue-shuttered house.

I never see Susan again.

Life was proving a great disappointment to me. At the age of fifteen it seemed to me that I had already exhausted most possibilities that life had to offer: pain, love, jealousy, anguish, loneliness, rejection, despair and failure were all mine. I had not only experienced all these emotions but had taken them to my heart as truly my destiny. Cast adrift I felt capable of achieving everything and nothing, with only 'the moment' being of any importance: neither the past nor the future but that one instant when one is suddenly blessed with the ability to see oneself entire and perfect in a restless and chaotic universe. Incapable of coping with the great events in life I would dedicate myself purely to the pointless and the insignificant.

With renewed hope I began again.

The death of my parents meant little to me. We had ceased to communicate with each other on any meaningful level many years previously. We lived in the same house, inhabited the same space and conversed with each other when necessary, but no real thoughts or experiences were ever shared. We neither hated nor loved each other, nor was it simply a case of toleration. Our whole relationship was defined by the fact that I was their child and they were my parents; that, to all three of us, seemed enough. Far from resenting this situation, I had come to welcome it as the natural order of things, and almost pitied those of my schoolmates who were forced to live in what was considered a 'normal' family relationship. No questions were ever asked appertaining to my well-being, my habits, my friends or my schoolwork. They gave me money, always more than enough, to buy clothes, books, food and anything else that I might desire or find necessary; an arrangement that suited all three of us and one of which I never felt inclined to take advantage. Strangely enough, the more freedom I was allowed the less disposed I was to make use of it.

I worked conscientiously, if not enthusiastically, at my studies (at least, up until the age of fifteen), co-operative in class and diligent in the completion of my homework. If I took any delight in my role as student it was not in the successful completion of the work set me, but in the persona that I had invented for myself as the 'good pupil'.

My mother insisted on dying at home, a decision that I found more than a little inconvenient. I was used to a routine of quiet and impersonal neglect of everything and everybody, and now suddenly there appeared, as if by divine intervention, a focus to my life. She would lie alone in my parent's bed, my father having moved into the spare room some weeks previously, no longer absent but a perpetual presence in my daily routine. Although there was no outside pressure on me to participate in any meaningful way in my mother's death I felt that it was only right and proper that I should visit her at least once a day. I would sit at the foot of the bed and watch her die. We exchanged very few words, not, at least at the beginning of her illness, because of her inability to speak, but simply through the custom of silence that had grown up between us which, even at that moment of ultimate crisis, we found impossible to break. We simply had nothing to say to one another.

My father continued much as before, apparently oblivious to or unable to accept the seriousness of the situation. He prepared all her meals himself, what little she ate, and carried them to her on a black, Japanese lacquer tray, not as if he were ministering to a sick woman but as if he were delivering breakfast to a new bride.

Perhaps it was only then that I began to understand just how close they were to each other, and how my presence, if not actually resented, was almost an irrelevance.

She died while I was at school. I came home early one day and the body had already gone, the windows were thrown wide open and the bed had been stripped. My first emotion was one of relief that my little life could now return to some sort of normality, and then regret that I had missed the actual moment of her departure. I felt frustrated and surprisingly angry that I had been excluded, even as a spectator, from the finale to such a dramatic series of events.

My father said nothing to me concerning her death, neither then nor during the next few days leading up to the funeral. We communicated on only the most practical of levels: arrangements were made, people informed, flowers and the room for the funeral tea ordered and booked.

And after?

With charm and a quiet dignity of which I had thought him incapable, my father began to drink himself to death. He had always exhibited an unnatural need and a somewhat larger than average capacity for alcohol, but he now approached this new role as the bereaved, desolate and perpetually grieving husband with a dedication and gusto that surprised even me. He no longer went to work: indeed, he seldom ventured outside the house at all unless it was to make one of his many trips to the local off-license, seemingly content to spend the rest of his days marooned in his favourite armchair, staring mournfully at the blank screen of the television set.

As for me, I continued much as before, quiet and introverted and content to live in my world and to allow my father to live – or rather, die – in his.

The end came surprisingly quickly, which was an important lesson to me in the immense power that a combination of drink and a mind set on death can have over the human body. He died in hospital: pale, unshaven, thin and still grieving for his dead wife. I visited him once, just before the end, my curiosity overcoming my natural indifference. His final words to me were: "Sod off", a sentiment with which I could only concur.

Being a businessman my father had left his affairs in good order. Being, I discovered, not a particularly good businessman there was much less money left, after all the debts and commitments had been accounted for, than I had expected or hoped for. Still, I reasoned that once the house was sold and the few assets that remained were realised, I should have enough to live on, if I were careful.

A few months later I dropped out of school and moved into a council flat, leaving the house with all its furniture behind me. I never thought of it or the life that I had led there ever again.

I was seventeen years of age.

In those days (the late 1960s) and in the small Northern English town where I was born and where I continued to live, most of the public houses were dark: not a darkness caused simply by an absence of light, but a darkness that seemed to emanate almost organically from the thick and heavily stained carpet, the dull, yellowing wallpaper, the heavy wooden furniture and the thin veil of cigarette smoke that seemed to soften and obscure the shape of everything. The only pool of light of any significance existed primarily around the bar, giving the impression, hard to resist, not of a meeting place or of a drinking establishment but of a theatre, with us, the patrons, as the audience. A perfect space, I reasoned, for me to live out the rest of my life.

I visited the same pub and sat at the same table every day. It is almost impossible to describe the pleasure to be gained from following such a routine: the welcoming security of familiar smells, sights, sounds and faces. I said very little to begin with, just enough to order my drink, but despite my natural reticence I soon became well known, almost but not quite establishing myself as one of the 'regulars'; my age and apparent unsociability telling against me. I drank only whisky. I delighted in drinking only whisky, a habit unusual in those days. I would hold the small, shallow glass containing the bright, golden liquid in one hand and my cigarette in the other, my two elbows resting on the table. It was a pose that suited me well, I believed.

Gradually, over the following weeks and months, I began to attract a small group of people to my table, due mainly to the fact that I bought drinks freely, reasoning that to buy a drink for a drunk was the ultimate act of self-promotion and frivolity. I was never so self-deluded as to believe that it was because of my personality. Colin, Diana, Kieran, Jackie and Vince were the most regular of my visitors: all slightly older than me but all equally incapable of functioning successfully in the life that was open to them.

Of these five drunks and misfits I found Kieran to be the most intriguing and perhaps the most potentially dangerous. He was not unintelligent, nor was his family background one of deprivation or neglect, but he had chosen to reject these 'benefits' with an almost careless disregard for his or anybody else's welfare; a decision that I could only admire and applaud. He moved with a pure, unconscious animal grace that fascinated and astounded me, his tall, lean and muscular body dominating any company or any place in which he happened to find himself. In his sallow cheeks and in his dark, hooded eyes and in the barely concealed fury that seemed always to play about his lips one could discern, already, the failure that he was to become. He carried a knife, an object of veneration that he would produce at the slightest opportunity, weighing it in his hand or twisting it expertly through his fingers, as if its mere presence brought him hope and comfort. We had learnt to ignore such moments of bravado, refusing to be either intimidated or impressed, but we were all aware that the irrationality and genuine violence of his personality and behaviour were not to be underestimated. One day, if only to be true to his nature, an act of real devastation would have to be performed. In an earlier age, as a warrior or an adventurer, he would have been lauded for his courage, but to us he was merely vaguely entertaining or, at his worst, a dangerous liability.

From Kieran I learnt the art of the unexpected, not the forced eccentricity of the surrealist or the carefully planned artificiality of the anarchist, but that sudden leap into drama, that spontaneous outburst of uncontrollable emotion of which only the truly deranged are capable. I basked in his aura of invulnerability and ultimate self-destruction.

In fact, far from being the self-controlled and self-reliant person that I appeared, it was only through my association with all five of my companions that I was learning exactly what it was to be a human being. There was no emotion, however deep or trivial, that could not be analyzed and copied. So adept had I become at this subterfuge that, as time went by, even I was no longer certain of what I really felt or believed. I would fall in love with any woman who paid me the slightest attention, irrespective of their character or appearance, with only the physical side of our relationship proving beyond me. I would become aroused and then, at the final moment of consummation, as if suddenly understanding exactly what it was that was expected of me and how ludicrously I was behaving, all passion and lust would subside, leaving me feeling nothing but disgust and regret. Only when drunk did I feel truly liberated: capable, without irony, of embarking upon the wildest and most irresponsible adventures.

At such moments, free from any bonds of personality or belief, what may I not have become: a thief, a murderer, a rapist, even a revolutionary? And when challenged and apprehended I could have truly said: 'But this isn't me; you are mistaken. Yes, I admit that I committed the act of which I am accused, but I am not that person who now stands before you: I am a stranger even to myself.' And how I would continue to profess my innocence even when found guilty and incarcerated; and rail, not against the injustice of the system, but my own indefinable nature.

My first attempted act of suicide occurred about that time, when I was eighteen or nineteen years of age. I say 'act' but, in truth, I had been working towards my own death ever since the day of Susan's betrayal. I had from that moment, and to all intents and purposes, ceased to eat, surviving on little more than a bar or two of chocolate a day. That reckless behavior, along with my ever-increasing dependency on whisky (seldom a single day went by when I was truly sober), had gradually begun to take its toll on my health, both mental and physical. My appearance had changed almost beyond recognition from the days when I had known Susan. I had become incredibly thin, weighing less than seven stone; my complexion was pale and sickly and my hair hung in long, curly strands well below the level of my shoulders. I looked into the mirror and I saw a stranger staring back out at me. I was striving, and of this I was only too aware, to become somebody else and, eventually, to disappear altogether.

I was very happy.

And then, not surprisingly, I fell in love again. Anna had wandered, as if by accident, into my life and expressed a mild interest in me, and I, remaining true to my nature, had wasted no time in convincing myself that I was in love with her. I never seriously doubted that, like Susan, she too would eventually desert me, but at that stage in my life I believed without question that that was my role and my destiny. Indeed, I almost welcomed the pain that such a relationship was bound to bring. "You must never ask me to do something," she used to say, "you must tell me." To follow such a command was so far beyond my understanding and my nature that I became almost powerless when in her presence; yet further proof, if any were needed, that I was incapable of living outside my life.

We were invited to many parties; Anna was popular and gregarious and constantly in search and need of entertainment. I would arrive already drunk or, if not, would waste no time in becoming so, attacking each glass of whisky with passion and commitment. Not only did I believe that such behaviour was necessary if I wished to function adequately in those situations, but I soon realized that other people had come to expect it of me. My glass was continually replenished while the other guests marveled at, and secretly mocked, my capacity for self-destruction. And while I drank, Anna mingled.

I would watch her from a distance, knowing even before she did which one of the guests she would take upstairs. I would pick him out almost as soon as we entered the room: invariably, the person most unlike myself. Where I was small, pale, thin and, if not actually effeminate then certainly imbued with a sort of sexual ambiguity, he would be stocky, muscular and uncompromisingly male.

Our relationship eventually reached such a complex stage of indifference, disgust and mutual dependency that Anna would ask my opinion on her latest conquest, in all seriousness and with the hope that I would approve and sanction her choice.

"So what do you think?' She would be excited, her eyes bright and her face flushed with the thought of the pleasure that was to come. "He's called John. He's a gardener. Well, actually, he's a musician, a drummer, but he's waiting to get a band together. He asked what you did and I told him that you were a writer but that you hadn't actually written anything yet. He's very nice, you'd like him."

Anna discussed with me with all the men she slept with, she said it would be hypocritical not to. "Why not," she would say, "it's not as if I'm trying to hide anything? You don't mind, do you?"

And she would kiss me lightly on the cheek, call me 'an angel' and then push her way through the crowd to take hold of her chosen partner's hand and lead him willingly from the room. Sometimes he, whoever it was, would glance round and throw me a look of mingled confusion, pity and triumph. She never looked back. She had an amazing ability to distance herself and her life from every individual action that she took, as if one event had no bearing on another: "When I'm with you, I'm with you, and when I'm with somebody else, I'm with them. I don't see the problem."

And who was I to disagree? What right had I to try and impose my will, my hopes or my desires on anything, even to the smallest degree? If Anna wished to behave in that particular way then that was her prerogative. She was an attractive woman, not beautiful in the accepted sense, but imbued with enough knowledge of the power of her own sexuality to attract the attention of most men. She seemed, at all times and in all situations, to offer the possibility of availability. Just to look at her was to understand that, once together, she would deny you nothing; everything would be open. Even when apparently engaged in the most mundane of tasks, you just knew that there would always be a part of her contemplating her own body and the pleasure that she could give and derive from it. How could I possibly interfere in a nature so perfectly formed and confident?

Sometimes, through an alcoholic haze, I would look round the room at the assembled guests; the furniture; the long, low table with its array of empty and half-filled glasses, bottles and overflowing ashtrays; the prints and posters on the walls; the imitation Indian rug; the Victorian fireplace now boarded over and at Anna herself, perched on the edge of the sofa, her legs drawn up beneath her short, multi-coloured skirt, and deep in conversation with some man or other. I would listen to the babble of noise and the relentless chatter of the record player and realize, as if for the first time, that my presence was unnecessary and that if I were not there then nothing would change and nobody would behave any differently. A proposition that brought me some comfort, I have to confess,

That is the mistake that so many potential suicides make, I reasoned. They believe that when they are gone everything will be different; how could it not be? "After all," they say to themselves, "I may not be important but am I not a presence, an entity in the world: a mass of flesh, bone and blood with a soul, a brain, an intelligence, a memory and an imagination? Surely when I am dead I will be missed and mourned? How they will suffer in my absence."

Which was the thought farthest from my mind when, in the late 60s and in a council flat situated in the centre of a small town in the North of England, I finished off the last of a bottle of whisky, swallowed 75 sleeping tablets and lay down on my mattress to die.

For those who have never embarked upon such a glorious adventure it is remarkably difficult to describe with any degree of accuracy the feelings, both physical and mental, that one experiences at just such a moment of crisis: it is neither life nor death but simply an intermission; a pause between one breath and another.

I opened my eyes and looked around me. It was late evening and the flat was illuminated by just a single, bare light bulb that hung from the centre of the ceiling. There was no movement and yet none of the objects upon which I tried to focus, nor their shadows, appeared static. It was as if everything had become imbued with its own particular rhythm: a gentle undulation or vibration that destroyed line and shape, giving each object a meaning and an importance as yet undiscovered.

I recognized everything and understood nothing: the long, low bookcase with its row of brightly coloured books; the single, wooden chair placed beside the window; the threadbare rug; the glass and the empty bottle of whisky by my side; the cracked and stained coffee cup and the half-spilled packet of tobacco; none of these things appeared to have any connection with me but to exist complete and entire and as living, breathing entities in their own right. I began to cry at the thought of the beauty and the stupidity of it all.

I believed I was dying – not like my mother, from no fault of her own but through the invasion of some indiscriminate and alien disease – solely through the arrogance and indifference of my own free will. And suddenly, confronted with the real and imminent possibility of my own death, I realised that *this* was enough to satisfy me, that it was not my actual death that I had desired, but only the decision to die and the gesture of dying itself that I had needed to experience, to prove to myself that I was truly alive.

I drew my knees up to my chest and hugged myself beneath the thin material of my blanket. 'At least I have done it well,' I thought. 'These drab and impersonal surroundings will tell nothing of my life to whoever discovers my body. I will have died in the most innocuous way possible: hardly a proper death at all, more of a performance in the art of dying. For that, and that alone, I can take some consolation and pride.'

And then I vomited, again and again.

Obviously I had failed in my attempt to kill myself; the proof lay splattered all about me: the bright, foaming liquid mess that spoke positively of life. I coughed up the last of the whisky and half-digested tablets and wiped my mouth with the back of my hand. I sat up on the mattress and pushed the blanket away from me. The surge of hope and expectation that I then experienced was almost overwhelming. This was not just relief at still being alive but an almost spiritual revelation of the power that I could exert over my own body. This was my life and I now knew for certain that I had the strength and capability to end it whenever I wished – probably the most liberating moment of my entire existence.

When the world proved to be too painful or too dull for me, I could die.

When I was betrayed in love (again), I could die.

When I had acted in a foolish or embarrassing manner, I could die.

When I ceased to find the people around me entertaining, I could die.

When I could no longer bear the responsibility of being me, I could die.

With such a possibility always open to me I now believed that I was capable of achieving anything.

I decided to become an artist, or, to be more specific I decided to live the life of an artist. I bought, from the local hardware shop, a large sheet of hardboard (three feet by four feet), six tins of paint and several brushes of varying sizes. I placed them on the floor of my flat where, almost immediately, they took on the same demanding presence as that blank sheet of paper that I had, many years previously, so comprehensively failed to fill with my thoughts and imaginings: a continual questioning of my competence and ability. I sat in the corner of the room, stunned into inactivity; too full of expectation actually to do anything.

Anna arrived. She was thrilled. "This is wonderful," she said, looking down at the hardboard and the paint, "just what I was hoping for."

"But what if I can't paint?"

"That doesn't matter," she said, nonchalantly dismissing my doubts with a wave of her hand. "You couldn't write either, and it's not as if you're a real artist anyway; you just have to pretend to be one. That's what's important. I mean, what else are you going to do with your life if you don't do this? But you must do it properly: continue to drink too much – and only whisky, you look so good when you drink whisky – and eat very little, and when you're in company say practically nothing at all and make it unintelligible or an insult or both. Oh, Jonathan," she continued, her voice rising in excitement, "I'm so proud of you."

She came and stood beside me, draping her right arm around my shoulders and pressing her body against mine. I reached out for her and pushed my right hand up beneath her skirt and down the front of her knickers, letting my fingers rest gently in between her legs. Slowly she hoisted up her skirt and opened her legs wider to allow me easier access. She was, as always, very wet and my first two fingers slid in easily. I rested my head against her waist and began, rhythmically, to move my hand back and forth, occasionally rubbing her clitoris with the tip of my thumb. Her breathing deepened.

"I'm so glad you didn't kill yourself, Jonathan," she said, "at least not in that dull and boring way; it would have been such a waste and not worthy of you at all. Now you can do it properly, like a real artist: slowly drink and starve yourself to death; and people will think that you did it because of your love for me. I will be so proud."

Her arm tightened its grip around my shoulders and her body began to rock steadily back and forth keeping in perfect time with the movement of my hand.

"So proud," she repeated, breathlessly, "so very, very proud."

Gradually I increased the speed and the pressure of my movement thrusting my fingers deeper inside her and slipping my other hand down the back of her knickers. These were the only times when I felt totally in control; when I had no fear of failure – I further increased the pressure and Anna began quietly to moan – but even at such moments I knew that none of it was real. This was not love, not even passion, but a performance as false and as forced as my belief in myself as an artist.

I looked at the blank sheet of hardboard and the six cans of paint arranged so neatly on the floor, waiting to be transformed into something substantial and exotic, and suddenly I was overcome with such a rage that if I could, if such a thing were possible, I would have strangled the whole world. If this was to be my life then I would live it without fear or apology; celebrate it as the wonderful, glorious failure that it obviously was.

I moved my hand more vigorously, almost violently, pushing my fingers deeper into Anna's cunt; my other hand forcing its way in between the soft, roundness of her buttocks. If this was what she wanted than I would be only too happy to oblige. Suddenly she came, her legs buckling slightly beneath her, her left hand grasping mine to stop the movement. She sighed deeply and rested the whole weight of her body against me. I was breathing as heavily as she, convinced that I, too, had participated in her pleasure.

"I have to go," she suddenly said. "I have a date."

She pulled away from me, rearranged her knickers and smoothed down her skirt. I watched her in wonder as, calmly and without the least show of emotion, she produced a small mirror from out of her handbag and began to reapply lipstick and eye shadow. Our brief encounter was over. I had provided a service no more significant than if I had made her a cup of coffee and now it was time to move on. She looked round the room.

"Why don't you get a mirror, Jonathan?" she said with obvious irritation. "I don't know how you manage without one." And then, turning to face me, "So, how do I look?"

In truth, she looked superb, so supremely sexual and confident that it was impossible to imagine anyone not loving and wanting her.

"You look amazing."

She smiled a wonderful, sincere smile of pleasure and then kissed me lightly on the cheek. (The first time since her arrival, I couldn't help registering, that she had actually kissed me.) "You're very sweet," she said, "but I really have to go. I'm late."

"Who are you meeting?"

"Just a man, you don't know him. I might see you later. Bye."

And she fled from the room, slamming the front door behind her.

I had an urge to laugh out loud. This was exactly how life should be: a perpetual moving towards adventure, an idiotic and ultimately pointless series of brief encounters and unexpected moments of pleasure and pain. How could I not love Anna when she was behaving so perfectly in keeping with her character? One could only applaud her dignity and her honesty.

I poured myself a large whisky and began to pace restlessly up and down the flat; I, too, needed movement. I wandered into the kitchen and looked out of the window at the block of flats opposite. I located the correct balcony and the correct bedroom window, but she wasn't there – perhaps later. Music began to play in the flat next to mine. Usually I would have resented such an intrusion, but now it seemed only fitting, and I welcomed the noise as an appropriate accompaniment to my particular moment of pleasure and pain. The sitting room was still heavy with the smell of Anna's perfume. I returned to my seat and looked down at the sheet of hardboard and paint. Anna was right: I was an artist and a writer, not because of what I did or didn't do, but simply because of whom I had chosen to be. I brought the glass of whisky to my lips and silently toasted the rightness of everything.

I was still drinking when Anna returned. I had consumed almost all of the bottle, steadily, without need or passion. After my initial restlessness I had fallen into some sort of quiet contemplation. I was not unhappy, not even agitated; everything seemed to make the most perfect sense. I sat on my chair, the glass in my hand, the bottle by my side and watched the last of the day advance into night. From my position next to the wide expanse of window I could see the top four floors of the flats opposite, and above that, the pale blue and grey of the watery, northern sky. Time passed, the music from next door ceased to play, the light faded and for one brief moment I felt myself becoming almost invulnerable.

Anna's sudden arrival came as a shock, the sound of the opening and closing of the front door breaking violently into my quiet imaginings.

"I'm starving. I don't suppose you have anything to eat?"

She passed quickly into the kitchen and switched on the light so that two thirds of the sitting room became suddenly, if faintly, illuminated. "And close the curtains, will you? I don't want to be watched."

I turned to look at the door leading into the hall. Another figure, short and stocky, had entered the room. He moved unsteadily, holding on to the doorpost for support.

"That's Karl," Anna shouted from the kitchen. "I think he's drunk."

Karl attempted to raise one hand in greeting, but thought better of it.

"I'm making some toast – do you want some?"

I knew instinctively that she didn't mean me.

Tentatively, keeping as close to the wall as possible as if he were pretending to be blind, Karl edged his way towards the light and disappeared into the kitchen.

In my own confused and uninvolved state I viewed all this with only the mildest of interest, still too deeply engaged in my own world to fully understand what was happening. I listened to the noises coming from the kitchen: the sound of cupboards and drawers being opened and closed, the clatter of crockery and the persistent hum of voices. Occasionally, Anna laughed out loud, strong and uninhibited. It was all as distant and foreign to me as the music that I had heard being played earlier that evening.

Eventually they came back into the sitting room, side by side and conspiratorial – I had not moved; the curtains remained open – and crossed to the mattress. Anna sat down first and then shuffled up to make room for Karl. They sat close to each other and began to eat their toast, balancing their plates on their knees.

"That's Jonathan," Anna said, drunkenly. "He's an artist, but he doesn't paint. He used to be a writer, but he didn't write either." She began to giggle and nudged her body against Karl."There's nothing that he isn't capable of not doing. Is that right, or do I mean there isn't anything that he isn't capable of doing? Oh well, it doesn't matter, you know what I mean. He's called Jonathan anyway – that I'm certain of. That's right, isn't it Jonathan? That's what you're called – Jonathan. And this is Karl." Her voice took on a sickly familiarity, and she briefly rested her head against his shoulder. "And he's very nice."

"They all are," I said.

"Yes, they are," said Anna, "but he's especially nice. Give me your plate."

Karl passed her his empty plate and Anna placed it with hers on the floor by the side of the mattress. Then, leaning back against the wall, she extended her legs and wrapped her left arm around Karl's shoulders. They kissed and Karl's right hand moved up to take hold of Anna's left breast. "Is he all right?" Karl asked, breaking away from her for a moment. "I mean, is he all right with this?"

"Who?"

"Him."

They both raised their heads and looked across at me, their faces pressed close together. There was no way that they could ever have been thought of as 'a couple'. Indeed, at first glance one could even have been forgiven for believing that they were two completely different species of animal: Anna's features were delicate, her eyes wide and clear, her skin a gentle shade of pink; while the overall impression one gained of Karl was of a brutish and ill-formed nature expressed only too clearly in the heavy brows, the thick set jaw and the large and fleshy lips. I longed to say to Anna, "Please don't do this, not with him. I understand your needs, your longing for satisfaction, but there are so many better men in the world; this one is not worthy of you." But of course she knew that; indeed, that was probably the very reason why she had chosen him in the first place. She, for whatever reason, needed to be brutalized herself; to lose or, at least, to deform whatever true nature she had been born with; to say to the world, "I have fooled you all. This is who I am and this is how I behave."

I think at that particular moment I had never before felt so much love for her.

"Just ignore him," said Anna, running the tip of her tongue across his lips. "In fact, to tell you the truth, I think he enjoys it – watching me – it's the only pleasure he gets, all he is capable of."

I smiled a faint smile, hidden from them in the half-light of the flat, and thought to myself, "Do whatever you have to do, Anna, become whatever you want. It concerns nobody else but you. You are responsible for your actions to nobody."

They kissed again, longer and deeper, and then slid away from the wall to lay full length on the mattress, their bodies pressed tightly together.

Anna was almost right: she *was* behaving in such a way for my benefit, but not for my pleasure. It was only her pleasure that she was thinking of. She needed me to be there to watch this moment of degradation and surrender: how else could she convince herself that she had behaved in such an appalling manner, had given herself, in whatever way he wanted, to such a man? She needed, later, to see the look of sadness and rebuke in my eyes, to suffer my condemnation and, perhaps, even my hate. This was not an act of passion or lust, but of sacrifice.

I turned away and looked out of the window at the flats opposite and the scattering of lights that lit up the skyline and the sky itself. Vague, shadowy figures moved behind closed curtains. Somewhere there would be the sound of music and conversation and people would be living out their lives together in trust and innocence. I rolled a cigarette and poured myself another drink. Behind me the sound of Anna and Karl's lovemaking had intensified, with their moans, sighs and grunts of pleasure now filling the heavy silence of the small, bare flat. I turned to look at them. They had thrown a blanket over themselves so that only their heads and naked shoulders were now visible.

Karl was on top, moving regularly and vigorously, every violent thrust of his body accompanied by a sudden expulsion of air or a soft and grateful moan of pleasure. I watched them without excitement or interest, only barely conscious of the act in which they were engaged.

Suddenly Karl stopped and, raising himself up on his two hands, looked down on the prostrate body of Anna lying beneath him. Her head was resting on the pillow with her blonde hair spread out on either side of her face and her large, full breasts clearly visible in the dim light from the kitchen. For one brief moment I thought he was going to spit on her. Slowly she turned her head and looked directly at me. The light from her eyes had vanished and her expression had become calm, almost waxen. She had become just as bored and uninterested in the act as I was and, for a split second, I even thought I could catch a glimpse of genuine sadness and regret in the way that she looked at me: a look of such loneliness and desolation that it almost broke my heart.

Silently I raised my glass and drank a toast to her, to the people living in the flats opposite, to the encroaching night, to the works of art that I knew I would never create and to the absurd life that I was living. God bless them all.

The next morning Anna left me for good. Nothing was said, no parting words of animosity or protestations of love: nothing to embarrass or disconcert either of us. Perhaps the events of the previous evening had finally proved too much, even for her: not in taking Karl to bed or in having sex with him in front of me, but in that one revealing look of hopelessness of hers that she knew I had seen and understood. She had nothing left to hide from me and she now knew that, no matter how outrageously she was to behave in the future, never again would she be taken seriously. She knew that the little comedy that had been our relationship had finally come to an end.

She left, and I truly felt nothing; my life was already being lived elsewhere.

We were becoming drunk, wonderfully, seriously drunk. No plan had been entered into, there was no particular cause for celebration nor was any reason thought necessary for our behaviour: only the excitement and the unpredictability of the moment. It was early evening but the pub was already busy. The jukebox was playing, people were talking far too loudly and there was something in the atmosphere, something almost bordering on the manic, that seemed to exist independently of the collective mood of the customers. We were drinking with passion and commitment.

Kieran demanded another round. "He can pay," he said, indicating me, "he's rich."

"That's not fair," said Diana, "he bought the last one."

"But he likes it," said Kieran, "it makes him feel important," and he pushed his empty glass towards me.

I tried to say that I didn't mind, but nobody was listening.

Vince staggered to his feet and wandered off to put some more money in the jukebox.

"And none of your blues crap," Kieran yelled after him.

"He's stoned again," said Colin, indicating Vince, "you can tell from his eyes."

"So fucking what?" said Kieran. "It might make him more interesting."

"I like him when he's stoned," said Jackie, "He makes me laugh."

"I don't like it when he pushes it on young kids," said Colin. "That's not right."

"No," said Diana, "I don't like that either."

"No, of course not," said Jackie, eager as ever to agree with Diana. "I just meant that he made me laugh, that's all."

"He's just trying to make a living," said Kieran, "same as the rest of us. There's nothing wrong with that."

A sudden burst of guitar music broke above the noise of the drinkers.

"I told you no fucking blues crap," yelled Kieran, lifting his voice above the surrounding chaos. "I can't stand it."

"Oi!" shouted the landlord. "Watch your language."

Vince, leaning over the glass top of the jukebox, waved at us, his floral shirt flapping about his wrists.

"Same again?" I asked, rising to my feet.

"About fucking time," said Kieran.

"Yes please," said Diana. "Do you want a lift?"

"No thanks, I'll manage."

I pushed my way to the bar and ordered the drinks. While I was waiting to be served I admired my reflection in the large Victorian mirror suspended behind the long row of brightly coloured bottles: I looked so beautifully pale and exhausted. The barmaid served me without smiling and I picked up the tray of drinks and made my way unsteadily back to the table.

"Oh my god!" shrieked Jackie. "He's dancing."

Vince had shuffled into the centre of the room and, almost incidental to the music, was performing strange and convoluted movements with his arms while rocking his body gently backwards and forwards and from one side to the other.

"Arse-hole," muttered Kieran, reaching for his drink.

"Leave him alone," said Diana. "He's not doing any harm."

"Even the landlord doesn't seem to mind," said Colin.

Kieran shrugged.

"We should have some crisps," said Jackie.

"I'll get some," said Diana.

"Do you think she fancies him?" asked Kieran, once Diana had left the table.

"Who?" asked Jackie.

"Him," said Kieran, nodding in Vince's direction.

"Good god, no," shrieked Jackie, obviously outraged at the very idea. "What makes you think that?"

"No reason," answered Kieran "just the way she looks at him."

"She looks at everybody like that," said Colin, smiling. "She can't help it."

"You mean like she wants to fuck them," said Kieran.

"You shouldn't talk about her like that," said Jackie. "It's not nice."

Kieran began to laugh. "Oh dear, is poor little Jackie jealous then. Fancy her yourself do you?"

"Fuck off, Kieran," said Jackie.

Diana returned and dropped several packets of crisps onto the centre of the table. "Help yourself," she said, "I've got enough for everybody."

"That's just what we were saying," said Colin.

"What do you mean?" asked Diana.

"Ignore them," said Jackie, "they're just being stupid."

Diana looked questioningly at me, as if she expected me to explain what they had been talking about. With her blonde hair and her perfect mouth she suddenly reminded me of Anna. They both had a similar reputation for being 'available', but whereas Anna thought only of herself, Diana's main concern, I suspected, would be the pleasure that she could give to other people: a service that, apparently, she was able and, at times, only too willing to provide.

"Don't ask him," said Colin, catching the look she gave me, "he knows nothing." The music came to an end and Vince returned to the table, his face flushed and shiny with tiny beads of sweat.

"Just in time," said Kieran. "We were just wondering who Diana would rather fuck, you or Jackie."

Vince looked confused, Diana unconcerned; only Jackie seemed genuinely angry: "You know, Kieran, you're such a twat."

Diana began to laugh and placed an arm around Jackie's shoulders. "Just ignore him," she said, "Kieran's just jealous that nobody wants to fuck him."

"I wouldn't touch you, anyway," said Kieran, his lips curling in disgust. "God knows what I'd catch."

"Who did you say wants to fuck me?" asked Vince, his expression more vacant than ever. "I don't really mind who it is, but I'd like to know."

"I do," said Diana, leaning across the table towards Vince and lowering her voice until it was heavy with emotion. "Didn't you know, I find you totally irresistible? At least, that's what Kieran thinks."

"Oh that's all right then," said Vince, rolling himself a cigarette, "but can I finish my drink first?"

Somebody banged into the back of Kieran's chair.

"Fuck off, will you!"

The man apologized and slunk away.

"Was that necessary?' asked Colin.

"What?"

"It was only an accident," said Colin. "One day you'll find yourself in trouble."

Colin was a large, muscular man: a builder by trade, although he seemed to do very little work. He lacked Kieran's need for violence, but he was perfectly capable of taking care of himself.

"I'm going for a piss," said Kieran, and left the table.

"I can't stand him when he's like that," said Jackie. "He frightens me.'

"He's all right," said Colin. "He's just a baby, really."

The barmaid came and began to clear our glasses away.

"Same again, Carol," said Colin.

"You know where the bar is," she said.

"Oh go on," pleaded Colin, taking hold of her hand, "just this once."

Despite, or possibly because of, his uncouth appearance and dubious manners he had a slight reputation as being attractive to women. The barmaid protested for a little longer, but you could see from her expression that she was flattered by his attention and had already given in. She shook her head and smiled at him.

"Oh all right," she said, "since it's you, but just this once and don't tell the landlord."

"Not for me," said Vince, his voice slow and almost incomprehensible, "I'm going."

The barmaid took our order and returned to the bar.

"Where are you off to?" asked Colin.

Vince shrugged and waved his hands in front of him. "Business," he said, in a pathetic attempt to be enigmatic. "It's better if you don't know."

We all nodded or adopted expressions of dubious understanding.

"There are things going on," Vince continued, conspiratorially, drawing up his chair closer to ours, "things that you wouldn't understand."

Diana leaned forward, resting her arms on the table. "Such as?" she whispered, enjoying this sudden diversion. "What wouldn't we understand?"

"Things," he said. "Things that *they* don't want you to know."

"And who's 'they'?" asked Colin, with barely disguised contempt.

Vince looked around him for a moment or two before drawing himself even closer into the centre of our little group. "They," he repeated; "the politicians; the businessmen; the teachers; the scientists; the pigs; the men in shiny suits; the landlords; the generals; the god-botherers; the evangelists and the judges. All of them. They're all in on it."

"Christ!" exclaimed Colin. "That doesn't leave many."

"That's it," continued Vince, suddenly becoming excited and looking furtively around him again, "you've got it. You shouldn't trust anybody. They all want to stop you thinking, man; keep you quiet, subservient. They put things in the food, man, and in the water. They want to abolish love."

This last was said with the breathless authority of a man who had just given voice to a great and hitherto unspoken truth.

"Oh, is that all?" said Jackie, sarcastically. "I thought it was something important."

"You don't understand," said Vince, nodding in my direction, "but he does. He's one of them."

Almost despite themselves, they all turned to look at me.

Colin laughed out loud. "Oh yes," he said, "That would be about right. And all this time I'd just thought of Jonathan as this ineffectual little drunk, when really he's the centre of some great world conspiracy. How stupid could I have been?"

Diana, however, was obviously enjoying herself and had no intention of letting the conversation go quite so easily. "I always thought there was something suspicious about him," she said, smiling at me but placing a reassuring hand on Vince's arm. "He's far too quiet."

"That's right," agreed Jackie, suddenly and with enthusiasm, obviously only too happy to pick up on Diana's artifice. 'I've noticed that. He says nothing but he's always listening."

"And have you noticed the way he's always watching us?" continued Diana. "Very suspicious. It wouldn't surprise me if he wasn't taking notes, or recording our conversations. Perhaps we ought to search him."

"I bet he has a book at home," said Jackie, warming to the subject. "A book with all our names in it, and everything that we say and do, and when the time is right he'll show it to the authorities and denounce us all."

"For fuck's sake," said Colin, whose tolerance for such fanciful conversations was notoriously short. "Don't encourage him."

"No," said Vince, becoming increasingly restless, "this is serious. He's very dangerous. You have to listen to me."

"Is that right?" Diana asked, turning towards me and adopting a voice and an attitude of grave concern. "Are you dangerous?"

"He could bore us all to death, I suppose," said Colin.

I wanted to treat Vince's words with the same amused contempt as the rest of them, but perhaps because of the amount of alcohol I had consumed or just because of the mood I was in, I found it impossible.

"We're all dangerous, aren't we," I said quietly, "in our own way?"

"Not like you," said Vince, his voice rising in anger. "You want to destroy love."

Diana pretended to be shocked. "Is that true, Jonathan, do you want to destroy love?"

"He'll deny it, of course, but don't believe him, it's all an act," continued Vince. "That's right, isn't it, Jonathan?" I said nothing. "You see, he can't answer. He has nothing to say." He was becoming more and more agitated, waving his arms about erratically, the words pouring out of his mouth in an increasingly incoherent torrent. "And if we don't have love then we don't have anything. That's right, isn't it? No love – then nothing, just violence. We might as well be animals fighting each other, for ever and ever; all nails and teeth and fangs, always biting and ripping away at each other's flesh. No, worse than animals, they, at least, kill for a reason." He made a sudden growl like an angry tiger, spattering the table with saliva. "We have to make a stand – all of us – now, before it's all too late. Root out the devil, overthrow the barbarians and let the new age of love begin."

Overcome by the power of his rhetoric, Vince suddenly threw out his arm in an expansive gesture of well-being, defiance and inclusiveness, and knocked over Colin's half full glass of beer, splashing the dark brown liquid from one side of the table to the other.

"For Christ's sake," said Colin, pushing back his chair and wiping away the splash of beer from the front of his jeans, "Just fuck off will you or I'll show you what real violence is."

The barmaid arrived with our drinks. "What's up with him?" she asked, nodding in Colin's direction.

"Nothing," said Diana, as keen as ever to keep things calm. "It's Vince, he's just had a bit too much to drink, that's all."

"He'll be going in a minute," added Jackie.

"Love!" said Vince, lifting his head and almost shouting the word in the barmaid's face. "You know what I'm talking about, don't you? We have to love one another."

"I haven't time," answered the barmaid, walking away. "I have a living to make."

Vince reached out for a drink.

"Do you mind?" said Jackie. "That's mine. You didn't want one, remember?"

"But we have to share everything," said Vince, "that's what I'm trying to tell you. We shouldn't own anything; everything for free."

"So you give your drugs away, do you?" asked Colin.

"That's different," said Vince. "I'm not like other people. I'm a visionary, a traveller in time and space spreading the word. I'm a bringer of joy, light and experience, and anyway, I have expenses to meet."

Colin, who hated anything to do with drugs, finally lost his temper: "Listen, dickhead, why don't you just do us all a favour and piss off?"

Even in his confused state, Vince understood the real threat in Colin's voice, and after taking in two or three deep breaths he clutched the edge of the table and hoisted himself unsteadily to his feet. "OK man," he said, "I can understand what you're saying. I have to go anyway," adding, as he was half way across the room, "but don't forget, he's dangerous. He has no love in him."

When any person, however popular or unpopular and however much their absence will or won't be regretted, leaves such a small gathering, those left automatically draw closer together as if to make up for the vacancy; as if to reassure themselves that the party will not be splitting up just yet, that there are things still to be discussed and fun to be had. Colin pushed Vince's empty chair to one side and we all, almost simultaneously, reached for our drinks.

"Don't worry, Jonathan," said Diana, offering up a wonderful smile of sympathy and reassurance. "He didn't mean it. He's just stoned."

"I know," I replied, dismissively. "I'm used to it."

In truth, however, I was not used to it, and Diana's obvious and apparently genuine concern for my feelings warmed and comforted me much more than I could ever have expected.

"The world," said Colin, in a voice no longer angry but calm and flat and heavy with a world-weariness of which I had thought him incapable, "is full of twats."

Kieran had not yet returned, but his voice, loud and strident, could still occasionally be heard, lifted high above the noise of the jukebox and the endless chatter of the other customers. The atmosphere in the pub was, if anything, growing more chaotic with more and more people arriving constantly and the air becoming heavy and foetid with the acrid smell of cigarette smoke and sweat. There was a certain air of desperation in the room which was more than just a striving towards pleasure or a mere search for entertainment, but something deeper and of greater significance, almost as if they had all decided, at the same time and for only for one brief moment, to live somebody else's life. People were talking far too loud, laughing without reason and hugging one another in exaggerated expressions of comradeship. To lose oneself completely in this surging and unpredictable mass of humanity seemed to be their only goal. A few of the tables and chairs positioned around the edges of the pub were still unoccupied, but the centre of the room was practically impassable. People hustled, jostled and rubbed up against one another in a seemingly disconnected and random fashion, except that, if one paid close attention to their behaviour there appeared to be a rhythm, a purpose and a synchronicity to their movements that defined explanation: an incomprehensible dance towards some sort of freedom and oblivion. From this maelstrom of activity Kieran emerged and swaggered his way towards our table, his expression dark and unforgiving. After looking down at us for a second or two and treating us to one of his most scornful looks, he took hold of his drink and, without saying a word, turned on his heels and pushed his way back into the heart of the crowd.

Colin said something, but I couldn't tell exactly what as his words were immediately swallowed up in the vast and endless chatter of the rest of the assembled throng. Words were coming at me from every direction, none of them intended for my ears but all assaulting my senses like the angry rattling of a metal cup against the bars of an iron cage. Conversations were begun and then ended suddenly without reason or completion, or interrupted, or whisked away to hang for a moment suspended in mid-air, vociferous and intense but barely intelligible.

"You can fuck off, I said. I don't do that sort of thing."

"But how was I supposed to know that's what she wanted?"

"No, I said. I'm fine. I've been accused of a lot worse."

"And he killed it. Just as it was about to attack him he took hold of its two front legs and pulled them apart, like a wishbone. It bursts their heart apparently. The police kicked the shit out of him when they got him to the cells."

"It serves her right. She was always a cow."

"No, I can get you one, but it won't be cheap."

"And don't forget the crisps this time."

"He just stood there laughing and it was pissing it down and all his money was all over the road."

"I mean, I told her not to do it, so what did she expect?"

"You can get them in blue or brown."

"You've got to hear this band, they're fucking amazing."

"If she wants him she can have him. I don't care any more."

"Together ... "

"Fucking idiot ..."

"Just for a couple of days ... "

"I never really liked her ... "

So many words. So much confusion. I was happy and sad, alone and with friends, desperate and joyful. Colin, Diana and Jackie were talking. I could see their mouths move and how they leaned towards one another to make themselves understood. I, submerged beneath all of this humanity, could only think of what Vince said to me. Was it true? Did it matter? I was without love, and he knew it. He knew how I existed. I was obvious in my loneliness but I never wished to be found out.

"I should go," I suddenly heard myself say, but not meaning it in the slightest, "I think I'm drunk."

There was, of course, no answer. I had spoken too softly, talking, as it were, to myself. I needed to make a greater effort if I were to be heard, destroying, simply by raising my voice, the effect I was hoping to achieve.

"I should go home," I repeated with just enough volume to attract Diana's attention.

Diana looked at me: "What?"

"I should go home."

"Why?"

"Because I'm drunk." I shouted out the words, suddenly overcome with a feeling of liberation at having at last made myself understood.

"Of course you are," Colin shouted back at me, his wonderful round, red shaven-headed face beaming at me. "That's why you're here."

"No," shouted Diana, "don't go. It's early, and anyway, you're not really drunk."

She was right, of course, and had said exactly what I wanted to hear. In her simple request for me to stay I had heard her say, "Please don't go, Jonathan. I know that you are not truly part of our group and that sometimes you can appear uncaring and that you say very little, but without your presence our lives and our time spent here would be so much less pleasant. You are important to make our day complete."

"No," said Jackie, her pale and empty face thrust towards mine and echoing Diana's sentiment, but with much less conviction, "don't go – and anyway, it's your round."

It didn't actually matter to me whether or not any of them truly meant what they had said. I had threatened to leave, for effect, and with a promptness that I could hardly have expected they had asked me to stay. I was more than satisfied. I had confirmed my presence as part of a group: a collection of individuals that, I believed, didn't seriously hate, patronise or mock me. And if it was my money and my generosity that helped to make me popular, then so be it. I was happy to be accepted on any terms. I just wished, suddenly and unexpectedly and with a strength of feeling that surprised me, that Colin, too, like Vince and Kieran would leave us alone and that there could be just me, Diana and Jackie left, huddled together around our little table; the three of us marooned, but safe and secure in the midst of so much chaos. Despite the failure of my earlier encounters it was only in the company of women that I felt truly able to relax, still vulnerable but confident that my behaviour and personality would not be questioned too harshly. I was even beginning to convince myself that given enough time and the right circumstances we could go some way towards revealing a little of the truth about ourselves, such is the deceptive power of the combination of a too-vivid imagination and copious amounts of alcohol. I would, for instance, have liked to ask Diana why, like Anna, she felt it necessary to sleep with so many men.

Colin managed, once again, to attract the attention of the barmaid and we ordered more drinks, for which I paid. She was wearing a low-cut blouse and as she bent forward to collect the empty glasses she leant perilously close to Colin, almost brushing his cheek with her breasts. For one glorious moment I thought he was going to make a grab for her.

"This is the last time," she said to Colin, in a voice that belied her rebuke. "From now on you'll have to get your own drinks."

Colin watched her greedily as she pushed her way through the crowd, the rolling movement of her buttocks plainly visible beneath her tight cotton skirt. "She's getting on a bit," he said, "and she's not what you'd call pretty, but she's got nice tits. I might have to fuck her later."

He said it as if he were joking, but we all knew that he was perfectly serious and that given any chance at all he would be only to eager to put his plan into action. As usual, the thought that the woman in question might not be exactly euphoric at the prospect of being fucked up against a wall in a back-street car park on a cold winter's night by an overweight, red-faced builder smelling of stale beer and tobacco seemed never to have crossed his mind. He would fuck her and she would be grateful.

"And what if she doesn't want to?" asked Diana, unable to resist teasing him. "What then?"

Colin pretended to be surprised. "What do you mean?" he said, smiling with self-confidence, sitting more upright in his chair and puffing out his chest. "Look at me, I'm gorgeous. How could she refuse? And anyway, she's all over me. Haven't you noticed? She's begging for it."

"And what about your wife?" asked Jackie, quietly, but in all seriousness. "What about her, or doesn't she matter?"

The directness of Jackie's question took none of us by surprise. It was well known that after a few drinks Jackie's desire, almost a need, to speak her mind irrespective of the consequences, often became too strong for her to resist. She was the only one among us who could lay claim, however much she tried to deny it, to having any sort of genuine moral belief or framework by which to live her life: not the invented and spurious morality that the rest of us sometimes adopted when feeling threatened or in need of justifying our actions, but a morality based on history, study, practice and devotion. She had been brought up a Christian, not crushingly so but with enough passion for it to have invaded nearly every aspect of her life. Her presence here, amongst us, was, of course, an act of betrayal: an attempt, futile in conception and in performance, to escape the person that she had become.

When drunk however, her true nature would break free and, perhaps, take even her by surprise by the depth of its commitment to a life that she had hoped to escape. Often she would lecture Diana, to no great effect, on the impropriety of her behaviour: on her careless disregard for her physical, mental and spiritual well-being. Diana, as usual, would take every well-intentioned rebuke with her usual calm and smiling acquiescence. "It's just me," Diana would say. "I don't know how else to behave."

"She shouldn't be here," I thought. "Jackie is not one of us. Oh, she would like to be, but her true nature will eventually win out and it is only because of her love for, and her friendship with Diana that she continues with this pretence at all. God will eventually find her out and then she will discover, at long last, something truly respectable to believe in: something to make her life worth while."

"I don't have a wife," said Colin, coldly, "at least, not when I'm out; and it's really none of your business, is it?"

"Of course it is," insisted Jackie, refusing, much to my surprise, to be intimidated by Colin's aggressive response. "It's everybody's business. We all have to live together, to treat everyone with respect. That's what makes us human. If one person is hurt then we all suffer." As Jackie became more and more animated her voice rose almost to a squeak and two tiny points of colour appeared on her thin and pallid cheeks, giving her the somewhat tragic appearance of a disappointed clown. "There are things we should and things we shouldn't do, for our own good and for our own peace of mind. Everything has to be paid for. Everything has to be accounted for. Don't you understand, Colin, when you betray somebody it's you that's being betrayed and it's you that will suffer the most." And she looked at Colin with such sadness and such pity and desperation in her eyes that I could almost have wept.

For a moment Colin did nothing, and then very slowly and very carefully he took a mouthful of his drink and then, with equal deliberation, returned the glass to the table. He leant forward and wiped his mouth with the back of his hand. For a split second I feared that he was going to hit her.

"Don't – you – ever – talk – to – me – like – that – again," he hissed, drawing out his words as if he were talking to an idiot.

"Who the fuck do you think you are to tell me what to do? I'll tell you who you are: a fucking nobody, that's who; a boring, pathetic fucking nobody who's too scared and too fucking ugly to do anything. Get yourself a fucking life or fuck off and leave us all in peace."

While Colin was speaking it seemed as if a hush had fallen on the pub, although his words could have been heard by nobody but us. This was Colin's moment, his one chance of the evening to offer up a performance of belief and character, and he had risen to the challenge superbly. He reached once more for his glass and then, in a final act of bravado, leaned back in his chair and turned his attention elsewhere. Jackie had been well and truly chastised for her temerity in commenting on Colin's behaviour and the whole incident was now considered over. For Colin, Jackie's feelings and beliefs, even her presence at our table was now no longer of any importance.

Jackie, too, reached for her drink and all but buried her head in the glass, while Diana placed a reassuring hand beneath the table on Jackie's knee. She moved closer towards Jackie and whispered something in her ear, causing Jackie to smile. Obviously Jackie was shaken by Colin's sudden outburst, but she was not totally crushed. In her head she still knew that she was right.

"Why do we always come to this place?" she said, directing her question to both Diana and me. "It's so boring. Why can't we do something different, something exciting for once?"

Diana and I exchanged a brief look of understanding. We both knew that 'excitement' was the last thing that Jackie really craved or needed, and that her only hope of salvation lay in a life of security and boredom.

"Where else would we go?" I asked.

"Anywhere," Jackie said, "just somewhere different."

"I can't think of anywhere I'd rather be," I said in all honesty. "Nothing is quite as ridiculous or as entertaining as this."

Diana smiled at me as if to say: "I understand exactly what you mean."

Kieran suddenly reappeared at our table, looking more distracted and agitated than usual. "Where's my drink?"

I passed him his glass. He refused to sit down but lurked above us, his eyes continually darting around the room as if he expected at any moment to be accosted by some unknown assailant.

"Why don't you sit down?" said Diana. "You're making me nervous."

"I only came for my drink," he answered without looking at her. "I'm mingling." The word seemed to give him some amusement and he couldn't help but repeat it: "Mingling," he said, his face breaking into a grin. "Just mingling."

"If you get into any trouble I'm not helping you out," said Colin, understanding Kieran's mood immediately. "I mean it, Kieran, this time you're on your own."

I expected Kieran to react angrily or, at least, to question Colin's rebuke, but he showed no emotion at all, merely continued to drink and to stare about him as if almost oblivious to our presence. I had seen him like this before, remote and apparently obsessed by some inner passion, and usually on occasions just like this one, when the mere sight of a group of people obviously enjoying themselves and drawn together by a common cause seemed to drive him almost to the edge of madness. He would need to strike first, just to defend himself and to prove himself capable.

"Is there going to be trouble?" asked Jackie, rather nervously. "Is someone threatening Kieran?"

"No, everything's fine," said Diana. "Nobody's threatening anybody."

"You have to watch these people," Kieran suddenly said, still looking around him. "They're not safe. They get a few drinks inside them and they think they're somebody else. It's because their lives are so fucking boring. They go on from day to day, following the same old routine, doing what they're told, yes sir, no sir, of course sir, it's a pleasure sir, a fucking honour sir. And then they come out for one night of the week with the wife or the girl friend or their mates, have a few beers and suddenly they think they're fucking Superman. They're fucking cowards, that's what they are, fucking cowards, the lot of them." This last was uttered so loudly that some of the people standing closest to us turned and looked in our direction.

"They're just people," said Diana, in an attempt to keep everything calm. "They're just having fun; they're harmless."

"No they're not," said Kieran. "They're fucking dangerous. They'd have us all the same as them. That's what they really want. They can't stand us being different. Turn your back for a second and they'll destroy you. Given half a chance and they'd kill us all."

"For Christ's sake, Kieran," said Colin, no longer able to contain himself. "What the fuck are you talking about? You think that everybody in this pub hates you and wants to kill you because you're not like them? Have you any idea just how fucking stupid you sound, how insane? Everybody in this pub hates you and wants to kill you because – what – they all envy you? Is that what you're saying?"

"I have freedom," said Kieran, his voice slow and steady, "and that's what they can't stand. I can do whatever I want and it frightens them."

"Kieran," said Colin, "why don't you just take a close look at yourself? You have no possessions, you live in a squat, any money you have you either steal or scrounge from your mates, you're a drunk and you take too many drugs. For fuck's sake, Kieran, your life's a mess. Most of the time you can't even feed yourself. What sort of freedom is that?"

"You just don't understand, do you?" said Kieran, draining the last of his drink. "None of you. But I'll show you. I'll show all of you. Then you'll see I was right."

He turned away from us and, using far too much force, pushed his way through the crowd, picking up a drink from somebody else's table as he did so.

For a moment or two we all sat in silence, too stunned and too preoccupied with our own thoughts to think of anything appropriate to say.

"I mean it," said Colin. "If he gets into any trouble he's on his own. I'm sick of helping him out. Fucking idiot."

"I think we should go," said Jackie. "I don't like it here any more."

"I'm not going anywhere," said Colin, lighting a cigarette. "If Kieran wants to act like a raving lunatic then that's his problem. It's got nothing to do with me."

Jackie and I looked at Diana, waiting for her response. If she said that she, too, wanted to leave then I would have to go with them, as there was no way that I could face the prospect of remaining there with just Colin. Amongst a group of people I could remain silent and watchful without drawing too much attention to myself, but with just the two of us the pressure on me to participate in some sort of dialogue would be almost too much to bear.

"I think we ought to stay," said Diana, again placing a reassuring hand on Jackie's knee, "just in case Kieran needs us."

"And what good do you think *you'll* be?" asked Colin. "He's off in a world of his own and he couldn't give a damn if you're there or not. If you're going to stay then do it because you want to, not because of him."

"He's right," said Jackie. "There's nothing we can do. I really think we ought to go."

"I can't," said Diana, more forcefully. "I know he's a fool and he doesn't care whether I'm here or not, but he's my friend and I can't just walk out on him. But if *you* want to go, Jackie, then that's fine. I understand."

The pressure now put on Jackie to reach a decision seemed intolerable, but we all knew that whatever the circumstances she would never willingly leave Diana.

"No," said Jackie, after only a moment's hesitation, but in such a way that it seemed as if it were Jackie who was doing Diana the favour, "if you're staying then so am I."

I felt extraordinarily relieved, not just because the possibility of having to spend some time alone with Colin had been removed, but because I could now continue to watch, until the final act, the sad little drama that was unfurling before me; for I was in no doubt that this was Kieran's show and that he had been intent upon creating just such a performance as this from the moment he had entered the pub. Silently, I congratulated him upon his timing and his choice of cast, audience and venue. I couldn't have done better myself.

The pub was by this time almost full to capacity, with all the tables occupied and even more people gathered in front of the bar and standing in little groups around the edges of the room, arranged around a small central, empty space. The noise was colossal and exhilarating: the continual crashing drone of the juke box, too loud and too distorted for any particular song to be differentiated from any other; the laughter, shouts, ordering of drinks and endless chatter of the customers, suddenly subsiding and then lifting again to full volume as if under the direction of some invisible conductor; the regular thump of glasses and bottles being banged down on beer-stained tables and the screech of chair legs being dragged and scraped across bare wooden floorboards. And the lighting, too, played its part: faint and shadowy in the half-hidden recesses and outer reaches of the room, but slowly gaining in power until it reached its full, glorious intensity directly above the bar, where it was reflected even more brightly in the long rows of shiny coloured bottles and in the large and highly polished Victorian mirror. The setting could not have been more perfect.

The conversation between Colin, Diana and Jackie as to the state of Kieran's mental health continued while I bought more drinks, with Colin again working his charm on the barmaid. As we drank and smoked and talked I kept my eye on the corner of the room where I knew Kieran to be, occasionally catching sight of him, apparently deep in conversation with three or four other men.

The violence, when it eventually came, was as sudden and as explosive as befitted such a place and such an occasion. The first blow was thrown (it was impossible from where I was sitting to see exactly by whom) and a space suddenly appeared around Kieran and his opponent: a stocky, well-built individual wearing a pair of baggy, blue denim jeans and a white, short-sleeved T-shirt, standing a good four inches taller than Kieran. Now I could see Kieran's face quite clearly: his eyes were bright, alert and sparkling, and he was smiling a wonderful, broad smile of liberation. This was the moment that he had worked so purposefully towards, and it was obvious that he had no intention of disappointing either himself or his audience. In one quick movement that almost took my breath away with its pure athleticism Kieran seemed actually to leave the ground and to hang suspended in mid-air for a second or two as he hurled himself forwards and upwards, smashing his head deep into the face of his opponent. The man, taken completely by surprise and with blood already pouring from a cut across the bridge of his nose, fell backwards, landing in a heap on the floor in the open space (left empty on purpose, it would seem, for just such an event as this) in the very centre of the pub. Exactly, I suspected, where Kieran had wanted him to be.

Now that he had attracted the attention of the whole pub Kieran could set to work in earnest. He took two strides forward. Without hesitation, in an act of violence that was almost frightening in its calm and calculated indifference, he swung his right leg backwards and then, with great force, forwards, kicking the prostrate body of his opponent deep in the pit of his stomach.

"Oh Christ," said Colin, shaking his head, "here we go again."

"I told you we should have left," said Jackie, genuinely frightened and shuffling her chair backwards, away from the scene of the violence. "Now it's too late."

There was only a moment's pause before Kieran struck out once more, this time aiming the blow at the head and face of his victim. Kieran's boot made contact with the man's face and he groaned and instinctively attempted to protect himself from further damage by drawing up his knees tightly to his chest and covering his head with his arms. Kieran took a step backwards and, like an artist viewing his latest creation, looked down critically at the defeated body of his opponent. Apart from the never-ending noise of the jukebox the whole pub had fallen silent; focused and expectant, both fascinated and shocked into inactivity. "It's not over yet," I thought. "How could it be when Kieran is the centre of so much attention?"

Kieran took a deep breath, wiped his mouth with the back of his hand and took another slow step forward. "He's never going to stop," I thought. "Not even when there remains nothing left of his victim but a shapeless and unrecognizable bloody mess." And I had a sudden vision of Kieran's leg swinging back and forth for ever like some demonic pendulum.

"Do something," said Jackie to Colin. "I can't bear it. Please make him stop."

"I don't think there's any need," said Colin, as two men suddenly broke away from the crowd and took hold of Kieran's arms, pinning them behind his back. "I think he's finished."

A third man approached the struggling group and stood for a moment before Kieran as if determined to enjoy to the full the sight of his incapacity, before he drove his fist with obvious pleasure and great force into the centre of Kieran's stomach. He hit twice more before Kieran was released and allowed to crumple inelegantly to the floor.

'Well, that was fun," said Colin, turning away dismissively from the action and reaching for his drink. "Perhaps now we can have some peace and quiet."

Diana made as if to stand up to go to Kieran's assistance but Jackie grasped her arm. "No – please don't – just leave him – don't get involved."

For a few moments more the crowd looked down on the two fallen figures, then their attention gradually drifted away and Kieran's opponent was helped to his feet by two of his friends. The landlord, a short, squat military-looking gentleman with a small grey moustache, obviously used to such incidents, sauntered casually over to Kieran. "Come on," he said, apparently without malice, and reaching down and grasping Kieran by the arm, "I think it's time you went home."

I was not convinced. Like any good production I couldn't believe that all this – the noise, the lights, the people, the whole dramatic situation had been brought together simply as a background to that one short and unsatisfactory episode; Kieran, I knew instinctively, would demand more. Brusquely, but not unkindly, the landlord helped Kieran to his feet and for a moment or two they stood facing one another while Kieran stretched and arched his back.

"Go home, Kieran," said the landlord. "Go home, sober up and stop acting like a bloody fool."

Kieran's expression was a wonder to behold: all the hate, despair and frustration that had raged within him were plainly visible in the fixed and distant glare of his gaze and the thin slit of his tightly drawn lips. I doubted if, at that exact moment, he even knew or cared any more exactly who or where he was.

The landlord turned and walked away, his mind already set on the next customer to be served and the next drink to be poured.

When Kieran produced his knife from his pocket I almost applauded, such was my joy at witnessing this obvious and ridiculous gesture of defiance. I just knew that he wouldn't let me down. However irrational Kieran's behaviour seemed to be,

I was under no illusion that at that precise moment Kieran intended to do real harm to somebody. With the knife held out before him he moved towards the landlord, seeing in him, no doubt, the last person to have caused him offence and therefore a genuine target for all his rage. A cry went up simultaneously from several of the customers; obviously I was not the only one unconvinced by Kieran's apparent defeat. The landlord spun round almost as Kieran was on him and managed somehow to grasp the hand that held the knife. Despite the landlord's desperate action there was no doubt that things would have gone badly for him had not two or three of the other customers intervened again. Kieran was grabbed from behind and held fast while the assault on him began; only this time, no restraint would be shown until Kieran had been incapacitated completely. A fight in a pub was a common occurrence, almost an accepted aspect of a good night out, but the use of any weapon was considered practically an act of terrorism: a savage blow aimed at the very heart of decency and correct behaviour. As such, the miscreant had to be dealt with severely. Kieran was held and hit again and again and again until he was forced to drop the knife, but even then the attack continued unabated, such was their appetite for revenge and justice. Nobody would object and nobody would interfere, so powerful a figure of hate and disgust had Kieran become.

"They're never going to stop," said Jackie.

"They're going to kill him," said Diana.

"It's his own fault," said Colin.

"This isn't right," said Diana.

"It's not fair," said Jackie.

Colin shrugged and the attack continued. "Perhaps they'll get tired," he said.

"Shouldn't the landlord do something?" said Jackie.

"He tried to kill him, remember," said Colin.

"We could call the police," said Diana.

"It's a Friday night," said Colin. "They'll be busy."

"Still," I said, "it does seem a little unfair." I was enjoying the show but I too was beginning to fear for Kieran's life. I didn't mind him being hurt, but I didn't want him dead; at least, not yet. There was still much pleasure and entertainment, I believed, to be had from Kieran's continued presence in the world.

"There must be something we can do," said Diana.

"There has to be," said Jackie.

"We can't just sit here and watch," said Diana.

"We could always look the other way," said Colin, "or order another drink. I still fancy that barmaid."

We continued to watch, unable to focus on anything else. Nobody called the police. Nobody turned away. Nobody left the pub.

"This is never going to end," said Diana, almost in tears. "This will last for ever."

"Oh for fuck's sake," said Colin, his patience at last giving out completely. "Why can't we have just a little bit of peace and quiet, just for one fucking night? I wouldn't mind, but I don't even like the guy." And in one swift movement he stood up and pushed the table away from him with such force that glasses were knocked over and drinks spilt. "O.K. that's enough," he shouted, pushing his way through the crowd. "Let him go. You're going to kill him." The three men holding on to Kieran hesitated. "Look," said Colin, "I couldn't give a fuck about this little twat. In fact, I'm almost tempted to join in. But he's not worth going to prison for. Leave him to me. I'll sort him out." Colin looked magnificent. His face bright red, his fists clenched by his side, his body stock-still and as solid as a block of granite. Perhaps relieved to have been given an excuse to retire with dignity, the three men let go of Kieran and slowly backed away. Gradually, sensing that the action was now well and truly over, the crowd began to lose interest. Soon only Colin and Kieran were left in the centre of the room, remote and ignored.

Kieran was on his hands and knees, his head hanging forward and his long, lank hair shielding his face. "Can you get up," asked Colin, "or do you want some help?" Kieran didn't move. "You never fucking learn, do you Kieran? I couldn't give a shit what you do, as long as it doesn't involve me. Do you understand? If you want to get yourself killed then fucking great, in fact it would be a relief, but do it somewhere else and preferably when I'm not around. I mean, what the fuck's the matter with you? Do you think you can beat everybody in the whole world? I'm not your fucking minder and if it wasn't for Diana whining on I wouldn't have helped you now. Do you want to die, is that it? Because if you do, why don't you do us all a favour and throw yourself under a fucking train? And if you can't do that then at least stop acting like a fucking moron. Now get up."

Kieran still hadn't moved, but a change had come over him. There appeared to be a slight trembling about his neck and shoulders as if he were in the throes of some sort of fit, and even as I watched his head fell further forward until it was almost resting on the floor. "He's really hurt," I thought. "They really have damaged him." And then I heard the noise: a deep, gurgling rumble like the slow closing of an old iron gate. "Jesus Christ," I thought, as the truth suddenly hit me, "he's laughing. I don't believe it. He's actually laughing."

Very slowly Kieran sat back on his haunches and lifted up his head so that his hair fell away from his face. He opened his mouth wide and began to roar with uncontrollable laughter. It was a sight both horrible and fascinating to witness. His face was battered and bruised and covered with blood; his top lip was torn and already bloated, and as he threw back his head in joy and merriment one could see a gap where his front teeth should have been. His laughter was so prolonged, so loud and so spontaneous that even Colin was stunned into inactivity.

"Get him out of here," hissed the landlord who had come to stand by Colin's side. "I don't care how you do it just get him out of here. He's not right in the head."

Colin nodded and moved forward to take hold of one of Kieran's arms. At first Kieran seemed only too happy to allow Colin to raise him to his feet, but suddenly he resisted and looked wildly about him. "My knife," he spluttered, spraying blood and saliva onto the front of his jacket. "Where's my knife? I'm not leaving without it. Who's got my knife?" Such was the desperation in his voice that practically everyone sitting or standing close by began to search the floor, probably against their better judgment. I, too, looked down at the floor.

It was, in truth, a beautiful object and for a moment I even considered keeping it. Trying not to draw too much attention to myself, I bent down and picked it up, and under the cover of the table began carefully to examine it, passing it from hand to hand and running my fingers gently along the handle and blade. The blade was some six or seven inches long and so highly polished that it seemed, whichever way I turned it, to gather and to reflect all the available light in the room. The handle was of a simple design and appeared to have been carved from a single piece of bone or ivory. Kieran called out again for the return of his knife, but still I was loath to let go of such a potent symbol of his power. Perhaps I believed that while I possessed his knife Kieran would somehow be under my control or that

I might even, by some magical transference of knowledge, gain some insight into his troubled mind.

"Keep looking," said the landlord. "It's got to be here somewhere, and the sooner we find it the sooner we can get rid of him."

Kieran had ceased to shout or even to say anything at all and had returned to his earlier posture of apparent defeat and desolation. I could no longer bear to see him in so much pain. Carefully I closed the blade, stood up and made my way across the room. Without saying a word I bent down and held the knife out towards him. He hesitated for just a moment before taking hold of the knife and lifting up his head to look at me. It was hard to tell on such a broken and damaged face but I like to believe that he might even have smiled at me.

"Right," said the landlord, "now fuck off and don't come back."

Colin half carried, half dragged Kieran out of the front door and I returned to my seat. The landlord, the barmaid and some of the customers began to pick up the upturned tables and chairs and to clear away the broken glass and spilt ashtrays. Within a surprisingly short period of time practically everything had returned to normal, except now there was a subtle change in the atmosphere. The relief that it was all over was obvious, but there still remained in the air a barely subdued sense of excitement. It was as if everyone somehow felt proud and privileged to have been involved, even as mere spectators, in such an outrageous episode. People began to laugh too much and too vigorously, and to go over the incidents leading up to the fight, and the fight itself, time and time again, as if it were thought necessary to lodge the event securely in their minds so as to be able to repeat the story later, with passion if not accuracy, for the benefit of friends and family. Even the landlord, long after he had retired, would no doubt continue to tell the story, placing himself at the heart of the action, of course.

"But weren't you frightened?" someone would ask.

"It must have been awful for you," someone else would say.

"You must have been glad to leave it all behind you," another would comment, placing a sympathetic hand on the landlord's shoulder.

And the landlord would puff out his chest and say, "Well, actually, it wasn't that bad. In their own way they were quite a good crowd; a little wild, perhaps, some of them, but it was just a case of knowing how to handle them. My army training helped of course. I quite enjoyed it, really."

I doubted if the landlord would remember me.

After a few minutes Colin returned and heaved himself into his chair in an exaggerated show of exhaustion. Almost immediately the barmaid appeared and, more affectionate than ever, handed Colin a pint of bitter. "Compliments of the house," she said, adding with a smile, "I think you deserve a treat after what you've done."

There was no mistaking her intentions and after she'd left Colin said, "I think this evening could turn out all right after all."

"Where is he?' asked Diana.

"Just outside," answered Colin, taking a large mouthful of his drink, "propped up against the pub wall."

"Is he all right?" asked Jackie.

"How the fuck should I know?" he said. "I've done my bit."

"You shouldn't have left him there, "said Diana. "Couldn't you have taken him home?"

"No," answered Colin, "I couldn't. He wouldn't have gone anyway. He said he just wanted to be left alone – which suited me fine."

"I think I ought to go to him, "said Diana, "just to make sure he's OK."

"Just leave him," said Colin, in exasperation. "Why do you always have to get involved? Why can't you just leave people alone? What the fuck's the matter with you?"

Diana fell silent. Now it was Jackie's turn to comfort Diana. "He's dangerous," she said gently. "There's nothing you can do. It's not that he's lonely or depressed or frustrated or anything like that. He's really ill. One day he'll have to be locked up, for his own good and for everybody else's."

"One day he will be," I said, almost in sorrow, "that's something I'm certain of."

Diana sighed heavily, and we looked sadly at one another. I never thought for one moment that Diana was physically attracted to Kieran for, despite her obvious concern as a friend for his well-being, she was only too well aware of his real nature and of the cruelty that he was capable of inflicting on those around him. But like me, although perhaps for different reasons, Kieran's life and presence brought a heightened sense of awareness to her own existence. In our own way we both needed Kieran to be there, to show us how not to live.

"I just want to help him, that's all," she said. "Is that so wrong? He's still my friend whatever he does, and friends help one another."

"Leave him alone," Jackie said. "There's nothing you can do, and you might get hurt."

"You're wasting your breath," said Colin spitefully. "If she wants to be a martyr, then let her. She won't be happy until she's suffered and we all have to comfort her and tell her how brave she's been. She pretends she's doing it out of love or friendship but really it's just a form of arrogance. She should be the Christian, Jackie, not you."

This little outburst managed to offend both Jackie and Diana and we all fell into an uneasy silence, each of us wrapped up in our own tiny thoughts. Jackie, no doubt, was wondering when she'd have the courage to leave Diana and all this chaos behind her and go in search of the life for which she was truly intended; Diana was probably imagining herself soothing away all of Kieran's troubles and being thanked for her patience and understanding; Colin, from the way his eyes followed the barmaid around the room, was thinking only of the fuck that was to come; and I could think only of the knife that I had held for that one brief moment, of its weight, shape and texture and of the damage that it could inflict.

We continued drinking for another hour or so, but my heart was no longer in it. From the heights of Kieran's violence and the excitement that it had engendered in me I seemed to have sunk into a sort of appalled lethargy, an abstract melancholy without any direct cause or reason. Nothing entertained me. Perhaps it was just the effects of the alcohol but everything now seemed beyond my understanding. The babble of conversation around me became just that: a babble, a continuous and indiscriminate growl and snarl of meaningless noises. For a brief moment I even failed to recognize my three companions. Their faces meant nothing to me: just a random arrangement of eyes, mouths, noses, cheeks and hair. They could have been anybody masquerading as people that I once knew. I longed to ask them who they were, what were they doing there and what had they to do with me, but even in such an advanced state of dislocation

I knew that any such question would be deemed ridiculous and, quite rightly, treated as such.

The evening had, for me, lost all purpose. I needed to leave. The show was over and soon the cleaners would arrive to sweep the stage clean. There would be no encore. I finished my drink and waited. Colin's, Diana's and Jackie's interest was directed elsewhere. Now was the right time to leave but I found myself incapable of movement. I measured the distance from my seat to the door. I imagined myself standing up, wishing everyone goodnight and striding towards the exit, but nothing happened. It wasn't just the effects of the drink but my own reluctance to leave one situation for another, however uncomfortable my present position seemed. I took a deep breath and lifted my empty glass to my lips, pretending to drink. Such an action, I reasoned would be the signal for me to start my journey. "Come on, Jonathan," I told myself, "keep moving. You know what it's like. Movement: that's the only thing that matters. You must keep putting one foot in front of another." I set my glass down and before I knew what was happening I had stood up and left the table, unnoticed and without saying goodbye, and was making my way unsteadily towards the door. I had in my head not the image of the world outside the pub, but of the interior of my own secluded flat. That would be my goal and that would be my reason to keep moving. As I left the pub I wondered if the landlord would note my departure with, if nothing else, just a nod of his head or a casual wave of his hand, but as usual he said and did nothing.

Once through the open door and out into the darkness and the rain, I took two or three deep breaths and then relaxed. I felt a surge of pride at having negotiated my departure so expertly. If I had not gone then, the moment would have been lost for ever and my sense of isolation and hopelessness would have steadily increased until it became the only emotion left open to me, governing and overriding everything else, and the evening would have been a complete failure. As it was, once I reached home, I could concentrate fully on Kieran's performance, reliving over and over again the events of the evening and the role that I had played in them.

In the dark and the rain I set off to walk the half mile home, noting as I left the pub behind me that there was no sign of Kieran, not even a splash of blood to show where he had been. Perhaps the rain had washed it all away.

I loved my flat, so lacking in personality that even my being there could add nothing to its general air of refined banality. I turned on the small lamp by the side of my mattress and made my way into the kitchen. Despite the vast amount of alcohol I had already consumed, I poured myself another large whisky. This was a different drink to the ones I had been drinking in the pub: then I had been drinking for the benefit of other people, now I was drinking purely for me.

I returned to the sitting room, carrying the bottle and the glass with me, and went to stand by the window. The curtains were drawn back and, standing a little to one side, I looked out into the darkness and across to the block of flats opposite.

She was still not there.

It seemed to me that my whole life had been spent in waiting for something to happen, waiting for others to entertain or to educate me. As a small boy, when not reading or marching my thin line of troops up and down the living room carpet, I would often play in an old, derelict mill set in two or three acres of waste land close to my home; a desolate spot (or so it seemed to me then), wild and overgrown with stunted hawthorn bushes, rose-bay-willow herb and rampaging fields of nettle and thistle. I spent so much of my spare time there that eventually I came think of it as a necessary part of my life: a place that helped to define me as a unique human being. I would look out from one of the high, mill windows, believing myself to be secure and invulnerable, and gaze abstractedly out on the world around me. It was there that I learnt that people could only be truly themselves when they thought they were alone.

In winter or when the days were cold and damp there would be only the bleak and abandoned landscape to stir my imagination; a landscape that I had grown to know so well that any deviation, however slight, in its composition would attract my attention immediately. The merest glimpse of a screwed-up empty cigarette packet, a broken bottle, a brightly coloured plastic bag or, more provocatively, a discarded piece of clothing was enough to send me into the deepest despair. I would be forced into imagining the type of person who could be capable of committing such an outrage, who could desecrate so carelessly what was, after all, my domain. How I loathed them all.

In summer, however, occasionally there were real people to keep me entertained, people who believed themselves to be unobserved: the girl, young and pretty, who lifted up her blue and white skirt and squatted down directly beneath my window; the man and the woman who lay down amongst the weeds and nettles, his hands slowly removing most of her clothes to give me my first glimpse of a woman's naked body; the woman who sat alone to read and to sunbathe, but whose hands continually strayed inside her blouse or beneath her skirt. Nothing seemed forbidden to me, and no act, however private or human remained hidden from my sight.

It was there and during those long and sometimes lonely days that I first began to masturbate with true passion, concentrating not just on my pleasure, on the regular movement of my hand, but on the pleasure that I could imagine being experienced by other people. And if I ever felt guilty at my voyeuristic behaviour, crouched on the filthy floor or secreted at the side of the broken window, then I absolved myself by telling myself that it was not I who went in search of such sights, but all that I had to do was to remain still and observant and that all such sights would eventually come unbidden (if not unexpected or unwelcome) to me.

I participated, if only vicariously, in so many similar episodes that it was only a matter of time before I began to believe that not only were they being performed solely for my benefit, but that without my distant presence such events would never take place at all. I was the centre around which the whole world seemed to revolve and at such times I had no desire to be anywhere else. To live one's life as a permanent spectator seemed to me, then, to be the most ideal form of existence: involved but untouchable.

Convinced that it was now too late for the woman in the flat opposite to make an appearance, I turned away from the window and went to sit by my collection of paints and my blank sheet of hardboard. I silently congratulated myself on the fact that I had created nothing, nothing of which other people could be dismissive or, god help me, congratulatory. I needed to live without expectation – even of failure.

I think I must have dozed or, at the very least, fallen into some sort of reverie, for when the knock on the door came I hardly realised it what it was for a second or two. Perhaps it was just a thumping in my head (I was used to such things) or the beginning of a dream or an incursion into a reality that wasn't mine and of which I had no knowledge. I waited with interest, still barely aware of where or what I was, just to see if the noise would repeat itself. When it came again I had to admit that there was something demanding my attention and that some sort of movement was necessary. People rarely called on me at such an hour (I had no idea exactly what the time was, I just knew that it was late) so, even in my befuddled state of half-sleep and drunkenness, my expectations of it being something of importance, perhaps even the beginning of an adventure, were high.

I opened the door and Kieran pushed past me. That was probably the last thing I had expected, as he had never called on me before. Quite dumbfounded, I remained for a moment or two staring out into the dark and deserted hallway.

When, eventually, I did return to the sitting room, it seemed that my flat had already ceased to be mine, such was the power of his presence.

He had already discovered the whisky and was drinking greedily from the bottle. I remained standing by the sitting room door, trying desperately to make some sense of his being there. It seemed a most grotesque and unwelcome intrusion into my life. My relationship with Kieran, such as it was, depended on my ability to pick and choose the moment of our meeting and to dip for an hour or two into *his* life and then return unscathed to the relative safety of mine. For him to be there, now, standing before me, apparently unconcerned about the chaos he was bound to bring seemed to me almost an act of sabotage. What possible reason could he have for calling on me? I wasn't even aware that he knew where I lived. What did he want of me? Had he confused me with somebody else? Was he so distraught by his recent beating that he had lost control of his senses? Nothing seemed to make any sense and I had neither the courage nor the composure to ask him such questions.

And then, as if aware of my agitation: "I had nowhere else to go." This was said neither in desperation nor as an apology, but stated simply as a matter of fact.

I moved hesitantly into the centre of the room. "I am the host," I thought, somewhat bizarrely. "Something is expected of me." I should make an effort and engage him in meaningful conversation. Ask him how he enjoyed being beaten up and did he consider it a worthwhile experience. Did he hold any grudges against his assailants and would he repeat the exercise. Was he in great pain and was his knife still safe. Instead, perhaps because I was trying too hard to please or just because I was so tense, I suddenly heard myself begin to babble. "Can I get you anything, a cup of tea or coffee or something to eat? I haven't got much in but I could do you some toast. I wasn't expecting visitors. Actually I don't get many visitors at all, which is odd since I live right in the centre of town. Maybe it's because I'm on the eighteenth floor and the lift isn't always working. Or it could be just me of course."

"Only with Kieran," I thought, as I continued to ramble on, "would I behave so out of character."

Slowly he turned to look at me. Even in the half light of the room one could see only too clearly the results of his violent encounter in the pub: blood was still smeared across his cheeks and beneath his nose, one side of his mouth was twisted almost beyond recognition and one eye was so badly swollen as to seem to be almost useless. When he raised his right arm to take in yet another great mouthful of whisky he gave off an almost overpowering smell of sweat, cigarettes, alcohol, blood and dirt. It was such a perfect vision, with his black leather jacket, tight blue jeans, long greasy hair and bloody face, of the lone street fighter, of the heroic thug and the rebel that, for a moment, I could hardly take him seriously. "He's made himself up for the occasion," I thought, "just to impress me." And as if to continue the deception he took another mouthful of whisky and said: "I think I've killed somebody."

I was so taken aback that I had no idea how to react. I don't think I understood his statement as having any basis in reality. It meant nothing to me. It was just Kieran being Kieran and telling me that he was Kieran. In a confused haze of remembrance I quickly went over the events of that evening. There had been a violent, nasty and bloody encounter, certainly, but nothing so particularly out of the ordinary as to result in Kieran having to make such an outlandish confession. Nobody, to my knowledge, had died.

I watched him drink. I watched the pressure of his lips, the suction of his mouth and the regular beat of his Adam's apple. His head was thrown back, his hair hung over his shoulders and his skin gleamed pale and damp in the glow from the single lamp positioned by the side of my mattress – and suddenly I knew that he was telling me the truth. "Who have you killed?" I said. "I don't understand."

He lowered the bottle. "You believe me then?"

"Of course," I said, "why should you lie?"

Slowly he wiped his mouth with the back of his hand, but made no reply. I suddenly understood that this teasing was to him a crucial part of the performance. He turned his back on me and crossed to the window. "Which flat is it?"

'What?"

"Which flat is it?"

"I don't know what you're talking about."

"The one where the woman walks around naked. Colin told me all about it."

It was true that one drunken night I had told Colin all about my neighbour's nighttime activities, but it was a confession that I had regretted making almost immediately and one that I had begged him never to repeat. She performed regularly for me, totally aware of my presence, pretending to try on clothes or to dry herself after a bath, posing before a mirror that might or might not exist. If we had ever met face to face, while out shopping or crossing the narrow expanse of concrete that separated our two blocks of flats, we would have made a point of ignoring one another. Ours, despite the obvious physicality involved, was primarily a relationship of the imagination, and despite or possibly because of that, it was a relationship of which I was immensely protective. I had no intention of sharing her with anyone, Kieran least of all.

I joined Kieran at the window, looked out and thanked god that her flat was still in darkness. "I don't know what Colin's talking about," I said. "I've never seen anything."

He turned and smiled his broken smile at me, almost fiendish in the half-light.

"If you say so," he said, knowingly. "It's a pity though. I could do with a wank."

I watched him as he moved away from the window, his shoulders taut and hunched beneath his crumpled leather jacket. If I was at all shocked it was not with the spontaneous use of such a word, that came as no surprise at all, but with the realisation that if the woman had been visible he would almost certainly have masturbated there and then, despite my presence. And suddenly I had a vision of Kieran in prison. There, I had no doubt, he would survive wonderfully, perhaps even thrive. The question of his sexuality or how he would satisfy his desires would never be an issue: shame and embarrassment were emotions unknown to Kieran and he would simply act as the situation or his nature demanded.

He took another mouthful of whisky and began idly to wander about the room, stopping every now and then to investigate some object or other, or to flick disinterestedly through the pages of some book whose title or cover had caught his eye. He returned nothing to its rightful place.

I was eager to know everything, but I knew better than to push him for an explanation. This was *his* show. "You look terrible," I said. "You ought to go to hospital."

"Right," he said disdainfully, "and why don't I go to the police as well? I'm sure they'd be glad to see me."

In truth, I cared nothing for Kieran's health and perhaps I was even a little bit thrilled to be in the presence of someone who had obviously suffered so much physical damage. I was waiting only for Kieran to tell me everything and, by implication, to bring me into his story.

"I might have to stay here for a few days," he said casually, adding, in a tone of voice that removed any possibility of disagreement, "that is, of course, if you don't mind."

"No, of course not," I said, "you're very welcome."

The politeness of my response seemed to amuse him. "Oh good," he said, "how kind."

Like a wild animal investigating for the first time the confines of a new lair, Kieran continued to wander around my flat, opening and closing drawers and peering into cupboards. I had, with great effort, to stifle my natural outrage at such an intrusion but if I wished to participate in this adventure I could hardly expect not to have to suffer such indignities.

Finally, apparently reasonably satisfied with his new lodgings, Kieran threw himself down on my mattress and began to roll himself a cigarette. "So," he began, speaking at the same time as his tongue flicked over the edge of the cigarette paper, "what's it like to have a murderer as a guest, then?"

"Is that what you are: a murderer?"

"Oh I think so. There was a lot of blood, not that that means anything of course. I've seen people bleed like a fucking fountain and there's been hardly any damage at all. But yes, I think he's dead."

"Who was he?"

"How the fuck should I know? We didn't introduce ourselves."

"Not somebody from the pub?"

"No, not somebody from the pub; I got thrown out of there, remember."

"I know, but you could have met up later."

"Well, we didn't."

"And you're sure this person, whoever he is, is dead?"

"For fuck's sake, Jonathan, what do you want me to do, take you there and show you the fucking body? He's dead and I killed him, and that's that."

"OK," I said, only too aware of his rising anger, "I'm sorry. I just wanted to be certain, that's all."

Kieran took another drink and we fell into silence. I sat on the chair close by the paints and the sheet of hardboard. We smoked and we drank and I waited. Soon he would have to tell me everything. How could Kieran, who had lived most of his life in public, not share with somebody else what was possibly the most important moment of his life? He needed to say these things out loud, if for no other reason than to convince himself that they had actually taken place.

"It was his own stupid fault. He wouldn't do what he was told. That's the trouble with so many people: they don't believe you or they think it couldn't happen to them. It's a complete lack of imagination. They see the news on the television or read about it in the papers and they sympathize, but really they think the victim, however seemingly innocent, must somehow have been at fault; must have played some part in their own downfall. Why was he out so late at night? What was he doing hanging around that place anyway? Why did he continue to see that guy when it was obvious he was a nut-case? All you have to do is live a clean life, be good to your parents and your wife and bring your children up properly and you will continue to live a long and happy life. So, when confronted by somebody like me, they don't believe it. They can't imagine their face splattered all over the front page of next day's paper." He paused for a moment to take another drink of whisky. "So he started off well. It was the shock, I suppose. I waited until I was sure the shop was empty, went in and asked for some cigarettes and when he turned round I jumped over the counter, grabbed him by his hair and put my knife to his throat. I wasn't vicious or anything. I mean, I was still a bit shook up after that pub thing, but I was in control. It's something I've done many times. And he seemed to be behaving himself. He sort of went limp in my arms, just like they always do. And I told him to empty the till, and he moved towards it, and I was still holding him, and I was already imagining being back outside and on my way home, and he just sort of lost it. That's where he must have thought 'This isn't happening to me.

I'm a good person and I don't deserve this.' Anyway, whatever the reason, he suddenly started to struggle. I must admit that took me by surprise. I mean, he was this short, fat bloke, and he thought he could beat me, or perhaps he just wanted to prove to himself that he wasn't a coward. Perhaps he could hear his wife saying 'And you didn't do anything. You just let him take the money.' So he started to struggle, and he managed to turn himself round so we were facing each other and I had my knife down here by his stomach, and he just sort of fell on me. I may have used a bit of force, but mainly it was all him. I couldn't believe it. I felt the knife go in and he gurgled and his face sort of sagged, and his eyes went wide and blank-looking and he started to collapse. I don't know why, but I tried to hold him up, but he was too heavy. He slid down me and I kept hold of the knife. And that was it. He was just lying there at my feet. In the end it was all too easy. I mean, I've always known that one day I'd have to kill somebody, but I always imagined it as something dramatic, you know what I mean: a street fight or a proper robbery, like in a bank or something, not some stupid little Paki in a corner shop. It's almost embarrassing. And you know what I got?" He reached into his jacket pocket and pulled out a couple of notes and a handful of silver. "Twenty quid, that's all, twenty fucking quid. I mean, would you get yourself killed for twenty fucking quid? What an idiot."

"Which shop was it?"

"What?"

"Which shop?"

"What difference does it make?"

"None, I suppose, I'm just curious."

"That one on the corner near the pub: the one that sells everything and never seems to close."

I knew exactly which shop he meant, and the person who owned it: a jolly fat man with greying hair and a large, bushy moustache. I'd spoken with him many times. He'd moved over here with his family from India some five or six years ago. "He wasn't a Paki," I said. "He came from India."

"Well, it doesn't matter now, does it? He's dead."

"It's a pity," I said, perhaps unwisely. "I liked him."

"What the fuck has that got to do with anything? I didn't go looking for him on purpose. All he had to do was behave himself and everything would have been all right. And all for twenty fucking quid," he said again. "What sort of an idiot would get himself killed for twenty quid? Even you wouldn't be that stupid."

"I don't know," I answered carelessly, still thinking of the jolly fat man with the greying hair and the large, bushy moustache. "You never know how you are going to behave."

"What the fuck are you talking about," he said. "Of course you do. If someone's holding a knife at your throat and asks for your money, and all you've got is twenty quid, you'd hand it over. It's just common sense."

"I know," I said, already regretting having involved myself in such a futile conversation, "but in the heat of the moment ..."

"What heat? Who the fuck's talking about heat? I was perfectly calm. It was just a business transaction, that's all. All he had to do was play his part and he got it wrong. I don't think he even panicked. He just forgot who he was for a moment. Look, I'll show you."

And to my horror I watched as Kieran placed the bottle of whisky on the floor and, staggering slightly, hoisted himself to his feet.

"No," I said, genuinely concerned for my safety, "that's OK, Kieran, I know what you mean."

"No you fucking don't," he said. "You think people should act differently than they are able to. You need to be taught a lesson." As he advanced towards me he pulled his knife out of his pocket and opened up the blade. I looked at his face, his bruised and broken face. He was incredibly drunk, but even more disconcerting than that, I could tell that he wasn't really here in my flat with me. A greater part of him was still back in the shop, reliving time and time again his encounter with the shopkeeper. "Stand up," he said. I hesitated. "Come on, I'm not going to hurt you."

"This is just a reconstruction," I told myself, "A necessary exercise or even a sort of exorcism to rid himself of the evil of the past few hours." But still I feared for my safety. He took hold of my hair and pulled me roughly backwards, pressing the point of his knife against my neck, just as he had described doing to the shopkeeper. "Take it easy," I said, in some discomfort but still attempting to keep a certain lightness to my voice, "this is only me, remember."

"Don't worry," he whispered. "I've already killed once today and I don't want to make a habit of it, do I?"

I could feel his breath hot and stale on the back of my neck.

"Now," he said, "if I asked you for money you'd give it to me, wouldn't you?"

'Yes, of course," I answered, desperate to get this over and done with as soon as possible, "straight away."

His grip on my hair tightened and he ever so slightly increased the pressure of the tip of the blade on my neck. "Of course you would," he said, "and especially if you only had twenty quid on you."

"Yes."

He fell silent, but still he held me fast.

"I agree with you, Kieran," I said, "you can have the twenty quid." Silence. "You can let me go now."

"You see," he continued at last, his voice sounding even huskier and more intimate than before, "there's no need for any trouble; no 'heat of the moment'; just you and me and a transaction to be done. You believe me, don't you, Jonathan? You believe that I'm capable of hurting you?"

"Yes, Kieran," I said, "I believe you."

"Now try and struggle."

"What?"

"Try and struggle; that's what the Paki did."

"There's no need, Kieran. You've made your point."

"I just want to show you what happened, so you understand I had no option."

"Look, Kieran, I believe you."

"For fuck's sake! Don't be such a coward. I'm not going to hurt you."

I could hear the anger and the frustration in his voice. I just hoped his desire to relive, as closely as possible, his murder of the shopkeeper hadn't erased completely his knowledge of what was real and what was imaginary. I began, half-heartedly, to struggle, to try to twist away from his grasp.

"Come on," he hissed, "you can do better than that. You're fighting for your life."

I wasn't sure whether it was because of my own sudden and unexpected burst of energy, or because of the slight loosening of his grip, but suddenly I found myself almost free. Then, in one quick and powerful movement, he spun me round and dragged me, once more towards him.

"That's it," he said. "That's exactly how we finished up."

I looked down. The point of his knife was now directed towards the pit of my stomach.

"Only, of course, it didn't end there," he continued. "That wasn't enough for him. He wanted more." He placed his left arm around my shoulders and pulled me towards him until I felt the tip of his knife come into contact with my stomach.

"I thought I could trust him, but I was wrong."

"I understand," I said, still trying desperately to maintain some control over the situation. "I can see how it happened. It was just one of those things. Nobody's fault, but you can let me go now. I think we both need a drink."

"Somehow," he said again, his voice now low and intense, "we finished up like this. I must have relaxed for a minute. I thought I could trust him, but I couldn't. Perhaps you can't really trust anyone."

I thought: "This is how the shopkeeper must have felt, not really believing that it was happening to him. Is this for real or just a joke or a test of some kind? This is an episode in my life that, eventually, I can look back on and perhaps feel proud of. I can tell my grand-children, like the landlord of the pub, that it was a time and a place through which I lived."

I tried, gently, to free myself from his grasp. I put my hands up to his arm, the arm that was wrapped around my shoulders. I tried, gently, to push him away. I tried, gently, to slip from his grasp. I tried, gently, without success to remind him of who I was. His hold on me tightened and I thought for a second:

"We are the same. We are both manufactured out of the same bone, marrow, sinew and muscle. What you can do I can do." I tried harder.

And then he took hold of me. It was almost as if up until then he had been pretending to be Kieran. "Now", he thought, "I shall be myself and you will understand just how powerful I am." He took hold of me and all my attempts at escape became laughable. I could have battered away at him for ever, and he would have absorbed every blow and turned it to his advantage. I became the shopkeeper and his final, futile attempts to retain some dignity. I was confronted with a being almost beyond my comprehension. And then, suddenly, I was overcome with an almost overwhelming sense of liberation. I could do nothing. I was defeated. Not only was there no point in continuing the struggle, but actually to continue would have demeaned me even more. I gave in. I yielded. What other options did I have? I felt myself hold on to him as if he were the rock that would save me from sliding into the abyss.

Kieran was not just stronger than me physically but also emotionally, and in his unquestioning belief in himself as a complete human being. He existed, he was Kieran, he behaved as Kieran ought to behave without doubt or hesitation, untroubled by conscience or regret. What was the death of one insignificant shopkeeper when weighed against such perfection? Here, if anything, was the true artist: the artist that I had always wanted to become.

I relaxed, wrapped my left arm around his waist and rested my head against his shoulder. I felt the roughness of his cheek against mine and took in, once more, the familiar smell of sweat, tobacco and alcohol. The pressure of his knife increased against the hollow of my stomach. I could die so easily. Almost, as it were, by accident; no other effort would be required than to take one slight step forward. I clutched the back of his leather jacket and pushed my free hand down between us, taking hold of *his* hand – the hand that held the knife. The position seemed so natural, so comfortable that for a moment neither of us moved. I closed my eyes and contemplated the bliss that was to come.

Suddenly he pushed me away with such force that I fell backwards and lay for a moment almost stunned, sprawled amongst the unopened tins of paint. I opened my eyes. He was looking down at me, his expression a mixture of anger and disgust. "I don't do it to order," he said, folding up his knife and replacing it in his pocket. "I am not an assassin."

Once one has decided to adopt a particular way of living and of looking at the world then nothing seems to be strange or unconnected. Meaning and a reinforcement of all one's beliefs are to be found in everything. Certain of one's failure, every meeting, every relationship, even the objects with which one surrounds oneself seem to conspire to convince one of one's inadequacies. "See," you say to yourself, "I knew it would be like this. I should have known better."

Kieran slept for most of the following day, sprawled fully clothed on my mattress, his face leaving tiny smears of blood on my pillow. Every time he moved I heard the dull creak of his leather jacket. Towards midday I crept from the flat and went in search of food. I avoided the main shopping centre and visited only the local corner shops; the type of shop that Kieran had attempted to rob the night before. I had no desire to see anybody that I knew or, more tellingly, to meet anybody who knew of my supposed friendship with Kieran. I had still not fully taken in the seriousness of Kieran's crime but, perhaps through some innate sense of self-preservation, I needed for the moment to distance myself from everything that Kieran represented. Once I had bought everything that I thought I required, I sat down on the small wooden bench situated directly opposite the entrance to my block of flats, and gathered my shopping about me. The day was dull and overcast, with a vague promise of rain or even sleet to come.

I looked up to the eighteenth floor and to my flat with its small concrete balcony. For a moment I could make no sense of what I was seeing. Did I really live there? Was that the place that I had come to think of as home? Now, when I considered the stark interior of my flat and my few pointless possessions, all I could see was Kieran. He was there, now, waiting for my return. My one place of refuge, where there had only ever been me and the life of the stranger who lived opposite, had been all but destroyed, possibly for ever. But there *was* Kieran: his presence; his grandeur; his greed, his selfishness and his animosity. He had chosen me to come to, and with him had come a past and an appetite for violence and chaos that both fascinated and repelled me; it was just this sense of otherness that I found so hard to resist. If he had, as it seemed, really committed such a crime then, however much I loathed the act, what difference did it make to me? I was not responsible. Whatever he had done I was confronted only with the Kieran that I knew. Who was I to judge another's behaviour? Why should I treat Kieran any differently today than I would have done a week ago? He was, after all, still my guest.

I returned to the flat. Kieran was still asleep. I moved quietly into the kitchen and unpacked my carrier bags. I made myself a cup of coffee and opened a packet of biscuits. I drew my chair up to the window and looked out. I would wait patiently for him to wake up. What else could I do?

About five o'clock that afternoon I heard him begin to stir. He sniffed once or twice, coughed and cleared his throat. I made him a cup of coffee and took it through into the sitting room. He was already awake, sitting up and rolling himself a cigarette. I placed the cup on the floor by the side of the mattress and went to draw back the curtains.

"Leave it," he said. "You never know who's watching."

I returned to the kitchen.

"You've been out?"

"Just to get some food and stuff."

"You didn't speak to anybody?"

"Like who?"

"I don't know; anybody."

"Don't worry, I didn't see anyone. I was very careful." (Why on earth I thought it was necessary for me to be careful was something that I hadn't, at that stage, considered.)

I opened a small tin of tomato soup and emptied the contents into my only pan.

"I don't want anyone to know I'm here," Kieran shouted from the sitting room. "And that means that lot at the pub. I don't trust them."

I sliced three thick chunks of bread from the loaf I had bought that morning, spread them with butter and placed them, with the bowl of soup, on the same black lacquered tray that my father had once used to serve my dying mother.

I carried it through into the sitting room and handed it to him. He took it without a word and began immediately to eat, greedily slopping soup over his chin and the front of his jacket. "Which is blood and which is soup?" I thought.

"How is it?" I asked.

He answered without looking at me or ceasing to eat: "It's soup."

I returned to the kitchen and, for want of anything else better to do, began to wash up the soup-stained pan.

"Did you get any tobacco and something to drink?"

"It's in the carrier bag – the white one by the door."

He wandered into the kitchen, a cigarette in one hand and a bottle of whisky in the other. "I think I might have to stay here for some time; at least until all the fuss dies down."

"You think it will?"

"What?"

"Die down."

"It's bound to. There'll be a bit of an outcry to begin with, but then people will forget or lose interest. I mean, after all, he was only a Paki, and there are other more important things to think about."

"But the police will have to investigate."

"And what are they going to do? They're fucking useless."

"As long as you weren't seen."

"It was late. I was careful. And, anyway, they still have to find me; and that's not going to happen, is it?"

I wondered for a moment if that was some sort of threat, if he thought me capable of betraying him. He had a way of speaking, especially when under pressure, that made every word and every sentence seem like a declaration of war. I finished washing the pan and dried my hands on the tea towel.

"You ought to clean yourself up," I said. "You look terrible."

"Do I?" he said, bringing his hand up to his face. "Do you have a mirror?"

"In the bathroom."

He was gone for a good ten minutes, but when he returned he appeared to have done nothing. "I like it," he said, opening his mouth wide to show off his broken teeth. "It makes me look interesting. Girls go for this sort of thing, you know: it's the sense of violence and danger they like. They pretend to want security and a man who understands them and all that shit, but that's only because they daren't say what they really want. I mean, look at Colin: he's an ugly fucker but he still gets the women. I bet he knocks them around a bit as well. They all love it."

In all the time I had known Kieran I had never seen him with a woman. Occasionally, one would tentatively approach him, perhaps fascinated by his reputation, but any such chance encounter would seem only to drive Kieran to even greater displays of childish excess and vulgarity. They didn't stay in his company for long.

"Can I get you anything?" I said, suddenly feeling uncomfortable in his presence.

"Such as."

"I don't know," I shrugged. "Something else to eat or a cup of tea or coffee ..." I quickly ran out of suggestions. "Anything."

"No, that's all right," he said. "I'm fucked. I think I'll go back to bed." He took another mouthful of whisky, stretched out his arms in an overblown gesture of tiredness and sloped off back into the sitting room.

"Should I say goodnight," I thought for a moment, "or sleep well" and almost laughed out loud at the inappropriateness of such an idea. He would think I had gone mad.

I listened to him moving around for a few minutes more and then the flat fell into silence. I remained where I was. I could, of course, have joined him in the sitting room, but for some reason that I couldn't explain, the thought appalled me. I needed to be alone and to regain some sense of my own identity. My flat, despite its distinct lack of personality, was all that I had to convince and reassure me of who I was, and if I were to lose that then I would have nothing. I pulled my chair up to the kitchen table and rested my head on my arms. Despite the earliness of the hour and my anxiety and my confusion I would try to sleep. This night, like everything else in my life, would eventually pass.

The next day we were both awake early. I had slept fitfully and uncomfortably on the hard kitchen chair, but I felt somewhat a hero at having undergone such a hardship. Kieran had hardly moved at all, with just an occasional bout of snoring to remind me of his presence. I had made toast and coffee and we were sitting at the kitchen table in a vague mockery of a normal family breakfast.

"I want you to get me a paper," said Kieran. "I doubt if it's made the nationals yet, but it should be in the local 'Observer.'"

'You think so?"

"What else have they got to write about? This is probably the most exciting thing that's happened in years. I might even be famous."

Overnight, a subtle change in Kieran's demeanor had occurred. Yesterday, although he appeared to be his usual arrogant self, I believed that now and then I could sense behind his bravado a certain lack of confidence, almost as if he had become involved in something that was beyond his understanding, something that had rendered him practically impotent. He had clung to his natural instinct for self-preservation as his only option, but blindly and without conviction. Now, he once more believed himself to be invulnerable. He had even washed his hands and face to reveal a Kieran less bloody but more intimidating than ever.

"And get me some dope," he said, finishing off the last of the toast. "If I've got to stay in this fucking place I'll need something to relieve the boredom or I'll go fucking mad. And remember: don't tell anybody where I am. Just for once, use your fucking intelligence."

Although it was not yet midday the pub was already open. I had had no intention of visiting the pub when I had left my flat, but where else was I to go? Simply to buy the paper and to score the dope that Kieran had demanded would have taken only half an hour or so, and I could hardly bear the thought of returning to Kieran so soon. I needed to see other people and to engage, even for a short time, in a world outside the confines of my flat. Nowhere, it now seemed, was safe.

Colin, Diana, Jackie and Vince, much to my surprise, were already sitting at our usual table. The rest of the pub was practically deserted. I knew as soon as I saw them huddled there, their heads bowed deep in conversation, that they were talking about the murder. What else could have brought them together so early in the day? I bought myself a drink and joined them. As I sat down I saw two copies of the local paper spread out on the table before them.

"You've heard?" said Diana, impatient to bring me into their little conspiracy.

"Heard what?"

"About the murder," said Diana.

"That Paki who runs the corner shop," said Colin. "He's dead."

"Kieran did it," said Jackie.

"We don't know that," said Diana.

"Yes we do," insisted Vince. "It says so."

"No it doesn't," said Diana. "It just describes somebody who looks like him."

"Somebody saw him?" I asked, genuinely surprised for the first time that morning.

"See for yourself," said Colin, pushing one of the newspapers towards me. "It's all there."

The story took up nearly all the front page and, for our local paper, seemed to be quite a well-written and in-depth article. There was even a photograph of the front of the shop. I read quickly, my eyes scanning the article for any reference, however oblique, to Kieran. The shopkeeper, apparently, had died not at the scene of the crime, as Kieran had believed, but in the ambulance on the way to the hospital. There were interviews with neighbours who extolled his virtues as a friend and a member of the local community: 'a wonderful man, always smiling and helpful', and with his wife who expressed her shock, sorrow and desolation that something so pointless and brutal could have happened to such a good husband and father: "He never hurt anyone; we moved here for a better life; who could have done such a thing; how are my three children going to manage without their father?" And towards the end of the article an interview with a detective inspector of police, who stated that a suspect had been seen leaving the scene of the crime and gave a description of the man who they were seeking. The description was so detailed and so accurate that anyone who knew him could have been in no doubt that the man they wished to interview was indeed Kieran. The policeman went on to say that an early arrest was expected.

"It certainly sounds like Kieran," I said, pushing the paper away from me. "There seems little doubt."

"I told you," said Colin. "It has to be. What a fucking idiot."

"He was very drunk when he left here," said Diana, who seemed at last to have accepted that it was Kieran who was the most likely suspect. "And he'd just had that awful beating. He probably didn't know what he was doing."

"But that poor man and his wife and children," said Jackie. "If it was Kieran he deserves to be caught."

"Don't worry, he will be," said Vince. "He's not the sort to remain hidden for long."

"That's true," said Colin. "He'll want to tell everybody about it. How it was the Paki who attacked him."

"With a knife," said Vince.

"Or an axe," added Colin.

"Or a shotgun," said Vince.

"And how he defended himself against a raving lunatic and only just managed to save himself," said Colin.

"When he's finished he'll want a medal for being a fucking hero," said Vince.

"I wonder where he is now," said Diana. "There aren't that many places where he could go."

"If he has any sense he'll be miles away," said Jackie.

"No he won't," said Colin. "He only knows round here. Anywhere else and he'd be just a nobody, and he couldn't stand that. Whatever he's done he needs this place to give him courage, to let everybody know he's Kieran."

I was only half listening to their conversation as I was still trying to take in everything that I had just read. Up until the moment when I had seen the newspaper there had only been Kieran and me. Kieran had told me a story and I, for reasons that I still didn't fully understand, had believed him and said I would help. But that's all it had been: a story, another aspect of Kieran's life. Now the story had become common knowledge and, somehow, taken on a life of its own; I was part of that story, perhaps an important part. I was suddenly overcome with an overwhelming sense of pride. I was innocent of everything but I could still participate in the spoils of war. I looked at my four friends sitting round the table and almost hugged myself with my secret knowledge. I was almost as much the subject of their conversation as Kieran himself.

"Perhaps he's sleeping rough somewhere," said Jackie.

"Has he any other friends," asked Diana, "I mean, apart from us?"

"I shouldn't think so," said Vince. "He's not what you'd call sociable."

"And what makes you think we're his friends?" said Colin. "Actually I couldn't give a shit about him."

"Well I could," said Diana; "whatever he's done."

"I don't know how you can say such a thing," said Jackie, "When he's murdered someone."

"We don't know that for sure," said Diana. "It could just be somebody who looks like Kieran."

"Yes we do," I said, quietly, unable to keep silent any longer.

"Don't be fucking ridiculous," Colin said to Diana, ignoring my words. "Why do you always have to defend him?"

"That's not fair," said Diana, "I don't always defend him."

"Yes you do," said Jackie, with a hint of sadness in her voice. "Always."

"We know it was Kieran," I said, raising my voice slightly. "I've seen him."

I took an almost physical delight in the silence that followed. All eyes were turned towards me. I slowly raised my glass to my lips.

"What do you mean you've seen him?" asked Colin.

"Where?" asked Diana, visibly excited.

"When?" asked Jackie.

"How is he?" asked Diana. "Is he all right?"

"What did he say?" asked Vince.

"He's all right," I said. "He came to me the night of the murder."

"Why you, for fuck's sake?" said Colin. "What use did he think you'd be?"

"Shut up," said Diana. "Let him speak."

"There's not much to say," I said, nonchalantly. "He came to my flat. He looked pretty terrible, and he told me he'd done it."

"Just like that," said Colin. "I don't believe it."

"No," said Vince, "I don't either. It doesn't make sense."

"But what did he say?" said Diana. "He must have given you some reason for what he'd done."

"He said it was a robbery and it all went wrong. The man fought back."

"So he stabbed him," said Jackie. "That's terrible."

I shrugged. "That's what he told me. I don't judge."

"No, of course you don't," Colin said, sarcastically. "That's not your style."

"I still don't believe it," said Vince. "You're making it all up."

"Actually," I said, determined not to be driven into a corner, "he's still there, at my flat." There was a moment's silence.

"You're joking," said Vince.

"You must be an idiot," said Colin. "Don't you realize the danger you're in?

"You have to tell the police," said Jackie. "You've no option. Think of that poor woman and her children. He can't be allowed to get away with this."

"I'm not saying he's going to get away with it," I said. "All I'm saying is that he came to me and I said he could stay for a few days, just until he sorts himself out."

"I can't believe you could be so stupid," said Colin, with surprising venom. "It's not even as if you like him."

I shrugged my shoulders. "I don't think that's got anything to do with it. He came to me for help and I said yes. What's wrong with that?"

"If you really believe that," said Colin, "then you're an even bigger fool than I thought you were. Is he really worth going to prison for?"

"He's a murderer," said Jackie. "He's murdered somebody, don't you understand that? You can't possibly want to help a murderer."

"How is he?" asked Diana, apparently oblivious to the discord going on around her. "Is he all right?"

"What do you mean, is he all right?" said Colin, exploding in anger. "Have you gone fucking crazy? Who cares whether he's all right or not? Am I the only one who understands what's going on here? Because of this twat, here," indicating me, "we're all in danger. We could all be arrested."

Vince, who seemed to have been becoming more and more amused by the whole proceedings, finally burst into laughter. "This is wonderful," he said. "And people wonder why I take so many drugs."

'Oh, that reminds me," I said, attempting to keep my voice casual, "I need to score some dope for Kieran."

"How much?" asked Vince, still laughing.

"You're not going to give him any, are you?" asked Colin.

"No, of course not," said Vince. "He'll have to pay for it like everybody else."

"I don't believe this," said Colin.

"It's just business," said Vince. "I have to make a living," and he threw a small packet of silver paper into the centre of the table. "There you go: two quid to you."

"That's it," said Colin, "I'm off, and you lot can go and fuck yourselves."

"Wait for me," said Vince knocking back his drink and picking up his money from the table. "I'll come with you. See you later," he said to us, as he sped after Colin, "and don't do anything I wouldn't do."

We could still hear the sound of his laughter even after he'd reached the street.

"Colin's right, you know," said Jackie." We shouldn't get involved."

"I want to see him," said Diana. "I want to make sure he's OK."

"That's such a stupid idea," exclaimed Jackie. "What good do you think you can do?"

"I think Jackie's right," I said, taken totally by surprise by Diana's suggestion and suddenly remembering Kieran's warning not to tell anybody where he was. "I'm not sure he wants to see anybody just at the moment."

"I'm sure he won't mind seeing me," said Diana, "and you never know, I might be able to help."

"I can't believe you want to help a murderer," said Jackie, "even if it is Kieran."

"But he might not have meant to kill anybody," said Diana. "Sometimes these things happen by accident. He might have just intended to frighten him."

"Actually," I said, unable to keep quiet, "that's exactly what he said: that he didn't want to hurt anybody at all; that all he wanted was the money from the till."

"There you are then," said Diana, relieved and proud that her trust in Kieran and, by implication, in the whole of humanity had been vindicated, "just as I suspected. But I have to know for certain, just for my own peace of mind. I have to see him."

"This is wrong," said Jackie, her voice heavy with fear and with sadness, "it's just too dangerous."

'You don't have to come if you don't want to," said Diana, gathering her possessions about her and preparing to leave. "After all, it's not as if you'd actually be of any use." Nothing that Diana could have said could have been guaranteed to hurt Jackie more, and Diana knew it. Even while Jackie's face sort of crumbled in on itself and she stared vacantly at her empty glass, Diana was already preparing her apology. For a brief moment I thought Jackie was going to cry.

"I know you don't think much of me," she said at last, her voice so small and pathetic that for one brief moment even I despised her, "and I'm not strong or pretty like you, but it's just that I care about you. You're my best friend and I don't want to see you hurt, that's all. If you're going to see Kieran, then of course I'll come with you."

Diana sighed heavily, whether out of affection or irritation it was hard to say, and placed an arm around Jackie's shoulders. "I'm sorry," she said. "I didn't mean to hurt you, but this is important to me. I have to see Kieran and of course I would love you to come with me." Jackie was immediately reassured and smiled gratefully up at Diana, only too happy, once more, to put her trust in Diana's friendship. I made a point of not looking directly at Diana, just in case her deception was covertly acknowledged by both of us. They stayed like that just long enough for Diana to be convinced that Jackie believed that their special relationship was once more established beyond any reasonable doubt and that they were as close as ever, then Diana bustled into activity.

"Right," she said, extricating herself from Jackie's embrace, "let's go."

We left the pub and began the short walk to my flat. It seemed to me that Diana was far too voluble and energetic for someone who was on her way to visit a self-confessed murderer. She flitted about me and Jackie like some small child on her first trip to the seaside, forever chattering and restless and asking questions with no intention of waiting for the answers: did I think that he needed anything? Should we buy him some food? How were his wounds? Should we stop off at the chemist? Did I think he would be pleased to see her?

I said nothing or answered only in monosyllabic grunts. I had my own concerns to occupy my mind. Slowly I was beginning to understand that my one moment of glory was now over. For a short time I had been the only one who knew of Kieran's whereabouts and the truth of his crime, and that knowledge had seemed somehow to grant me a special place in the universe, almost as if I were blessed. Driven by frustration or ego, I had used that knowledge to glorify my own part in the whole sordid affair. I had divulged everything I knew, and in so doing had reverted ignominiously to just another ordinary human being. Diana's request to see Kieran had taken me completely by surprise but, having brought her into my confidence, how could I possibly refuse her anything? Up until the confession of my knowledge of his whereabouts, there had been just Kieran and me, linked as it were by our common iniquity. Now I was totally irrelevant.

We walked on, Diana buzzing with excitement and Jackie and I quiet and totally absorbed within our own isolation.

The lift was working and empty. I ushered them in and pressed the appropriate button. The door closed and we moved upwards. I tried not to count the floors.

We stopped with the usual heart-stopping judder at the eighteenth floor. There was the usual two-second pause and then the door opened. I led them towards my front door, my keys in my hand. I put the key in the lock, turned the key and pushed the door slightly open, but before progressing any further I turned and said to Diana and Jackie, "Let me go in first. "He won't be expecting visitors."

I entered my own flat. I tried to be confident. I left Jackie and Diana to close the door behind them. While still in the hall I heard Kieran shout out, "About fucking time, too. Where have you been?" Kieran was in the kitchen, but as I entered the sitting room he staggered out to greet me. The curtains were still closed, but even in the half-light I could see that he was drunk; a state of affairs that did nothing for my peace of mind. For a split second, despite his angry words of rebuke, he seemed almost pleased to see me; then he caught sight of Diana and Jackie. The change in his attitude was immediate but subtle, so subtle that I doubt if anyone who didn't know him well would have noticed any change at all. Diana put on her best smile and said, "Hello Kieran."

"Just a moment," Kieran answered, his voice as soft and as soothing as Diana's, "there's just something I have to talk to Jonathan about." Taking hold of my right arm he propelled me with apparent affection but with great force into the kitchen where, out of sight of the other two, he pushed me up against the wall and placed his hand around my throat.

"I thought I told you," he said in a spitting whisper, "not to tell anybody where I was. So what have you done, you stupid fucking moron? Is there no end to your stupidity? What do I have to do to make you take me seriously?" His whisky breath was so hot on my face, and I felt so exhausted and defeated by the lives of other people that I could barely stand, let alone give a reasoned response to his question. I suddenly thought I could collapse now into his arms. Abdicate, again, from all responsibility and let fate and the passing of time decide all. "Hit me," I thought, "just hit me and exhaust yourself of all rage, frustration and inadequacy and then the world will continue on its way as usual and, perhaps, we can both get a good night's sleep."

"Well," he persisted, "why did you do it? Why did you disobey me?"

I felt the pressure of his fingers around my throat. Did he really expect an answer? I doubted it, but what did it matter? It was a ritual he had to go through to prove that he was still the Kieran that he needed to be, and for one glorious, uncontrollable second I thought that I was going to burst into laughter, right there in his face, for the stupidity and absurdity that he and I and the whole human race stood for.

"Don't blame Jonathan. It's not his fault. I made him bring us."

Diana's intervention was perfect: her voice and attitude expressing neither panic nor over-concern, merely a wish to explain, in as logical and as calm a manner as possible, the fundamental truth of the situation. Who could possibly have resisted such an innocent call to reason? But just in case, Diana placed her hand on Kieran's arm and looked up at him with the same expression of surprise and vulnerability that I had seen her use on so many people so many times before. She smiled her perfect smile and her teeth shone snowy white and her eyes seemed to glow an even deeper blue than usual. "I was worried about you," she continued. "I just wanted to make sure you were all right."

Not even Kieran could resist such a look of innocent contrition. He let go of my throat and attempted to echo Diana's angelic smile with his own lop-sided grin. "Don't worry," he said, throwing me one last glance of disgust, "it's just a little game we play. Jonathan pretends he's an idiot and I pretend to be angry. Sometimes, of course, we get a little carried away and I actually have to hit him, just to make the game seem that little bit more real, but there's never any actual harm done. In fact, if the truth were known, he rather likes it."

"You look terrible," Diana said, raising her hand to his face and running the tips of her fingers over his cuts and bruises. "Have you been putting anything on them?"

"Not so as you'd notice."

"Right then," she said, obviously rather pleased that she had, somehow, managed to take total control of the situation, "let's see what we can do for you." And, with no murmur of dissent from Kieran, she led him into the sitting room and sat him down in front of the window. Only when she attempted to draw back the curtains did Kieran object. "Leave them," he said, "there's no need for an audience."

For the next few minutes Jackie and I watched in fascination while Diana bustled about the flat, obviously determined to refuse all offers of help even if we had volunteered. After some searching she eventually discovered, hidden beneath the sink, a small washing-up bowl which she filled with hot, soapy water, and, screwed up at the back of the cupboard, a reasonably clean hand towel. Holding these two objects out in front of her as if they were imbued with some sort of religious significance she slowly crossed the sitting room floor and placed herself at Kieran's feet. "This might sting a little bit," she said, dipping the cloth in the water and reaching up towards Kieran's face, "but you'll feel and look a lot better by the time I've finished with you."

"Did you get a paper?" Kieran suddenly asked brushing away Diana's hand and leaning eagerly forward on his chair. "Today's paper, did you get it?"

"Of course," answered Diana, "Jackie's got it. Now just sit still"

"And?"

"And what?" said Diana.

"Am I in it?"

"Of course you are," answered Diana; "the front page, no less. You're almost a star."

"Let me see," he said, more agitated than ever and holding out his hand and beckoning Jackie towards him. "Come on, I want to see it."

"You'd better show him," said Diana, "or we'll never get this done."

Jackie produced the folded newspaper from out of her bag and handed it to Kieran. Kieran brought the page close to his face and began to read, while Diana squatted back on her heels and waited patiently for him to finish.

"Fuck!" he exclaimed. "They know it's me."

"Right, now hold still," said Diana. "I can't do it properly if you keep moving."

"Fuck," he said again, "I wonder who saw me. I can't believe it. I was so fucking careful."

"They don't actually name you," I said.

"No, but it's me, isn't it? I mean, it's so fucking obvious. The police must know it's me. Even they're not that stupid."

"But what does it matter," asked Diana, "just as long as they don't know where you are?"

"Of course it fucking matters," said Kieran, jerking his head away from her hand, "and watch what you're doing, that fucking hurts. It means that instead of wasting time interviewing lots of other people it'll be just me they'll be looking for – just me. Christ! This is a fucking nightmare."

He turned his attention once more to the newspaper.

"There," said Diana, realizing that any further effort would be futile, "that's the best I can do. Tomorrow I'll bring some proper ointment and plasters, but it's going to be sore for quite a while. Now, how about something to eat? You must be hungry."

Diana disappeared into the kitchen and for many minutes nobody said anything while she clattered about, noisily opening and closing drawers and cupboards and Kieran, his head bowed in concentration, continued to read and re-read the description of his crime and of himself. Jackie, at last realising that this was to be no fleeting visit, sat herself down on the edge of my mattress, neatly tucking her pale, thin legs beneath her cheap, black skirt and resting her hands politely on her lap while she attempted, with admirable concentration but with very little success, to become invisible. I remained standing by the door to the hall, only too aware that my presence in my own home was no longer strictly necessary.

Eventually Diana reappeared carrying a plate of bacon and eggs and a mug of coffee that she placed, along with herself, on the floor at the foot of Kieran's chair. She crossed her legs and looked around her. "Don't just stand there," she said, patting the floor by her side, "come and join us. You do live here, you know." Reluctantly I did as I was told.

Kieran suddenly threw the newspaper to one side with a look of disdain that seemed to me to be just a little too contrived, picked up his plate of food and began, noisily and greedily, to eat.

"That's what I meant about not telling anybody where I was," he said, shovelling in great mouthfuls of food. "One word in the wrong place and I'm fucked."

"We all are," said Jackie, quietly.

"Well excuse me if I don't burst into tears," he said, "but I do think I'm just a little bit more important than you. And nobody asked you to get involved anyway. It was your choice."

"So what are you going to do now?" asked Diana, keen to keep the peace between Kieran and Jackie. "I mean, you can't stay here for ever."

"I don't see why not," he said. "Now I've got you to look after me. And Jonathan doesn't mind me staying here, do you Jonathan? In fact," he continued, lowering his voice and leaning even closer towards Diana, "between you and me I think he quite likes having me here. It makes him feel important."

"Yeah, that's right," I said, attempting to strike the right note between humorous contempt and calm acquiescence, "I've always wanted a murderer as a house guest."

Perhaps it was the first time that the word 'murderer' had been used dispassionately in Kieran's presence, but for whatever reason, the atmosphere in the room seemed suddenly to change, to darken and to become more concentrated. We all knew, instinctively, that only Kieran could break the silence. He continued to eat until his plate was wiped clean. He placed it on the floor in front of him, sat back on his chair and rolled himself a cigarette. "You're right," he said. "That's what I am: a murderer. Who'd have thought it? And yet it's still me. Amazing isn't it? How can one simple, stupid act define who you are? I am no longer just Kieran, but -" his voice dropped to the deep, tremulous tones of a mock Victorian actor engaged in some cheap melodrama "- Kieran The Murderer, and that's how I shall always be known."

"But we know different," said Diana, misunderstanding his meaning completely and placing a comforting hand on his knee. "We shall always know you as just Kieran."

I cringed inwardly for Diana's trust and her naivety.

"Don't get me wrong," Kieran said, hurriedly. "I'm not complaining. That's just the way things are, and if people want to see me like that then that's fine by me. At least people have heard of me."

"Of course," said Diana, eager to adapt to Kieran's way of thinking, "and I'm sure that's very important. I just meant that we know the real you: the Kieran that existed before all this … fuss."

I looked at Diana in amazement. I could make no sense of her words or of her behaviour. This '…fuss', was the death of another human being and yet Diana was behaving as if it were no more than a slight aberration in an otherwise blameless existence: an accident; a misjudgment; an unfortunate choice between two similar opportunities. Was she really that close to Kieran; so close that she had become blind to his true nature? Was she in love? Was she desperate to become part of his life however sordid that life appeared to be? I couldn't believe it – none of it. And yet Diana's hand remained on Kieran's knee.

"Perhaps this *is* me," said Kieran, blowing out another great plume of smoke and adopting an almost ridiculous attitude of self-satisfied condescension: "the Kieran that you have always known, and the death of that shopkeeper was no more than just a way of me becoming truly honest and complete. Now, at last, I have become the Kieran that I should have always been."

I could have laughed out loud, or at least snorted my contempt, but Kieran's expression was one of such intense concentration and seriousness that I felt myself stunned into silence. After all, who was I to pass judgment on another person's delusions?

"And the man?"

"What?"

"The man," repeated Jackie. "The man you murdered. What about his life, his chance to become the person that he always wanted to be? What about him?"

The question was obviously pointless. Kieran had always been and would always be incapable of believing that any other person's life could possibly be as important, as significant or as grandiose as his own. I watched him carefully as his eyes glazed over in confusion.

"I didn't know him. How can you expect me to feel anything? His answer was so reasonable that it seemed to be bordering on the insane.

"But you ended his life," persisted Jackie. "That's your responsibility."

I expected Kieran to explode into anger, as was usual whenever he believed his opinions were being questioned, but to my amazement he merely shrugged his shoulders. "All victims aren't saints. How do you know he didn't beat his wife or fuck his children? Perhaps I did society a favour."

It was obvious that Kieran was enjoying himself. He had never considered Jackie to be of any importance, physically nor emotionally, and her words of criticism were, for the moment, simply a form of amusement. He smiled smugly down at Diana, confident that he had impressed her with his wit and this sudden demonstration of self-control, but Diana, too anxious to know exactly how to react, only shifted uneasily and slowly removed her hand from his knee. Kieran immediately noted her change of mood and let the smile fade from his lips.

"That's an appalling thing to say," continued Jackie, unaware of the danger she was in. "I can't believe that you really mean it."

"I mean everything I say."

"Then nobody's safe. You could find a reason to kill anybody."

"Sometimes you don't need a reason."

"This is silly," said Diana, desperate to restore some sort of peace between the two of them. "We know that Kieran didn't mean to do it. It was just an accident."

"Nobody forced him to go into that shop," said Jackie. "Nobody forced him to carry a knife or threaten the shopkeeper. It was all his choice and he has to take responsibility for his actions."

I watched as Kieran began to grow more and more restless. Not only were his motives and, by implication, his whole personality being questioned, but he was in danger of becoming a mere bystander to the most important event of his life. Perhaps he really had been furious at the article in the newspaper, for a moment, but now that he had been all but named as the murderer I had no doubt that he wished, if not actually to celebrate his notoriety, then at least to have the seriousness of his crime treated with the respect that he believed it deserved. He had become important and had no intention of being ignored or analyzed as if he were an ordinary human being.

"We all do stupid things," said Diana; "things that we regret."

"But that's the point," said Jackie: "he doesn't regret it. He talks about it as if it was an unfortunate accident, something trivial like knocking over a cup of tea, or even worse, as if the poor shopkeeper deserved it and we should all be grateful."

"You're exaggerating. I'm sure he doesn't think like that at all. This isn't easy for him either, you know. You, of all people, should be more understanding."

"Go to his wife and his children," said Jackie, ignoring Diana's reference to her latent Christianity, "and see how understanding they are. See if they are prepared to forgive him."

Kieran made a sudden grunt of anger and disgust. "I don't care. Do you understand? I don't fucking care."

Both Jackie and Diana fell instantly silent.

"I don't want understanding and I certainly don't want forgiveness. I went into the shop and I stabbed him, and the stupid fucker died. I did that – nobody else – just me, and I don't fucking care. All that matters now is that I don't get caught. What you or anybody else thinks about me has got nothing to do with anything. In fact, I don't know why you're here anyway. What do you want from me?"

"I don't want anything," began Diana. "I just thought that – "

"Not you," interrupted Kieran. "Her. What does she want?

"I came with Diana," Jackie said. "She's my friend."

There was such an unexpected innocence in her answer that I could have fallen in love with her there and then.

Kieran let out a snort of derision. "Oh, of course," he said. "I should have known: Jackie the faithful, the caring and the submissive. Give us a bark, Jackie. Go on, get on your knees and give us a bark. I'm sure we could find a collar and a lead for you. You'd like that, wouldn't you? We could drag you around. Give you a slap now and then just to let you know who's boss, and keep you well fucked. You wouldn't have to think at all, just keep your mouth shut and your legs open. I'm sure even you could manage that."

Her response was so dignified, so courageous that I was forced to look at her in a new light. Her physical appearance had always seemed to me to give a perfect insight into her character: a pale and undernourished body and a face so drained of all animation that one believed that even the lightest of rebukes would reduce her to tears. This time, I believe, she took us all by surprise, even Kieran. She waited for a moment to see if Diana would come to her aid, and then very slowly she raised herself to her feet. "I'm leaving," she said, her voice calm and steady. And then, turning towards Diana: "Are you coming with me?"

Diana hesitated, but only for a moment. "No, I don't think so, not just yet. But you go on. I'll see you later."

"I think you're making a big mistake," Jackie said, moving towards the door, "and you're going to get hurt. You're not as strong as you think you are."

And much to my amazement, as it was probably the first time that I had ever seen her act independently of Diana, she left the flat, closing the door softly behind her.

"Thank Christ for that," said Kieran, "she was really beginning to annoy me. I don't know why you hang around with her."

"Oh, she's OK," said Diana. "She just worries about me."

"She fancies you, you mean," said Kieran. "I don't know why you just don't let her fuck you and get it over and done with. Or perhaps you already have."

"No, certainly not," responded Diana, her pale complexion turning a delicate shade of pink. "I'm not like that, and neither is she."

"Yeah, right," said Kieran, "whatever you say."

Diana took hold of Kieran's empty plate and mug, struggled to her feet and moved towards the kitchen. "You have a dirty mind," she said. "I think you need help." But there seemed to be genuine affection and laughter in her voice.

As soon as she had left the room Kieran leaned towards me, enveloping us both in the smoke from his cigarette. "Jackie's right, you know," he whispered.

"About what?"

"About Diana: she's not as strong as she thinks she is. In fact, she's pretty stupid."

"She seems to think a lot about you."

"You think so? Then you're a bigger fool than she is. It's not me she wants to be with, but Kieran The Murderer. I'm dangerous, and it's *that* that she wants to be a part of. They all love it: this sense of danger and excitement. They need people like me to live their lives for them. You too: you're just the same. I'm not your friend, never have been and never will be, but you let me stay here. You bring me food and Diana. Why else would you do that if you weren't proud of me?"

"I didn't bring you Diana. She came because she wanted to."

"But you told her where I was, despite me insisting that you told nobody. Why was that?"

"I was drunk. We were talking. I had to put people straight."

"Bollocks. You just couldn't resist letting people know that you were now a part of me. You were proud, and you brought me Diana as a way of thanking me."

I focused on the yellow dribble of egg adhering to one side of his mouth. I could make no sense of anything he was saying or, rather, each utterance when taken in isolation seemed to strive towards some sort of ultimate logic, but when taken as a whole, all of his ideas, insights and comments upon the vagaries of human existence seemed to flounder into a mass of contradictions. I had not brought Diana, as he put it, but I had. She was here, now, in the kitchen, and if not because of me then why else would she be here? "And what about Jackie," I said. "I suppose I brought her for a reason as well?"

He shrugged, took a mouthful of whisky and lit another cigarette. "It never happens the way you imagine it," he said. "I enter a shop with nothing but good in my heart; you bring me Diana and Jackie. You must always think very carefully before you enter on any course of action where the outcome is not already known. Things happen, things over which you have no control."

He was wrong and he was right, and all I could think of was Susan and Anna and my parents and my long line of soldiers and my desire and my need never again to be involved with somebody like Kieran.

"You know, Jonathan," he continued, with an intimacy that I found almost repellent, "it was all so easy, that's what I can't get used to. Nothing was planned. I didn't think 'now I'll go and kill somebody' – I was far too pissed for that – it just happened, and it was all so fucking easy. And now I can do anything I want. One simple little act and now I feel free to do anything. That's what you have to understand, Jonathan, I'm not the same person. You have to be very careful."

I looked into his eyes. There was no emotion, no expression and no passion, just Kieran being Kieran. I stood up and moved towards my blank sheet of hardboard and my paints. No doubt he believed that I had moved away from him through an overwhelming sense of fear or disgust or simply because of an inability to cope with the sheer power of his presence. In truth, it was his attempt to use me as his confidant, as a repository for his all his thoughts, that I had found so repulsive. I was still uncertain why I was helping him, why I was letting him use me and my flat – perhaps through simple inertia or curiosity – but whatever the reason I had no desire to be dragged into his world, to enter into the madness that was Kieran.

It was a relief when Diana re-entered the room. She was drying her hands on the same soiled towel that she had used to clean Kieran's cuts and bruises. She paused for a moment and looked around the room as if she expected it somehow to have changed in the short time that she had been away, and then slumped down once more at Kieran's feet. She opened her handbag, produced a packet of cigarettes and, in a moment of simple and obscene intimacy, lit two cigarettes: one for her and one for Kieran. They began to smoke together, contentedly, a caricature of two close friends meeting after a lifetime of separation. They said nothing. For once even Kieran seemed, for the moment, happy simply to be part of an experience over which he had no immediate control.

I watched. What else could I do? I watched. In my flat, two people whose lives, desires and thoughts were a complete mystery to me were sitting and smoking and, apparently, delighting in each other's company. Incapable of making any sense of the situation in which I now found myself, I knew then that I would do nothing. Whatever happened I would do nothing. If my life was in any way connected to theirs then it was purely as a spectator and a witness, and I had no desire to be or to do anything else.

Diana and I met up the following afternoon. We were sitting alone at our table in the pub, the others having yet to arrive. It was quite clear that Diana was still very much exhilarated after her encounter with the 'new' Kieran. She was talking far too much and too rapidly, and her eyes seemed to shine with an unexpected passion and enthusiasm. She was wearing a tight, floral dress of pale blue and yellow flowers and her long, blonde hair was pulled away from her face and fastened at the nape of her neck by a bright red ribbon. She looked exquisite and surprisingly vulnerable, like a young girl on her way to her first 'grown up' dinner party. As she spoke her eyes darted continually around the room and her hands fluttered nervously in front of her as if all the danger and excitement of Kieran's life had, somehow, been transferred directly to her. "I'll do all the shopping, of course, that's no problem – if you give me the money – and the cooking. I know you've done your best, but if it were up to you two you'd just live off whisky and cigarettes. I've already been to the chemist and I've bought some bandages and antiseptic and stuff, he's not badly hurt – it looks much worse than it is and it's not as if he's not used to being hit – but still, it needs looking after. I was thinking that once he's cleaned himself up it might be a good idea if he grew a beard or maybe just a moustache. And, obviously, he can't stay with you forever, so I thought he could stay with me, just for a while until things calm down, or perhaps we could share him – one week with you and one with me."

"The police are everywhere," I said.

"Yes I know. Have you seen a copy of today's 'Mirror'? He's made the nationals."

"The shopkeeper was well-liked and his children are cute, they look good in photographs."

"I can't understand why they haven't been to see us," Diana said.

"Who?"

"The police, of course: who else? They must know about us. We were always hanging about together."

This last comment came as quite a shock to me, so much so that I had to stop myself from exclaiming: "but what can we tell them? We are innocent, we don't know anything."

Diana, sensing my confusion, leaned across the table and took hold of my hand. "Are you OK?" she asked.

"Yes, of course," I said. "Just thinking, that's all."

It had been four days since the night of the murder and it was true to say that in all that time the role of the police in this whole affair had barely entered my consciousness. I was, of course, aware of the gravity of the situation and that the involvement of the police was necessary and to be expected but, for some reason, I had found it impossible to link the two events: the murder and its aftermath. For me the position was clear: Kieran had committed an appalling act of destruction, perhaps the worst that I could imagine. And not just for money, although that may have been the initial spur, but simply to show his disdain of and his power over the 'normal' rules of existence. "I am different from you," he had declared. "I am stronger and braver and will not be confined by your petty morality." But once the deed was done, what then? What more was to be said or undertaken? Naturally I grieved over the death of the shopkeeper and the pain and loss that his family was now suffering, but any consequent act of revenge or retribution seemed to me to be almost an irrelevance, practically an insult to the dead man's memory.

"May I ask you a question?"

"Of course," answered Diana; "anything you like."

I paused for a moment before continuing. "Why are you helping him? I mean, you know what he's done and what he's capable of. Why do you want to be involved?"

Diana smiled. "Why do you?"

"I don't think I do. He just arrived, that's all. It was almost as if he had established his presence before I really understood what was going on. I don't consider myself to be involved, not in the same way that you are."

"And which way's that?"

"Emotionally."

"Ah," and she smiled her beautiful smile again, "is that what I am – emotionally involved?"

"Aren't you?" (I longed for her to deny it).

She paused a long time before answering. "I don't think I know any other way to behave, Jonathan. I'm not like you. I can't cut myself off from what's happening around me. I'm a part of it, of everything. I don't have degrees of involvement. I don't think, 'this is acceptable but this isn't', or, 'yesterday I cared but today I don't'. I always have to be true to myself. How else do I know who I am?"

I suspected her of lying. No, that's probably too strong. I listened to her words and thought, "She is exaggerating her importance as a human being. She has to believe that she is capable of behaving at all times with dignity and consistency or else she really will have nothing. How could she possibly admit to herself that her motives for looking after Kieran were the simple, human ones of selfishness, pride and arrogance?"

"How can you live like that?" I said, only half in jest. "You must be exhausted."

"Oh, I am," she said, laughing and wiping her forehead with the back of her hand, "can't you see what a wreck I've become? I hardly dare show my face in public."

I thought she looked more wonderful than ever and longed to tell her so, but I couldn't help but believe that this deepening and transfiguration of her beauty was due solely to Kieran's influence, and that any compliment I was to pay Diana would naturally reflect upon him.

"You should hate him," I said, revealing more of my thoughts than I had intended. "Hate him for what he's done."

She moved away from me, leaning back in her chair and letting go of my hand.

"I don't understand," she said. "I don't understand what you want of me."

"I don't want anything."

"Yes you do, but I don't know what. You seem to want me to be somebody different, to act according to your beliefs. And yet, you're the one who is hiding him and protecting him from harm. I know the seriousness of his crime, Jonathan, what he has done. I'm not stupid. But so do you. Who do you think the police would consider the more guilty, you or me? You seem to think that because you really don't care what happens to Kieran that somehow makes you less culpable. It's what you do that matters, Jonathan, not what you think. You should really look at your own behaviour before you start criticising mine. Our relationship is not close enough for you to be able to tell me what to do."

The vehemence of her attack took me completely by surprise, and seemed only to add weight to my belief that she cared much more for Kieran than she was actually admitting. But in one thing I knew she was right, although to hear it from her own lips caused me much more pain than I could ever have imagined: our relationship, such as it was, depended only on the superficialities of a distant friendship, and any deeper or more meaningful contact between the two of us would remain, for ever, an impossibility. And yet, even as my heart seemed to heave downwards, I could still believe myself in love.

"I'm sorry, Jonathan," she continued, perhaps sensing my dejection and softening her tone a little, "I care for you deeply but you are a child. You have no idea what love or commitment is. You have never experienced anything; not truly. You filter out anything important from your life until you are left with only memory, and it's those false memories that keep you believing in yourself as someone who is living a reasonable life. Before you can move on as a human being you must decide on what you believe, and put your trust in those beliefs." Her words, however kindly meant, did nothing to alleviate my sense of irritation and alienation.

"Thank you," I said sarcastically. "Thank you for showing me where I was going wrong. Here I was, in my naivety, believing that I was living a satisfactory and generous life, keeping myself to myself and doing no hurt to anyone. But it seems I was wrong. How you must have all laughed at my childish behaviour. How easy it must have been to use me."

I knew that I was being ridiculous and that in the context of our conversation my words were striving so hard to impart a sense of drama that I was in danger of sounding like the child that she apparently believed me to be. Inwardly I despised myself, but I could not stop. "Without me, no, to be more exact without my money, I don't know how you would have all managed. Who would have bought all your drinks for you? But that's OK, I don't mind being used. In fact, as you have just said, I welcome it because I have nothing else in my life – but that's my problem and I don't expect gratitude."

"Gratitude." She repeated the word slowly and with emphasis as if the mere sound of it filled her with disgust. Her cheeks were flushed and her eyes were bright with anger and outrage. "You don't deserve gratitude, Jonathan. I suspect everything that you have ever done in your whole life you have done just for yourself. Oh, maybe you've had no choice and it's just been the only way that you've known how to behave, but that just makes it all the more insulting that you should now be seeking praise or even thanks. Why should anybody be grateful to you for doing only what gives you pleasure? You use people just as much as everybody else, even Kieran. But at least he knows his true nature and is prepared to own up to it. You can't even do that."

The conversation had taken on a life of its own. The words spoken seemed to come neither from me nor Diana but to exist independently of both of us. I had no desire to say what I had said, and I hoped that Diana, too, was merely responding to an attack that was both fictitious and self-absorbed. But I still couldn't help continuing: "You are in love with a murderer. You know that, don't you Diana, you are in love with a murderer?"

For a brief second I was proud of what I had said. "You are in love with a murderer." It had a poetic ring to it. This was what I had always longed for: a moment of pure, real life drama. Now I was really living. This was life made into something more important than life. Something that, at last, I could take seriously. And then I saw her face. Her expression had changed, almost instantaneously, from one of pride and confrontation into one of defeat. What, up until then, I had considered to be no more than an exercise in linguistics, however important its final conclusion was to prove, had suddenly become something of weight and importance. She was hurt. Not in the sense of the game that I believed we were both playing, but in truth and reality. I was ashamed, ashamed for being so careless in my use of words, and for my arrogance and cruelty.

"I'm sorry," I heard myself say. "I didn't mean it."

"Is that what you really think?" she said at last, ignoring my futile attempt at reconciliation. "That I am in love with a murderer?"

I tried desperately to make amends: "No, of course not; I'm sorry, I'm just being stupid."

"No, Jonathan," she said quietly, "you can't get away with it that easily. You meant it, I could tell from your eyes. I can't believe that you think me capable of such a thing. Do you really hate me that much?"

I was truly outraged. "I don't hate you Diana; far from it. I'd never do anything to hurt you. It's just that since the murder everything seems so complicated that I don't know what I think any more; and you've changed, you have to admit that. When you're around Kieran you seem different."

"Of course I do," she said with passion, "but that's because of the situation. I'm just as confused as you are, Jonathan, and I've had to change just to try to make some sort of sense of it all. I know exactly what Kieran's done and what he's capable of doing, but does that mean I should desert him? If I do that, then what does it make me? If you were in trouble, Jonathan, I'd do exactly the same for you. It's just the way I am. I thought you, as my closest friend, would understand that."

The phrase 'as my closest friend' anchored itself in my brain. Never before had she referred to me in such terms. Never before had she singled me out for such special praise. Did I believe her? Could I allow myself to believe her or was I being seduced? If she had used the phrase 'as my closest friend' as a deliberate attempt to gain my understanding and my sympathy then how could I believe anything she ever said again? But how could I think her capable of such deception, of such manipulation? Surely such deviant behaviour was beyond her? Her head was slightly bowed but her eyes were on mine: soft and vulnerable, but challenging, as if to say, "Doubt me if you wish, but you know it's true. You know that you are my closest friend."

I needed to trust her. I longed to say, "I understand why you are behaving the way you are, but please think, your innocence and your vulnerability will not protect you. You are excited by being in such close proximity to somebody like Kieran, but this is no fantasy. A real crime has been committed; a real person has been murdered; real people are grieving and yet you look better and seem happier than ever. Do you not think you should question your own behaviour before you question mine? If you are not in love with Kieran the person, then are you sure you are not in love with Kieran The Murderer?"

Instead, I said, "I'm very sorry. Things have happened that have taken me by surprise. I don't really know how to react. I don't want to hurt you. I don't want to hurt anybody. I think, probably, I just want to be left alone."

Her expression softened even more and her eyes became almost translucent dragging me towards her; and I suddenly realized that she was looking at me in the same way that I had seen her look at Kieran: with that same sickening mixture of condescension, pity and, god help me, invented love. And at that moment I loved her so much that I wanted to kill her.

Eventually we entered into an arrangement. We both knew, without admitting it openly, that we could not continue as we were; that it was impossible for us both to be in Kieran's presence at the same time; that the tension between the three of us would be almost too much to bear. Diana and I would have to organize the time we spent with Kieran very carefully so that we could continue to live our lives almost independently of him. I, naturally, would have him in the mornings and at night, while the afternoons would belong to Diana. In this way we hoped to fulfill the strange obligation that we felt towards Kieran, and to maintain the tenuous link that we felt still existed between the two of us.

As much as I still regretted the relationship that was forming between Kieran and Diana, my time spent alone with Kieran now became almost tolerable, thanks to the knowledge that I was no longer the sole recipient of Kieran's nightmare vision of the world. I would listen politely and patiently to his drunken outpourings, to his ramblings and his railings against the stupidity and vindictiveness of a society incapable of fully understanding him, knowing that relief would soon be at hand. The knock on the door would come and Diana and I would exchange places, unsure for a moment whether we were Kieran's companions or guards. And later, when we met up in the pub, we would say nothing of our time spent alone with Kieran. Perhaps we both understood, instinctively, that any conversation relating to Kieran would cause us more pain than we were prepared to bear. For three days this arrangement seemed to work so well that I almost began to forget what a ridiculous, dangerous and serious world I had been drawn into. Routine, of whatever type and however repugnant, had always been a great comfort to me.

And on the fourth day:

It was late afternoon. It had rained steadily for most of the day and the clouds were hanging low in the sky, bringing on an early darkness. I was, unusually, the only customer in the pub.

The landlord was sitting at the far end of the bar reading the sports page of the local newspaper. I had been there for almost an hour and had hardly touched the single measure of whisky that I had placed on the table in front of me. I was not unhappy, nor was I particularly thoughtful. I was simply content to be there, alone and ignored. Despite the silence and the gloom, or perhaps because of it, I felt myself to be part of something inexorable, something above and beyond me. I gained comfort from the knowledge that I was no more and no less significant than a thousand other people who had sat in exactly the same spot where I was now sitting. The lights of the one-armed bandit flashed off and on noiselessly and the rain occasionally spattered against the window pane behind me. Despite the best efforts of the cleaner, the pub still smelt of the previous night's excesses, of sweat, alcohol and cigarette smoke, and that too brought me comfort. This time I had no need of alcohol to bring on that familiar and incongruous feeling of inclusiveness and dislocation that I so loved. I was a part of the pub and the silence and the rain, and yet I experienced everything as if through a thin sheet of frosted glass; as if I were my own ghost watching my life unfold about me.

The door opened and Diana entered the pub. I recognized her immediately, of course, but she seemed somehow different, less substantial as if she, too, were simply a part of the life that I was inventing for myself. I watched her carefully as she bought her drink and came towards me, desperate to put some sort of shape and form to the entity that I knew as 'Diana'. She sat down opposite me and placed her drink on the table next to mine. For a moment I couldn't take my eyes off the two drinks, of the way the juxtaposition of clear and golden liquids caught what little light there was and reflected it back onto the table, the packet of tobacco, the dark blue of the cigarette lighter and the ashtray. Everything seemed perfect.

I followed her hand as it took hold of her glass and slowly raised it to her lips. One side of her face was bruised a deep, violent red, and there was a cut, not too deep but still bloody, just below her bottom lip. As she opened her mouth to drink she uttered a tiny, involuntary cry of pain. I could make no sense of any of it. This vision of Diana was not what I had expected, imagined or wished for. I turned away from her and looked around the room, just to confirm that everything was, indeed, as it should be. Slowly she returned her glass to the table and raised her eyes to look me full in the face. "He hurt me," she said in a voice no louder than a whisper. "He hurt me very much."

The landlord at last finished reading his newspaper and closed the last page with a violent crackle. The lights of the one-armed bandit continued to flash on and off, and the rain continued to splatter against the window pane.

"It wasn't my fault," she said. "I did nothing." A single tear formed at the corner of her right eye, which she quickly wiped away with the back of her hand. "I did nothing," she said again. "Nothing." She opened her handbag and rooted about inside for a second or two before producing a small packet of pink tissues.

I had absolutely no idea what to say or do. I imagined taking hold of her hand. I imagined reaching out for her and enveloping her in my arms. I imagined telling her that I was sorry and not to worry and that everything would be fine. I imagined saying "You don't look that bad and the bruises will soon disappear." I imagined offering her a cigarette or another drink, but everything seemed either pointless or vaguely ludicrous. Even the simple act of reaching for my own drink seemed to be an act too disruptive, too mundane to be acceptable in such a situation. I turned in on myself and waited expectantly for something else to happen.

She took hold of one of the tissues and began, tentatively, to dab at her face, wiping away the thin smear of blood from beneath her bottom lip. She investigated the tissue for a moment before screwing it up into a ball and depositing it in the ashtray – an act that, unfairly, caused me a fleeting moment's irritation. The silence between the two of us became more obvious and more intense, and yet it wasn't a silence that I found particularly uncomfortable. I had the distinct impression that she expected me to remain silent and that she knew I would be incapable of saying one thing of value. Again she looked me full in the face. "He raped me."

I understood that she had just told me something important, something that demanded a positive reaction, but still I found myself unable to connect with the Diana who was sitting opposite me, or the words that she was saying. Diana had been raped by Kieran, but I had no idea what that actually meant. I tried, almost despite myself, to imagine the act, but I could find nothing substantial to hold on to. I was almost on the point of saying, "are you sure?" when Jackie entered the pub. Neither Diana nor I had seen Jackie since she had walked out of my flat some days previously, and I had always suspected that our first meeting would be far from easy. But this was different. Diana caught my eye and turned to see Jackie approaching our table. "Oh god," she said, lowering her head and arranging her hair to cover as much of her face as possible, "why now?"

For a moment or two Jackie hovered by the side of our table as if waiting for permission to sit, before easing herself down next to Diana. Diana kept her face averted and I concentrated on my drink. I attempted a vague smile in Jackie's direction, but that was all. I could think of nothing relevant to say.

"You're both very quiet," Jackie said after a while. "Is everything OK?"

"Yes," I said. "Fine. And you?"

"Yes, fine," she answered. "A bit dull, but yes, everything's fine."

Still Diana had said nothing, nor even acknowledged Jackie's presence, and eventually Jackie realized that it was up to her to make the first move. "I haven't seen you for a while," she said, lowering her voice in a tentative attempt at intimacy. "Are you OK?" Diana still said nothing. Jackie looked across at me, her expression a mixture of sadness and confusion. I shrugged my shoulders in a gesture of complete hopelessness. She tried again: "Look, I'm sorry for walking out on you, but I didn't know what else to do. Kieran was being so rude, and it was only you I was thinking of. I just didn't want you to get hurt, that's all. I care about you Diana, and if I've let you down in any way then I'm sorry. I hope you can forgive me."

I longed for Diana to raise her head and to look at Jackie. I couldn't believe that anybody could miss the opportunity to participate in such a wonderfully dramatic moment as this.

Diana slowly raised her head and looked at Jackie: a performance even better than I had hoped for. There was an audible intake of breath, and Jackie raised her hands to her own face as if it were she that had been damaged. "My god," she said, "what's happened?"

"Oh thanks," said Diana, attempting a faint smile and dabbing once more at her face with a tissue, "do I look that bad?"

"No, I mean yes. Diana, you look terrible."

It was as if this verification of the state she was in permitted Diana, finally, to admit that something horrendous had occurred. She began, quietly, almost imperceptibly, to cry. Jackie didn't hesitate, but took Diana in her arms and pulled her towards her. "Oh Diana," she said, burying the side of her face in Diana's hair, "I'm so very, very sorry."

I didn't doubt for a second that Jackie's show of concern and compassion was spontaneous and genuine, "but how convenient", I couldn't help thinking, "how convenient for Jackie that she should now return in shame and trepidation only to be welcomed as Diana's one true friend and saviour". And "It should be me holding her like that. I should be the only one capable of bringing her such comfort." Perhaps my reaction was one of pure jealousy, but at the time I had almost convinced myself that I was acting out of the best of intentions, and that my only motive was one of pure altruism. "It's Kieran," I heard myself say. "He raped her."

Diana cast me a glance of such withering contempt that I immediately felt ashamed. Jackie released Diana from her embrace and looked deeply into her eyes. "Oh my god," she said, "it's true. It's true."

"Please," said Diana, sinking once more into Jackie's arms, "don't be cross. It wasn't my fault."

"No, of course it wasn't. How could it be? I just don't ... I mean how could ...?"

Stunned, for a moment, into silence, Jackie could only shake her head in disbelief.

"It wasn't my fault," Diana repeated, her voice now broken by sobs. "You have to believe me. I did nothing. Nothing. I just wanted to help."

"Shush," said Jackie soothingly, holding Diana even tighter, "I know. I know."

I looked at the two of them, brought together by a moment's recklessness. How I wished I could have been a part of their suffering.

"We must do something," said Jackie, still holding on to Diana. "We must do something to stop this. He must be made to pay for what he's done."

"No," said Diana, vehemently, wiping away her tears and extricating herself from Jackie's embrace. "No, we will do nothing."

"But he can't be allowed to get away with this," persisted Jackie. "I can't bear it."

"I mean it," said Diana, surprising even me with the force of her words. "It's all over. It's finished. There's no point."

"But it isn't," said Jackie. "He could do it again. Surely you don't want to be responsible for that?"

"Please don't shout at me," said Diana. "I just couldn't go through with it. Who would believe me? Nobody forced me to go and visit him: a man wanted for murder. I did his shopping for him, looked after his wounds and cooked his meals for him. I'd just look like a fool."

Jackie fell silent for a moment, pondering Diana's words. "OK," she said at last, "if that's what you want. But we can still tell the police where he is. We don't have to mention you at all."

"But what about Jonathan?" asked Diana. "They'll arrest him, too."

They both turned to look at me.

I envisaged, for a moment, the police forcing their way into my flat, the struggle with Kieran, and the two of us being handcuffed and bundled into a police car. There would be an audience, no doubt, and the press, and a flashing of cameras, and shouts of abuse and, later, the trial. My role in the whole affair would be secondary, but still important. And yet it all still seemed something of an anti-climax. I needed something more substantial.

"It's up to you, of course," I said. "You must do what you think is right."

"But you must have an opinion," said Jackie, her voice rising in frustration. "Are you prepared to let Kieran get away with what he's done to Diana? Don't you care? Don't you want him to suffer?"

"That's not fair," exclaimed Diana. "This has nothing to do with Jonathan."

I was so grateful for Diana's intervention. I genuinely had no idea what I felt or how I should respond. Murder? Rape? Such acts of destruction were so alien to my nature and understanding that I felt myself more cut off from the rest of society than ever.

"I give up," said Jackie in despair. "I just hope you both know what you're doing, that's all. You didn't listen to me last time, Diana, and look what happened. But whatever you decide I'll stand by you. You know you can always trust me."

"I know," said Diana. "I always could." And although she smiled gratefully at Jackie she couldn't disguise the hint of sadness in her voice. "Look after my drink will you?" she continued, giving Jackie's arm one final squeeze. "I have to go to the toilet."

We watched her carefully as she struggled to her feet and made her way awkwardly towards the door marked 'Ladies' at the far corner of the room. She moved so slowly and with such difficulty that I began to realise for the first time just how seriously she had been hurt. As soon as she had disappeared from view, Jackie turned on me, her face creased and flushed with anger and frustration. "This is ridiculous," she said, spitting out the words with such venom that I was taken by surprise. "You can see how much pain she's in. You can see what he's done to her. How can you be so calm, so disinterested? Don't you care? She thinks a lot about you, and you're supposed to be her friend but now, when she needs you the most, you do nothing. What's the matter with you?"

In some strange way I found her attack on my character almost reassuring; yet further proof that I was beyond reproach.

"But what can I do?" I asked, my voice remaining calm and unresponsive. "It's Diana's choice. She's the one who's been hurt, and if she doesn't want to do anything about it, then how can I interfere?"

"You can tell the police where Kieran is. You don't have to mention Diana at all. Just get him locked up where he can't do any more harm."

"But that's not what Diana wants."

"What's that got to do with anything? Just do it! I'm sure she'll forgive you, eventually." I remained silent, my head bowed and my eyes focused on the drink in front of me, as if I were taking her suggestion seriously. "Because if you don't tell the police," she continued, "I will."

Her threat seemed genuine and, for a fleeting second, the perfect solution to all our problems. Diana would be revenged, Jackie would feel virtuous and Kieran, a vicious and dangerous criminal, would be out of all of our lives forever. We could all congratulate ourselves on acting so correctly and with such honour. There would, of course, be the small matter of my aiding and abetting a man suspected of murder, but I had no doubt that I could, eventually, convince the police of my innocence: "I didn't want to do it, but he gave me no option. I feared for my life." So why did Jackie's threat to hand Kieran over to the police fill me with such a deep feeling of dread? I tried to imagine returning home to an empty flat and continuing with my life as if none of this had ever happened. It was almost impossible. The mere thought of it plunged me into such a state of dejection that, for a moment, I could see no future in anything.

"You must listen to Diana," I heard myself say. "You have no right to go against her wishes. Being a best friend means you have to respect the other person's point of view, even when you don't agree with it. I don't understand how you can be prepared to risk losing Diana's friendship, all because of Kieran. He will have won again and you will be left with nothing. It's Diana who matters, not Kieran. What's done is done and if you make the wrong decision now Diana may never forgive you. Are you sure that's what you want?"

I felt as if my words had had some effect. Jackie looked at me long and hard, incapable or unwilling for the moment to pursue her line of argument, before sighing heavily and reaching for her drink. "Be careful," I said, eager to press home my advantage. "By condemning Kieran, you might be condemning yourself."

Before she could answer, Diana returned from the toilet. She had applied fresh make-up, too much lipstick, powder and eye shadow, in a vain attempt to cover up the worst of her bruises. Far from returning her to some sort of normality, the over-use of make-up seemed only to emphasize her disfigurement. One's eyes were drawn irrevocably to the mask that her face had become.

"That's better," she said, attempting a smile only with her mouth while her eyes remained dead, "now I can face the world."

"I'll get you another drink," said Jackie, "unless you want to go home."

"No," said Diana. "I'm tired but another drink would be good. Thank you." Her gentility and politeness after having suffered so much brutality seemed almost unnatural.

"So," Diana said, as soon as Jackie had left us, "what were you two talking about? Jackie doesn't look at all happy."

"We were talking about you," I said. "She was threatening to tell the police where Kieran's hiding."

"You talked her out of it, I hope."

"I think so. I told her you might never forgive her. She didn't seem to like that."

"No," she said, "she wouldn't." And then, leaning closer towards me: "You understand why I don't want anybody to know, don't you Jonathan? Why I just want to forget the whole thing."

"Of course," I said, "and I think you're right. Kieran is untouchable. If we sent him to prison he wouldn't care. I don't mean he wants to go to prison, but he would just accept it as another part of his life. He would regret nothing and neither repent nor apologize. Prison, for Kieran, would be totally inadequate as a form of revenge."

"I don't want revenge," said Diana. "I shall never forget what he did to me, but slowly the details will fade until I can almost convince myself that it happened to somebody else. Perhaps a film I saw or a book I read. I need to continue to live my life as if none of this ever happened. It's the only way I know how to survive."

I nodded in agreement but, to be honest, I found her unquestioning acceptance of her situation somewhat unsettling. Deep down, I wanted her to rage against the unfairness of it all, to shout and to rave and to despair. How can one judge the seriousness of any act except by the way that people respond? Where others may have seen in Diana's stoicism an example of the bravery and grace of the human condition, I was in danger of seeing only delusion and cowardice.

I longed to say "Apart from the bruises and the cut to your face that are obvious to everyone, are you sure that you have been seriously hurt, and that your show of condescension and dignity is not a simple form of self-aggrandisement?" Instead, of course, I said nothing.

"Are you OK?" asked Jackie, as she passed Diana her drink. "You look very pale."

"Yes," answered Diana, "I'm fine; just a little tired, that's all." And once more she smiled her thin, unresponsive smile.

"Right," said Jackie, switching almost immediately into the role of nurse and protector, "we'll finish our drinks and then I'll take you home. You need looking after."

Half-heartedly, Diana attempted to shrug off Jackie's concern, but Jackie was insistent. "No," she said, "this time I won't take no for an answer. I understand why you won't let me tell the police about Kieran, although I still think you're wrong, but at least I can do this for you. Drink up and I'll take you home and cook you a meal. I bet you haven't eaten for hours. And your bruises need seeing to and you need a good long rest. You should really go to the hospital or at least see a doctor, just to be safe, but I don't suppose you want to do that either. You're probably still in shock and won't really begin to understand what's happened to you until later. But don't worry, I won't leave you. You're sure you don't hurt anywhere else? You've no other pains, I mean, inside? You can't afford to take any chances. You must tell me if you start to feel worse. Promise me, Diana. Promise me you'll tell me if you start to feel really ill or if you have any other pains anywhere else. I'll never forgive Kieran for what he's done to you. People like him only know how to destroy, but we won't let him destroy us, will we Diana? We're much stronger than that. We'll show him."

"Jackie," Diana finally exclaimed, placing a restraining hand on Jackie's shoulder, "stop it. You're making me nervous." But she was smiling fondly at her.

Jackie stopped talking and took hold of Diana's hand. They were together, their bodies leaning affectionately towards each other. Jackie, despite her earlier disagreement with Diana, was obviously happy. This was the role that she had always envisaged and desired for herself: Diana's friend, confidante, protector and saviour. She had long known that if only Diana would be guided by her then the lives of both of them would be enriched beyond measure. As she saw it, the flaws and failings inherent in each other's character would be more than counterbalanced by the good points that, she believed, they both possessed. Her love for Diana, for in any accepted use of the word it *was* love, was, if she would only admit it, almost indistinguishable from the pure and self-sacrificing love that she had once offered up to her god. The only difference, and one that Jackie was only too ready to embrace, was that in Diana she was confronted by a being far from perfect and, therefore, somebody more in need of her advice and guidance. "If you would only listen to me," she longed to say to Diana, "then together we could attain that level of perfection that is the true destiny of all right-thinking people. You are kind, thoughtful and honest but your generosity is wayward, lacking in direction or discretion. Too often you demean yourself by the company you keep and by the irrelevance of your compassion. You need me to be your judge and severest critic." She had a vision of the two of them living together somewhere bright and isolated: a whitewashed cottage overlooking the sea where the light would soften and blur their individuality until they merged into one perfect entity. How she longed for Diana's beauty, and how she despised herself for the triviality of her ambition. Jackie's face expressed pure bliss: her eyes were half closed and she was smiling a faint, beatific smile of victory and contentment.

Diana, too, looked content. For once she seemed totally willing to give herself emotionally to Jackie. They were still holding hands and Diana's head had fallen slightly forward. She seemed on the point of falling asleep. As her expression relaxed and softened, the light in her eyes seemed gradually to fade and she appeared more vulnerable than ever. Suddenly I envied Jackie, her proximity to, and the trust that she obviously engendered in Diana. And yet I knew instinctively that it would have been impossible for me to replace Jackie in Diana's affections. My self-doubt and sense of alienation would have made even the simple gesture of holding Diana's hand seem like an act of betrayal. I could never have responded so naturally and unthinkingly to Diana's distress.

"Are you OK?" Jackie asked once more, brushing the hair away from Diana's face. "Can I do anything for you?" Diana looked up at Jackie, opened her eyes wide and smiled. It was almost as if they were already alone and my presence had become a total irrelevance. Suddenly I felt terribly ashamed of my inactivity. But what else could I do? I had no knowledge of how else to behave.

"We can leave whenever you like," said Jackie.

"Soon," said Diana, letting go of Jackie's hand and reaching for her drink.

"I'll get a taxi," said Jackie.

"Don't be silly," protested Diana. "It's not far. We can walk."

"It's pouring down," said Jackie. "I don't want you catching a cold on top of everything else."

"All right," said Diana, "whatever you think is best."

"I won't be a minute," said Jackie, "I've got the number somewhere." She picked up her handbag, stood up and made her way to the phone situated at the far end of the bar.

"She seems very happy," I said.

"What do you mean?" asked Diana.

"Nothing," I answered tentatively. "Just that she seems very happy, that's all, now that she's got something to do."

"She cares," said Diana.

"Yes, I know," I said, without conviction. "She's a very caring person."

"You shouldn't mock," said Diana.

"I'm not mocking," I said. "But you have to admit, this couldn't have happened at a better time for her."

"I don't understand."

"Well," I said, sensing Diana's mounting resentment and trying to choose my words carefully. "You two had a falling out, and now you're the best of friends again. It's all very convenient."

"So you're saying the rape was a good thing."

"No, of course not, how could it be? It's just that Jackie can now feel that she's being of some use to you. She can feel wanted."

"But she is of some use to me. She always has been. You don't understand us at all, do you?"

"Oh come on, Diana, you have to admit that there have been times when even you have found her irritating."

"At least she was prepared to do something."

"I don't understand."

"When she heard I'd been raped, she was angry. She wanted Kieran to suffer for what he'd done to me."

"But we agreed that you didn't want the police involved. You said so."

"Yes, I know," she said, "and I was right. But that doesn't change the way I feel. I have been hurt badly, Jonathan, and just because I don't want to go to the police doesn't mean that I can forgive or forget. Jackie understands that, whereas you ..."

"What? I don't understand what you want of me."

"Nothing, Jonathan, I don't want anything from you."

"But you obviously do, that's why you're talking to me like this. What do you want of me?"

She fell silent for a moment, but she continued to look at me long and hard, her eyes scanning my face as if she were searching for something as yet undiscovered, some distinguishing mark that would give her a new insight into my character. "I want you," she said at last, drawing out her words for maximum effect, "to feel."

I was stunned into silence. To feel what? The pain, happiness and love of other people? How is that possible? One can empathize, but actually to feel ... Such a show of emotion must surely be no more than a device, a stance that one adopts to appear acceptable. I would not play the hypocrite. "I can only be what I am," I said. "Anything else would be a lie."

Diana leaned forward in her chair and took another mouthful of her drink. When eventually she spoke, her voice was calm and almost totally devoid of all emotion: "Shall I tell you what

Kieran did to me, Jonathan? Would you like to know? Would that help you to understand what I am feeling?"

I was horrified. How could she possibly contemplate saying such things? I began to speak, but could find no words to complete the sentence.

"You don't seem very keen," Diana continued. "What are you afraid of?"

"I'm not afraid," I managed to say, "it's just that I don't see the point."

She smiled: a vague smile of victory and condescension. "There's every point," she said. "I don't believe that you think I've been raped at all; that it's all in my head. Oh, he may have slapped me around a bit, but rape? You can't imagine such a thing, can you Jonathan? You need to be told."

I looked across to where Jackie was still on the phone. I couldn't understand what was taking her so long. I thought of my blank sheet of hardboard and my paints waiting to be turned into something extraordinary. I thought of Kieran and my dead parents, and it seemed to me that despite what Diana had just said, truth and reality were to be found only in my imagination.

Suddenly Diana burst into laughter. "Don't worry," she said, "and don't look so frightened. I've no intention of telling you anything. I just wanted to know how you'd react, that's all. I wouldn't dream of destroying your little world. After all, it's all you've got."

I turned away from her. All I wished for was to be alone. I had done nothing and yet I was constantly being made to feel so guilty. How dare people expect anything of me? On another occasion I would have scuttled off to my flat clutching a bottle of whisky, locked the door behind me, drunk myself into a stupor and waited for the woman in the flat opposite to perform for me. But Kieran was there and I had nowhere else to go. Even the life that I thought I was living now no longer seemed to belong to me.

Jackie returned to the table. Without sitting down she reached for her glass.

"Sorry it's been so long," she said, "they're very busy. But they can fit us in now, if you're ready."

Diana picked up her glass. "Ready when you are."

Jackie helped Diana to her feet and placed a protective arm around her shoulders.

"Don't forget, Jonathan," said Diana, just before turning away from me, "he hurt me. He hurt me very much."

I watched as they headed towards the door, arm in arm. I half hoped that Diana would turn round and look at me for one last time before she left the pub, but I knew she wouldn't.

It was later than usual by the time I returned to my flat. I knew that Kieran would be angry at my prolonged absence, but still I had delayed my journey home for as long as possible. I was reluctant both to leave the warmth and security of the pub and to spend any more time than was absolutely necessary in Kieran's company. I was still slightly uncertain as to what exactly had taken place between Kieran and Diana (Diana's apparent resilience and lack of any desire to seek revenge, serving, in some strange way, only to trivialize the reported brutality of the act) but whatever had occurred I knew that I would be faced with a new Kieran: a Kieran more triumphant and arrogant than ever. I made my way home slowly and with an ever-increasing feeling of dread. I even, despite my belief in nothing, offered up a little prayer that I would find my flat empty.

He was waiting for me.

The first thing I noticed was a new scar running the full length of one side of his face, not deep but still open and raw. He was sitting in his usual position by the window, a half-empty bottle of whisky by his side and a cigarette in his hand. There was loud music playing on the record player.

"You took your time," he said, as I entered the room, but he was smiling and his manner was relaxed.

"Yes, I know," I said. "I'm sorry. I got talking. You know how it is."

"That's all right," he said. "These things happen."

"Do you want anything to eat?" I asked, as I made my way into the kitchen.

"No, I'm fine," he answered, his voice suddenly taking on a smug and unpleasant edge. "I've had everything I want."

I clattered about in the kitchen, without reason and to no purpose. I simply wanted to avoid being in the same room as him for as long as possible.

"Who have you been with?" he asked, lifting his voice above the sound of the music. "Anybody interesting?"

"No, not really," I answered, "just the usual crowd."

"Was Diana there?"

I hesitated for just a second: "Yes," I answered, "and Jackie."

"How is she?"

"Who?"

"Diana, who else?"

"Yes, she's fine."

"Are you sure, was she OK?"

"No ... well ... yes, how do you mean?"

"The bruises on her face – didn't you notice? You must have noticed. You're not blind are you?"

"No, of course not, she did look as though she'd had a little bit of trouble."

"It's what she wanted," he said, his voice still coming from a long way away and lifted high above the sound of the music. "Some women are like that. It's the only way they can come. They need a little bit of violence. They have to be shown who's boss. She kept telling me to hit her. God, you should have heard her moan. Every time I hit her the more she moaned. But you probably know that. I presume you've had her. You're a fool if you haven't. She's always available."

Perhaps it was the association of my name with his and Diana's, or the amount of alcohol I had drunk, but I suddenly felt tired and sick and disgusted with the whole affair and especially with my role in it. Almost before I had decided upon any deliberate course of action I found myself leaving the kitchen, crossing the sitting room floor and switching off the record player.

"What did you do that for?" he asked. "That was the best track."

"You have to leave."

"What?"

"You have to leave. You can't stay here."

It was obvious that my words came as a total shock to him: he remained seated, his glass of whisky held half way to his mouth, his forehead creased in concentration. "It's the police," I continued, "they're interviewing everybody. It's only a matter of time before they come here. You have to leave."

He lifted his glass to his lips and drank slowly, his eyes never leaving mine. I took a step towards him and waited patiently for his reaction. Now that I had spoken I felt remarkably calm. There was nothing that he could do to me that could alter what had been said. I felt strangely liberated.

"Who have you been talking to?"

"What? I haven't been talking to anybody."

"Yes you have," he insisted. "You've already told me you were with Jackie and Diana and the rest of them. What have they been saying?"

"Only that the police have started to interview everybody who knows you, and that it was only a matter of time before they got round to me. In fact, they were surprised that I hadn't been interviewed already." I was aware that I was talking far too quickly, and without conviction or precision.

"You're lying," he said, "I can tell by your eyes. This has got nothing to do with the police, has it? It's Diana. Whatever she's told you about me, it isn't true. You shouldn't believe a word she says. She's a lying cow."

The mere mention of Diana's name threw me into a panic. I had no desire under any circumstances to discuss or even contemplate what had happened between the two of them. "Just think about it, Kieran," I persisted, "the police know who your friends are. Of course they're going to come here."

He lit up another cigarette and let the smoke drift out from his mouth and nose.

"And you say the police have already started interviewing people."

"Yes."

"Colin, Vince, Jackie."

"Well," I hesitated, "I don't know if they've seen everybody, but we must all be on their list. They must have considered the possibility that one of us might be hiding you. They're not that stupid." He continued to smoke and to drink, but said nothing, and for the first time I began to believe that I might actually have succeeded in convincing him of the rightness of my plan. "I'm only thinking of you," I began, eager to press home my advantage.

"OK," he said, interrupting me, "you've made your point. Just let me think."

I wandered off into the kitchen, and it was only when I attempted to fill the kettle that I realized that my hand was shaking. I laid out two cups on the work surface, I brought out coffee, and milk from the fridge and listened to the boiling of the water in the kettle. Kieran joined me in the kitchen. I could sense his presence behind me, but I could also sense his confusion. Eventually he spoke, his voice sounding surprisingly lost and abandoned: "So where should I go?"

"Don't worry," I said, desperate to hide the indecision in my voice, "I'll find somewhere safe for you to stay. You can trust me, I won't let you down."

"You better had," he said, threateningly, "or we're both in trouble."

"Everything's fixed," I said. "Colin will pick us up in his van in about an hour. He'll be waiting for us in the basement."

It was late the following evening and I had, for once, acted with vigour and precision. Colin had taken some convincing to help until I pointed out that if Kieran were caught then Colin, along with the rest of us, was sure to be implicated. "Do you think Kieran would hesitate to give us away?" I had said. "He would find it amusing and only fitting to see us on trial beside him."

"Where are we going?" Kieran asked.

"Somewhere safe," I replied, loath at that point to give too much away. "It's not far."

I was busy and, surprisingly, almost elated to be so organized and active. Kieran stood in the middle of the room while I worked around him. I opened cupboard doors and stuffed bags with clothes, blankets, toiletries, a sleeping bag, whisky, cigarettes, cooking utensils and anything else that I thought could be of use to him.

"I hope you don't think I'm camping out," he said, watching me closely. "It's not my style."

"Not quite," I said, careful not to give too much away and enjoying my sudden power over him. "At least you won't be out of doors."

"I'm glad to hear it," he said. "It's fucking freezing out there."

Eventually all was ready and I stood back to view my efforts. "Right, I think that's all we can manage this trip. There's more stuff in the van. We're bound to have forgotten something, but that's OK. I can bring what you need later. Are you ready?"

"This better be good," he said, picking up two of the bags, "or you'll regret it."

"Don't worry," I said, "you know you can trust me."

The trip down the stairs (we thought it safer than risking the lift) was uneventful – we saw nobody. Colin was waiting for us in the basement, the back doors of the van already open. We were safely inside in a matter of seconds, me in the front seat and Kieran in the back.

"So where are we going?" asked Colin, his voice flat and unresponsive.

"Just head towards town," I said. "I'll give you directions as we go along. Don't worry, it's not far."

"Aiding and abetting a suspected murderer," Kieran said, as we turned out onto the main road, "you could get five years for that."

"I'm helping Jonathan," said Colin, "not you."

"Well that's all right, then," said Kieran, his voice coming out of the darkness behind us. "I'm sure the police will understand. They're good like that."

"Listen Kieran," said Colin, "I don't have to do this. I couldn't give a shit whether you're caught or not, and if you don't shut the fuck up I'll stop the van and leave you right here by the side of the road. Just see how far you'd get then."

"I don't need you," Kieran answered, his face suddenly appearing between me and Colin, "and I don't need him either. So don't expect me to be fucking grateful."

Colin slammed on the brakes of the van so violently that Kieran almost toppled over into the front seat. As Colin took hold of the door handle I reached out and grasped his other arm. "Don't, Colin," I said. "He's doing this on purpose. You know what he's like. Let's just get this over and done with as quickly as possible and then you'll never have to see him again. And you," I continued, turning towards Kieran, "just try and be quiet for ten minutes will you? You may not like this, but just think of the alternative. There isn't one. And sit down, for Christ's sake. You're too fucking obvious."

Kieran hesitated for a moment, and then, with one final growl of disapproval, disappeared from view.

"Right," I said, "can we carry on now?"

Reluctantly, Colin shifted into first gear and the van moved slowly forward.

"If he says one more word," Colin whispered, "I swear I'll do it. Either that or I'll hand him over to the police myself."

"He won't," I said. "He knows this is the only hope he's got. You know what he's like. He can't help himself."

"Yeah, well," said Colin. "He should make more of an effort and realize just who his friends are."

In the darkness I smiled quietly to myself. How little Colin understood Kieran and, unlike Colin, how much I wanted Kieran to remain exactly the same as he was. I think it was at that precise moment that I realized that everything was going to be fine. I turned and looked out of the side window, content and relaxed in the familiarity of my surroundings.

Following my directions we left the town centre and climbed Town Mill Rise, heading towards Kirklees Estate and the house where I had once lived. Although not far from my flat, I had never (simply through a lack of interest or curiosity) returned to the area where I had spent most of my life, and much to my surprise very little seemed to have changed. I recognized without trouble the shops, houses, cul-de-sacs, avenues and streets where I had played and that I had travelled practically every day in my journeys to and from school and in the infrequent visits to the houses of my few friends. As we approached my old house I asked Colin to slow down, and gazed abstractedly at the iron railings surrounding the small front garden, and the red-brick façade with its four sash windows, now painted white, and its central front door, so much like a child's drawing of an ideal family house. And I felt nothing. So alienated had I become from my past that I could hardly remember living there at all. Not one incident of any real significance could I bring to mind to help me to anchor my childhood to a definite sense of time and place. I had become truly homeless and almost revelled in this sudden surge of anonymity. It was only as we left the main thoroughfares and headed towards the outskirts of the estate did I begin to experience some definite feelings of anxiety and anticipation. Gradually the houses became fewer and more and more dilapidated, neglected or even abandoned altogether, and the roads became less and less well maintained. Eventually we turned sharp left and found ourselves on a narrow, cobbled street that soon petered out and became nothing more than a rough boulder-strewn and pot-holed lane, reminiscent of an old farm track or walkway.

"OK," I said, as the van plunged for one last time into a particularly deep and vicious depression, "this will do."

"Thank Christ for that," said Colin, "I don't think the van could stand any more."

"Where the fuck are we?" asked Kieran, his face looming once more out of the darkness. "Is this some sort of joke?"

We peered out through the windscreen and the side windows, straining our eyes against the diffused glow of the headlights, and searching in vain to discover one recognizable object or shape to give us confidence that we were in the right place. A thin and peevish rain had begun to fall.

"There's nothing here," said Colin, shaking his head from side to side. "Nothing."

"Yes there is," I said, "you just can't see it. I thought it best if you didn't know exactly where I was taking him; much safer that way."

"Suits me," said Colin, "the less I know the better. Right then – everybody out."

Battling against the rain and the darkness, Kieran and I dragged the bags out of the back of the van and threw them onto the damp and pitted ground. As soon as we had finished unloading and slammed the door behind us, Colin began to move off, maneuvering the van slowly and with some difficulty backwards and forwards until he was facing the way we had come. I thought he might say something before leaving us, but he drove away without even a glance in our direction.

"Now what?" asked Kieran.

"Come on," I said, hoisting one of the rucksacks onto my shoulder, "this way."

I was determined to keep moving and to give no chance for Kieran to question or to doubt my intentions.

I remembered the route so well, even in the half light of a late January evening. I strode out confidently and without hesitation. We walked steadily for about twenty minutes, following a narrow, stone-strewn path as it meandered and dipped and cut its way through rampant fields of hawthorn and thistle. The rain intensified and I heard Kieran curse and swear behind me as he stumbled and slipped his way forward. Turning right and leaving the main path behind us, we struggled up a short, sharp incline and came, at last, to a flat expanse of scrubland that fronted the remains of the old, half-derelict mill where, as a

154

child, I had spent so much of my time. I stopped to take in the view: the scattered and broken remains of masonry and rusting metal, and the vast frontage of the mill itself, a symmetrical and brooding presence glowing a dull silvery grey in the gathering gloom. It was, for me, a moment of almost religious intensity, as if I were suddenly confronted by a place of such mythical significance that I had come to believe that it existed only in my imagination. Kieran came and stood next to me, his breathing harsh and erratic and almost deafening in the heavy silence of the night. I moved quickly forward, giving him no time to recover or to say anything.

We didn't stop again until we had reached the main entrance to the mill. We stood close together and strained our eyes into the darkness. I reached into one of the bags and produced two torches. "I'll go first," I said, "but be careful – some of the steps might be rotten."

We crept forward, the light from our torches picking out and illuminating the crumbling walls, the broken and splintered floorboards and, half way along the corridor, the wide, wooden staircase that wound its way steeply upwards and into the very heart of the building itself. As we began to climb I breathed in deeply, savoring the long remembered smell of dust, damp and decay. Despite the trepidation with which I approached each new step, I felt myself to be in some sort of spiritual ecstasy, striving to return to the only place where I had ever truly felt at one with the world. "Nearly there," I said, as we reached the top floor of the mill. "Just down here and then we can relax."

I took Kieran to my room. I led him slowly, determined to experience to the full the memory of past adventures and delights. I entered the room, hesitated for a moment and then dropped my bags to the floor. Kieran did the same. I looked around me, directing my torch quickly from one side of the room to the other, desperate for reassurance that everything was as it should be, that nothing had changed and that my memory had not played me false. A full winter moon was shining brightly through the broken widow frame and the few remaining panes of cracked and distorted glass, illuminating one wall and a greater part of the rough, wooden floor. "Well," I said, incapable of keeping the pleasure and excitement out of my voice, "what do you think?"

"You tell me, Jonathan," he answered, his voice cold and flat. "What should I think?"

"Don't worry," I continued, ignoring his obvious lack of enthusiasm, and beginning to unpack the bags. "I'll make it comfortable for you. And with a little bit of luck you won't have to stay here long. You'll soon get used to it. And you never know, you might even get to like it."

In truth, I was so caught up in the strangeness of the moment that I had almost convinced myself that it was me and not Kieran who was going to spend some time there. I worked rapidly and enthusiastically, totally absorbed in the distribution of our meagre possessions. Kieran, much to my relief, showed complete disinterest in the whole scheme, crossing to the window and staring mournfully out into the surrounding darkness. In one corner of the room I unrolled a small woollen rug, on top of which I placed a thin rubber mat and a sleeping bag. Over that I spread a heavy woollen blanket. By the side of this, within easy reach, I arranged, neatly and in some sort of order, his tins of food, coffee, water, whisky, cigarettes, crockery and cooking utensils. The small gas stove with a box of matches and five large candles, two of which I lit, I then placed in the centre of the room. I dragged the empty bags to one side of the room and then stood back to admire my work. I thought it perfect; an escape from everything that could cause hurt, fear, loneliness and despair. "OK," I said, "I think that's it."

I was eager for Kieran to share in my pleasure, for him to turn away from the window and, almost despite himself, to congratulate me on my efforts. He didn't move. His whole body remained totally immobile, his back and shoulders hunched towards me. I liked to believe that he hadn't heard me. I spoke again, raising my voice slightly. "OK, Kieran, I've finished."

Slowly he turned round and cast his eyes over the scene set out before him.

"Well," I asked eagerly, "what do you think?"

He reached casually into his jacket pocket and pulled out a packet of cigarettes.

"Very pretty," he said, flicking open his lighter, taking in a deep breath and letting the smoke drift out from his nose and lips. "And just where am I supposed to take a shit?"

His comment was so unexpected, and seemed so brutal and mundane in, as I saw it, such magical surroundings, and yet so typical of him that I almost burst out laughing. "There are the remains of some toilets down the corridor," I said, pointing in the right direction, "just opposite the staircase. They don't work, of course, but as each one fills up you can just move on to the next. There's a roll of toilet paper over there by the whisky."

"You seem to have thought of everything," he said, in a voice far from congratulatory, "but there's just one problem: I won't be here." He picked up one of the torches and strode towards the door.

Without thinking I moved to intercept him and took hold of his arm.

"You can't –" I began.

"Can't?" he said, breaking free of my grasp and gripping me by the throat. "Can't what? Don't you fucking dare tell me what I can and can't do! I could kill you, Jonathan, do you realise that? Here and now I could kill you and nobody would know or care. If this place is as safe as you say, it could be weeks, even months before you were found, and by then I would be long gone. So just be very careful how you talk to me."

"I'm sorry," I managed to gasp, "but I'm only thinking of you. The police are everywhere. If you leave here you're bound to get caught. I'm trying to help you."

"Look at this place," he said, spinning me round but still holding me tight. "Go on, look at it! Do you really think I'm going to stay in a shit-hole like this? What's the matter with you? I can't believe you could be so fucking stupid, or are you doing this on purpose? Is that it, Jonathan? Did you think, it's only Kieran so it doesn't matter; just stick him anywhere; just get rid of him? Is that it, Jonathan? Are you hoping I'm going to die in this place?"

I was genuinely shocked. I truly believed that I had made the room as comfortable and as habitable as possible. "I don't know what you want from me," I said, half in anger and half in despair. "Without me you'd probably already be in jail. But if you don't want to stay here, then that's fine. Just fuck off and see how far you'll get. But just remember, Kieran, however bad you think this is it's still better than prison. But it's up to you. I don't fucking care any more."

As always when I felt myself losing control, I suddenly became aware of the futility and idiocy of my behaviour and, even while speaking, my true feelings seemed to evaporate in a haze of indecision. I watched myself reacting to his words and immediately lost all sense of purpose. But still I continued: "You wouldn't stand a chance. Your picture is everywhere. Everybody knows what you look like. I know it's not brilliant here, but it's the only chance you've got. You should be comfortable enough once you get used to it, and I'll come and visit you every day and make sure you've got everything you want. You never know, it might only be for a day or two. The police are bound to lose interest sooner or later. Why don't you give it a try? What have you got to lose?"

For a moment his grip around my throat and chest tightened even more until I could hardly breathe, and then suddenly, as if he had only just realized that he was in contact with something deeply unpleasant, he pushed me violently away from him. He hesitated briefly, then strode purposefully to the far side of the room where he reached down for the bottle of whisky, scattering my carefully arranged pile of tins, utensils and boxes all over the floor. He raised the bottle to his lips and took a long drink, his eyes never leaving mine.

"Why are you doing this?" he asked. "What's in it for you?"

"I don't know," I answered. "Maybe it's just something that friends do for one another."

"That's what Diana said," he said, "and I didn't believe her and I don't believe you." He took another drink of whisky. "You're a fucking liar."

I shrugged, knowing that it would be pointless to say anything. His expression was still hard and unforgiving, his thin lips drawn into a tight slit of almost ungovernable rage. He clutched the bottle of whisky to his chest and began slowly to wander around the room, peering out through the entrance and along the corridor, following the contours of the walls, scuffing up tiny clouds of dust with his boots and returning finally to the window, where he stood motionless, his back turned towards me. "It's fucking freezing," he said, wrapping his arms tighter about himself. "I'll probably die of pneumonia long before the police find me."

Still I said nothing. I waited in silence, listening to the drip of rain falling on the remains of the broken and dislodged roof tiles. A slight gust of wind blew across the room and set the flames of the candles in motion, throwing our shadows into obscure and unrecognizable relief.

"I'm not staying long," he said.

"No."

"Just a couple of days and then I'm off."

"Yes," I said. "I understand."

"And you'll come every day?"

"Every day. Without fail."

We fell once more into an uneasy silence.

"I'm hungry," he said.

I crossed to the stove. "I'll make some soup." For the next few minutes I busied myself happily, content to have something useful to do at last. I lit the stove, emptied the contents of a tin into the pan, brought out two bowls, two spoons and two knives and placed four large chunks of bread and butter on a plate. As the soup began to bubble Kieran came and joined me, sitting close to the stove and holding out his hands towards the warmth.

"You love this, don't you?" he said.

"What?"

"All this," he said, indicating the whole room. "All this camping out crap, this 'roughing it'."

"I don't mind," I said, "when it's necessary."

He dipped his bread into his soup and plunged the soggy mass into his mouth, smearing his chin with the bright red liquid. "You ought to thank me," he said, speaking and chewing at the same time.

"Thank you for what?"

"For giving you something to live for."

I smiled and thought of the murdered shopkeeper and his wife and children and of Diana. "Thank you," I said. "I'm very grateful."

"You're welcome," he said, stretching out his hand for another piece of bread. "I aim to please."

We continued to eat and to drink whisky for the next half an hour or so, saying little, marooned in our tiny pool of light, our bodies huddled towards the warmth of the stove. I knew that I should leave, that my job was done for the time being, but I was finding it almost impossible to move. I thought of my long, cold walk home and I almost shivered with disgust. Even Kieran's unwelcome presence failed to encourage me to go. Indeed, for that one brief moment I could have almost convinced myself that he and I were friends; that we were both outcasts, brought together in adversity by a cruel, uncaring and vindictive world. We continued to smoke and to drink in silence, becoming more and more aware of the noises around us: the creak of wood, the spatter of rain falling on floors and ceilings, and the distant groan of the wind blowing through collapsed masonry and the deserted rooms and corridors. The tiny gas stove hissed between us.

Kieran leaned forward to light his cigarette from one of the candles.

"You'll be OK," I said. "Nobody ever comes here." He said nothing. "I think this was one of the offices. Most of the machinery was housed on the first two floors, but I wouldn't wander around too much, it's not safe." Still he said nothing.

"And I wouldn't spend too much time at the window if I were you, especially during the day. It's pretty deserted round here, but people do occasionally pass by. And try and keep the light down to a minimum. You'd be surprised how easily it can be seen, even from a distance. And try not to go outside, even for a second, you never know who's watching."

"Jonathan," Kieran said, bringing me to a halt, "why don't you just fuck off home?"

"You're right," I said, rising to my feet and attempting to hide my irritation at being so summarily dismissed. "I've been here long enough."

I picked up the empty bags and my torch and made my way towards the doorway. "Is there anything you want?" I asked.

"Like what?"

"I don't know – anything."

He thought for a moment. "Bring me some dope."

"OK."

"And a radio."

"A radio? I'm not sure that's a good idea – the noise."

"Just do it," he snapped, "or I'll go out of my fucking mind."

"OK, whatever you say." A pause. "Right, I'd better be going. It's a long walk home." But still I didn't move. I finished my cigarette and stubbed it out on the floor. He was watching me intently.

"You sure you'll be O.K?"

"Just fuck off, will you," he said, "and don't forget the radio."

The police, in an act of almost sublime timing, called round at my flat the following morning. So opportune was their visit that I could have almost convinced myself that they had been waiting for Kieran to leave. I was still in bed when the knock came. I answered the door with no idea who could be calling at such an early hour. There were two of them: one in plain clothes and one in uniform. They politely introduced themselves and I, in some confusion but without hesitation, invited them in. I had invoked the fictitious presence of the police so many times in my dealings with Kieran that I had almost begun to believe that they existed only in my imagination, and that this encounter would never actually take place. At that moment I could, in all truth and with genuine amazement, have asked them what they wanted with me, and believed that I was totally ignorant of everything. I followed them into the sitting room, closing the door to the hallway behind me.

They turned to face me. The first thing that struck me was the complete incongruity of their appearance in such surroundings. Compared to the people I knew and with whom I mixed and the life that I lived, they could have been representatives of a completely different species of human being. Their sheer physical presence seemed to dwarf my meagre frame and every aspect of my tiny flat. I felt as if I were suddenly living the life of a child. I was wearing a soiled and ill-fitting short sleeved T-shirt, and a pair of blue and white striped pyjama bottoms.

"Please sit down," said the man in plain clothes, "we just want to ask you a few questions."

I hesitated for a moment, unsure whether he had the right to ask me to sit down in my own flat but, still only half awake, I obeyed and immediately regretted it. Perched uncomfortably on the edge of my little chair I felt myself shrink even more in importance.

"You know why we're here," he said, "what this is all about."

I had no desire to appear a fool. "Yes, of course," I said. "It's about Kieran. I've been expecting you."

"Have you?" he said. "Then I presume you've had enough time to get your story straight?"

If I had ever imagined this confrontation, I had seen myself as struggling under pressure but always calm, confident and ultimately victorious. The reality was proving far less predictable. I had failed to take into account my natural desire to please and to confess all in the vain hope of forgiveness and redemption. I longed to tell him everything. I said, "I have no stories to tell. I don't know anything."

He smiled, and I realised that I could tell him nothing that he didn't already know, and that this visit was a pure formality. He knew I was guilty and wished only for my confession. "At another time and on another occasion," I thought, "We could have been friends."

I continued to answer all his questions to the best of my ability, allowing my mind and imagination to dwell elsewhere. This, like everything else, I reasoned, would pass.

"Would you say you and Kieran are friends?"

"Yes, of a sort."

'What does that mean?"

"He's not that easy to get to know."

"But you'd help him out if he was in trouble."

"I suppose so."

"There's nothing wrong with that. I'd probably do the same; up to a point." He reached into his pocket, pulled out a packet of cigarettes and offered me one. I shook my head. "You don't smoke?"

"No – I mean yes, but I'm fine thanks."

He wandered across to the window and peered out through the drawn curtains.

"He was seen, you know."

"Who?"

"Kieran, the night of the murder. He was seen round here."

I looked across at the other policeman who was half-heartedly opening drawers and cupboards, and who seemed totally indifferent to the whole affair.

"Why do you think that was, Jonathan? I mean, what do you think he could have been doing round here so soon after the murder?"

"I don't know. Perhaps they were mistaken and it wasn't Kieran at all."

He closed the curtains and came and stood in front of me.

"Oh, it was Kieran all right. There's no doubt." He took a drag on his cigarette and leaned towards me, allowing the smoke to encompass both of us. "Where is he, Jonathan? Just tell me and then we can leave you in peace. You seem a bright lad and I'm sure you want this over just as much as we do. Perhaps he threatened you. I can understand that. Is that what happened, Jonathan? Did he come here and threaten you? Nobody can blame you for being afraid. He's a very violent man."

"I don't know where he is," I lied, surprising myself with the power of my denial. "If I knew I would tell you."

Again he smiled. "Listen, Jonathan, he was only a Paki. OK, I know that. But I've still got my job to do. We're going to get him, sooner or later, and then you'll be on your own. You'll go to prison, Jonathan. Is that what you want? Just think about it for a minute. I'm trying to help you." He had brought his face so close to mine that if I had so wished I could have easily reached out and stroked his cheek. I had a sudden desire to tell him everything, just to make him happy.

"I'm sorry," I said, attempting to make my voice sound as apologetic as I could, "there's nothing I can tell you."

His eyes narrowed and for one brief moment I thought he was going to hit me. "He hates me," I thought. "This man really hates me and he doesn't even know who I am."

He had a large face, almost perfectly round; the skin was pale but of a purplish tinge, the sort of skin that however often he shaved one would always be able to discern the beginnings of a beard; the lips were full, the eyes small and of an indistinct colour, and his hair was cut so close to his head that naked patches of his scalp were clearly visible. It was a face so in keeping with his occupation and his character that it was practically impossible to think of him as being anything other than what he seemed. I almost envied him his inability to escape his personality. "I'm sorry," I said again, "but I really can't help you."

He continued to stare at me for a few moments more, his expression fixed and his eyes unblinking, before he suddenly straightened up and turned away from me. "OK, Sergeant," he said. "That's it. We're done here."

I was shocked and, despite the pressure I had been put under, not a little disappointed. I had almost begun to believe that I was someone of importance.

"Is that it?" I said, unable to keep the sadness out of my voice.

"I think so," he answered, "unless you've got anything else to tell me."

I thought hard. Surely there must be something I could say to delay his departure. "No," I said, eventually, "nothing."

"Don't worry," he said, as if he understood exactly what I was feeling. "We'll be back. We still have a lot to talk about."

I remained seated while they left. I heard the front door close behind them.

There was, the more I thought about it, something pleasantly satisfying about the policemen's visit, as if a circle had been closed or a destination reached. "This," I thought, "is the interval between two acts. I must reflect on what has gone before. There appears on the surface to be no discernable plot, only a mismatched collection of various incidents that could hardly add up to what one could call 'a life'. But there is a structure and, if one looks hard enough, an elementary interplay of cause and effect. In fact one could, if one felt so inclined (and ignoring the accusation of hyperbole) use the word 'destiny'. From the moment of my birth and throughout my childhood; from my solitary play and the benign indifference and eventual death of my parents; from my abortive relationships with Susan and Anna; from moving into this flat and meeting up with Diana, Jackie, Colin, Vince and Kieran; from the night of the murder and Kieran's sudden arrival at my flat; from the rape of Diana and Kieran's occupation of the room at the mill (my room) and the recent visit from the police, I believe that I can discern a thread (however erratic and indistinct) of direction and possibility that could give some meaning to my life. Remove any one incident, however seemingly insignificant, from the whole and the entire construct would be plunged into chaos. Everything is and has been necessary to bring me to this one specific point in my life."

The policemen left and closed the door behind them. I discovered that my hands were shaking, just as they should have been. The blank sheet of hardboard was still waiting to receive its first splash of paint, just as it should have been. The young woman in the flat opposite was waiting to undress for me, just as she should have been, and Kieran, alone and, no doubt miserable and anxious, was waiting impatiently for my next visit, just as he should have been.

Everything was almost perfect.

TWO

I can live like this for a week or two – if necessary. I am not the sort of person to give in so easily. That's something that people don't fully understand about me: I am strong, much stronger than they realise. All they see is Kieran the renegade, the outlaw and the fool; a man out of control using, exploiting and threatening all those around him. But for me to behave in such a way I have to believe in the rightness of my cause, in my invincibility. In another time or in different circumstances I would be applauded for my bravery and strength of character.

And yet, as Jonathan left me, almost before he had disappeared from view, I was suddenly overcome with an almost unbearable sense of desolation. I crossed to the window and watched the thin ray of light from Jonathan's torch as it flitted from one side of the path to the other, illuminating and highlighting various obscure and unrecognisable shapes and forms, until it was swallowed up in the darkness. The moon shone fully into the interior of my room.

I blew out all but one of the candles and crawled into my sleeping bag fully dressed, throwing the blanket over me. My whisky and cigarettes were close to hand. I was tired, but the strangeness of my situation made sleep impossible. The rain was still falling and the wind blowing, bringing me, strangely enough, some comfort in such desolate surroundings. Out there, there was a world that continued to exist as it always had, irrespective of whatever life I was now leading, a world that I could rejoin whenever I wished.

For, despite the loathing and disdain I feel for Jonathan, and the anger that seethes within me for him having brought me to such a place, I am aware that this is not a prison; that the limitations on my freedom are self-imposed and that I can and will leave whenever I wish. I will not be forced into any form of behaviour that is unnatural to me, neither by Jonathan, the police, nor by my own past indiscretions.

Tomorrow I will explain to Jonathan exactly what is expected of him if he wishes to continue to be honoured by my presence.

*

I wait a good four hours after the police have left my flat before I venture out. Despite the unpleasantness of my encounter with the detective, I can't help but feel thrilled at the thought that now I am considered a person of importance and that the people that I see, the words that are said and how I behave matter.

I meander slowly into town, occasionally stopping in front of various shop windows that hold no interest for me, just to take the time to look about me. I don't really believe that I am being followed, but the possibility that I might be under some sort of surveillance is not totally beyond the realms of possibility.

I buy all the provisions that I think are necessary to keep Kieran relatively comfortable and catch the first bus out of town that is heading vaguely in the right direction. Two changes of bus later and I find myself standing outside the entrance to the mill. It is already late afternoon but it is still light. As I approach the mill I almost expect to see some sign of Kieran's presence, perhaps a wisp of smoke curling above the half-collapsed roof, or even a glimpse of Kieran himself: the vague, shadowy outline of a lone figure peering out through the high, broken window. I see nothing.

I enter the building and begin slowly to climb the long flight of stairs, becoming more and more certain with every step that I take that I will find the room abandoned and Kieran long gone. The thought appalls me more than I could ever have anticipated.

Over the last few weeks our lives have become so inextricably linked that I doubt that I could go on living in any meaningful way, without his presence.

As I enter the room Kieran is squatting over the primus stove attempting, without success, to light the gas and carelessly discarding one spent match after another. His back is turned towards me, but his every action, even his very posture speaks of anger, resentment and frustration: so much so that I am tempted to believe that, aware of my imminent arrival, he has adopted such an attitude solely for my benefit. "You're late," he says, without turning round. "I was just about to come looking for you."

I place my rucksack full of shopping on the floor and squat down by his side. Without comment and with no resistance from Kieran I take the matches and light the gas. There is a pan half-filled with water close by.

"I was just about to make some coffee."

I place the pan on the stove. "How did you sleep?"

"How do you think?"

"Were you warm enough?"

"You're late. Where have you been?"

"The police – I've had a visit."

I feel his body stiffen. "You're joking. What did they say? What did you tell them?"

"Nothing – you were seen on the night of the murder – near the flats."

"Shit."

"Don't worry, they can't prove anything."

"But they must know I was with you. What did they say?"

"They told me I have to tell you to give yourself up; that it was only a Paki and that with a good lawyer you'll be out in a couple of years."

"Fuck that. They'll crucify me. Are you sure you weren't followed?"

"No way, I was very careful"

I tip one heaped teaspoonful of coffee into his mug and add the boiling water. I pass him the mug, handle first.

"Did you bring any milk?"

My heart sinks. "No, sorry, I forgot."

"For fuck's sake, Jonathan, what's the matter with you?" His rage seems to be out of all proportion to the offence. "It's not that difficult. Make a list or something. Just remember, you brought me here – I'm your responsibility. If you can't look after me properly then just fuck off and I'll take my chances out there. Just think, will you? Try using that." And he reaches out with the first finger of his left hand and prods me three times on my forehead. "So what did you bring?"

He crawls across to the shopping bag and tips the contents out on to the floor. Ignoring the bread, eggs, soup and the other foodstuffs he gathers up the whisky and the cigarettes. "At least you've done one thing right," he says grudgingly. He opens the whisky immediately, raises the bottle to his lips and begins to drink.

While he's drinking I pick up the groceries and arrange them neatly by the side of his sleeping bag. I don't know why, but it seems important to me to maintain some semblance of order, to give the appearance of a room that is cared for and not one that is used simply as a convenience. I smooth out his sleeping bag and tuck in the corners of the blanket.

"Have you seen anyone?" I ask.

"Like who?" he answers.

"I don't know – anyone."

"I thought the whole point of coming here was not to see anyone, or have you got that wrong as well?"

"No, of course not, but you never know, somebody might walk past. We're not that far from civilization."

"Well I haven't," he says, taking another drink. "Seen anyone, that is. Not a fucking soul. Only you." And he half sniggers and laughs and spits out a thin spray of whisky over the front of his T-shirt and jacket.

"Why are you so angry?" I suddenly ask. "What's your problem?"

He stops drinking and turns to look at me. "Why am I so angry?" he says, tilting his head slightly to one side in an attitude of mock concentration. "Well, let me think. I've just murdered somebody, even if it was only some stupid Paki. The police know it was me and are looking for me everywhere. I've no money and I'm freezing my bollocks off stuck in a fucking shit-hole that isn't fit for a dog. Oh, and I nearly forgot, the only person who could possibly help me is a fucking moron. Will that do, or should I go on?"

"Well just remember, Kieran," I answer, with as much passion as I can muster, "that if it wasn't for this moron, you'd have been caught long ago. You came to me for help. I didn't want anything to do with this, but I'm doing the best that I can, and if that's not good enough then I'm very sorry. But I haven't had much experience at dealing with murderers."

He raises the bottle once more to his lips, but he never takes his eyes off mine.

"Oh, by the way," he says at last, his voice reverting to its usual icy calmness, "where's the radio?"

"Oh shit," I think. "Oh shit, shit, shit."

"Listen Kieran," I say, apparently with genuine regret, "I'm really sorry. I meant to bring one but with one thing and another it went clean out of my head. It must have been the visit by the police. It obviously upset me more than I thought."

"Tomorrow," he says, maintaining that same slow and ponderous tone, "bring it tomorrow, and the milk and more whisky and cigarettes and dope. And bring me a change of clothes. I'm beginning to smell like a pig."

"Where should I get the clothes?"

"This may come as a revelation to you, Jonathan, but you walk into a clothes shop and you fucking buy them. Do you think you could manage that?"

"But how do I know what to ...?"

"Just do it, Jonathan. Use your common sense. Christ, I'm thinking of turning myself in just to be rid of you. And make sure you're not followed, and don't tell anybody where I am. Do you understand – nobody? And this time don't be late. I'm rapidly running out of patience."

Despite the sense of exhaustion that I feel after having spent nearly three hours in Kieran's presence, I am almost elated when I finally leave the mill. Nothing has changed. Kieran is still Kieran and his anger and his arrogance is as uncontrollable and as great as ever. If my relationship with Kieran is not only to continue but also to deepen and to thrive then it is necessary for him to remain exactly as he is. A Kieran suddenly acquiescent, compliant, grateful or (god help us) even apologetic would be almost unbearable. How then would I know how to behave? What strategy could I then employ to keep his interest, and to maintain his dependency on me? His anger is necessary to both of us.

*

I think I can congratulate myself on an inspiring and convincing performance. Jonathan needs to be controlled, to be "lead by the nose" . He can't help it – it's a necessary part of his character. I could almost pity him if I were blessed with such an emotion, but as it is I find him pathetic.

I had been waiting for him all morning, saw him approach the mill and prepared myself accordingly. I began in my usual way: an invented insult, an over-reaction, an apparent loss of control but, as is invariably the case, I found myself believing in the irrationality of the moment. Why shouldn't I be angry? Why shouldn't I castigate him for his stupidity and lack of care? His impotence and lack of involvement make it all too easy for me. Like the shopkeeper and Diana and everybody else I meet, Jonathan can only truly be himself when he devolves to somebody else all responsibility for his character and actions.

I became genuinely angry and if he had said one more thing to provoke me I could have seriously hurt him, but fortunately for him he remained true to his nature: he became meek, intimidated and apologetic. Tomorrow and the next day and the next he will learn exactly what I expect of him.

Despite my isolation and the bleakness of my surroundings I believe I might actually find something in this situation to amuse and entertain me. I shall wait eagerly for his daily visits and in the meantime I shall attempt to live to the full the life that I have chosen for myself. I am a murderer, a thief and a rapist and recognised as such by society. Perhaps it is only right that I should have to suffer some indignities for the crimes I have committed; how else can I fully understand and celebrate the type of human being that I am.

My room and its contents are satisfactory but not perfect as a hideaway for such a dangerous villain as me. The crumbling, red-brick walls; the splintered and heavily stained floorboards; the tiny, broken and discoloured window panes; the overall impression of filth, grime and neglect form a wonderful backdrop against which I can play out my little subterfuge, but the arrangement of my provisions and possessions leaves a lot to be desired: everything is too neat, too artfully arranged. There is still too much of the smell of Jonathan about the place.

It is necessary, if I am to remain sane, to destroy the fictitious order that Jonathan has inflicted on me. I stride about my tiny domain, kicking cans, packets and bottles (opened and unopened) from one side of the room to the other and back again. A carton of vegetable soup splits open spilling its green and slimy contents all over the floor while a bottle of orange juice is smashed wonderfully and spectacularly splattering the bright orange liquid high on to the walls and ceiling. Forgetting for a moment the real object of the exercise I begin to play, reverting to the childish excess and total concentration of a ten year old. The noise must be immense in the echoing silence of the old mill, but I don't care, I'm having far too much fun. And when finally I've finished, brought to a halt not by my satisfaction at the devastation which I have caused but by simple exhaustion, even I am surprised at the chaos that surrounds me. I start to laugh, outrageously, uncontrollably, until even I become frightened by my apparent complete lack of control.

"This has to stop," I say to myself. "I have been here only one night and already I am behaving like a lunatic. What appears sensible to me would to somebody else, to somebody incapable of understanding the need I have to impose my presence on everything about me, seem like the behaviour of a madman."

I take hold of the screwed up bundle of material that is my sleeping bag, drag it into the centre of the room, smooth it flat and sit myself down. I light a cigarette and take another drink of whisky. This is more like it; this is the way I wish to spend my days: surrounded by the physical manifestation of the chaos that exists within my mind.

I can hardly wait to see Jonathan's reaction.

*

I arrive early next morning. I wish to vary the time between my visits as much as possible; to encourage Kieran to live in an almost permanent state of expectation and anxiety. The room is almost unrecognisable from the day before with food and drink splattered and thrown everywhere. I am shocked and outraged, but I say nothing. He is watching me closely, almost slyly, smugly, willing me to say something, anything to give him the opportunity to hurl himself once more into one of his ungovernable outbursts of rage and feigned indignation.

I clear a space with my feet and drop my carrier bags on to the floor.

"I've brought you what you asked for:" I say, "a pair of jeans, a couple of T-shirts and a jumper, just in case you get cold."

He is sitting cross-legged on his sleeping bag, and his expression is now an almost total blank. He looks terrible. Even in so short a time the change in his appearance is quite remarkable. His unwashed hair hangs long and lank, and clings unpleasantly to the sides of his unshaven face. His eyes, which seem to be permanently veiled behind some pale watery liquid, have sunk even more into his skull and his skin has taken on the colour and texture of ancient parchment.

"I don't know whether you'll like them or if they'll even fit," I say. "I'm not used to buying for other people."

"What do you think of the room?" he says. "I've made some improvements."

Ignoring his question I up-end the second carrier bag and tip the contents on to the floor. "I'll just leave these here then, shall I?"

His eyes quickly scan over the usual collection of boxes, cans and bottles. "I don't see a radio."

I was expecting this: "I couldn't get the right batteries – I'll sort it out tomorrow – but I have brought you this."

I reach into my pocket and produce a tightly wrapped package of silver paper. "A little present from Vince."

"You didn't tell him where I am?"

"No, of course not."

Carefully he unpicks the small shiny package to reveal the black, sticky lump of dope hidden inside.

"It's good stuff," I say, "the best."

He holds it to his nose for a brief moment and then, without comment, pushes it into the right hand pocket of his jacket. I wasn't expecting any words of thanks, but there is something in Kieran's attitude that is even more surly and insular than usual. The fact that he didn't make more of a fuss over the radio I find worrying and confusing. This is not like him.

We sit opposite each other in silence. Usually, to maintain some sort of feeling of optimism and of the world continuing to turn as normal, I would make myself useful, busy myself about the room, rearrange his possessions, tidy his food store or fill a pan with water, light the stove and make coffee. But surrounded by such chaos and apathy I can't think of anything to do that would not seem out of place or trivial and pointless. We continue to sit and to say nothing. Slowly, and seemingly without enthusiasm, he reaches for the bottle of whisky.

"I'll bring you another bottle next time I come," I say, trying to maintain some sort of contact, "perhaps even two."

He doesn't answer.

"Is there anything else you want?"

"Such as?"

"I don't know – anything."

"Surprise me."

Again we fall into silence.

"You haven't tried your clothes on," I say, the sudden brightness of my voice failing to convince even me. "If they don't fit or you don't like them I can easily take them back. I've kept the receipts. It's no trouble."

"Listen, Jonathan," he says, speaking very slowly but apparently without anger, "you've done your duty, proved what a caring human being you are. Now why don't you just fuck off?"

Again he lifts the bottle to his lips. That's it. I have been dismissed. I suppose I should feel content and reassured that his ego is as strong and unassailable as ever, but my immediate reaction is one of irritation. How dare he speak to me like this? Whatever my motives, all this is my doing. I am the one who has worked hard to procure all that is needed to maintain some sort of civilized existence and to secure his safety. There are times when even I desire some sort of recognition of all my efforts.

I stand up and walk purposefully towards the door, but just before leaving I turn and say, "I might be late tomorrow. I have things to do."

And I don't wait for an answer.

*

Perhaps I was a little too hard on him, but I just couldn't help it. He was so fucking annoying, just sitting there and looking so smug and righteous. So he brought me some clothes and stuff – so what? That's what he's supposed to do. It's because of him that I'm stuck in this shit-hole. He owes me. He's just like Diana; he deserves to be hurt. But not yet, not until the police have grown bored with me and I can finish with him once and for all.

And he still hasn't brought the radio. If I didn't know him better – if I didn't know him to be a coward – I'd think he was doing it on purpose. But, basically, he's just an idiot. Still, he does keep me supplied with whisky and drugs, so he can get something right. If he'd just bring me a radio I could forgive him almost anything -

almost.

Tomorrow I think I'll start a new regime; expand my horizons a bit. It's time I explored my surroundings properly. You never know, I might even find something to entertain me.

He didn't come. Yesterday. He didn't come. I remember that he said he might be late, that he had things to do – but he didn't come.

I woke up early. In fact I'd hardly slept all night; too many dreams; too much dope. I woke up just as it was getting light. I was cold and put on my new jumper under my jacket. It made me look like a fucking bank manager, but at least it was warm. I wiped away the condensation from the window and looked out. There was nothing moving; nothing alive. There was a sun, but

182

it was too thin, too watery to give any sense of hope. I think I may have even shivered a little.

I lit the stove and put on some soup to warm. I wasn't particularly hungry but I felt the need to engage in some sort of activity, to do something that could be thought of as vaguely normal. I sat hunched in front of the stove and drank the soup from a white, chipped mug that I held tightly in between my two hands. There was no discernible taste, just the heat of the liquid on my lips and mouth. I looked around me and, probably for the first time since I had arrived in this place, I felt lonely. I even caught myself looking forward to Jonathan's visit, but I refused to accept such feelings as having any sound basis in reality. It was the cold, the lack of human contact, the squalor of my surroundings and my own erratic nature that had driven me to such extremes of self-indulgence. I would continue with my plan of the night before and become, once again, master of my own fate. I would start to explore.

I placed my cigarettes and lighter in my pocket and took up my torch. I set off, but with much less enthusiasm than I had experienced the night before. In my imagination my journey through the interior of this building had seemed predominantly an act of bravery, an adventure, and yet another example of me, the ruthless and courageous outsider, confronting and eventually overcoming the dangers that constantly beset me. But, as I tentatively stepped beyond the confines of the room and turned to view the long, half-derelict and shadowy corridor stretching out to the right and left of me, I came to a halt. I switched on the torch and let the thin beam of light flicker over the walls, floor and ceiling. Almost without realising it I held my breath so that in the intermittent light and shade I seemed hardly to exist at all. I strained my ears into the silence until eventually sounds, tiny and sporadic, became magnified and intense, hinting at a world alien and unknowable. I was not afraid. I refused to admit that such a disarming emotion as fear could be responsible for my indecision. Perhaps I was more tired than I realised. Perhaps it was just boredom or indifference. I turned and looked back into my room – the room that I had detested but despite all my misgivings had managed to make my own. Everything that was necessary for my survival lay scattered about the floor. Despite the cold and the discomfort it was there, for the time being, that I felt most safe and in control.

The time was not right. I would wait until I felt more inquisitive, more confident of discovering something of interest. I had been led astray before, convinced myself that "out there", somewhere beyond myself, there existed something, a person, a place or an event that could possibly change my life for ever, only to be left more disillusioned than before. It was all shit. When or if I eventually left my room it would be without hope or expectation, simply an extension of and a natural elaboration on my daily routine. I would hardly be aware of moving at all.

I returned to my room and sat down cross-legged before the stove. I rolled myself a joint. I would sit as still as possible and wait for Jonathan.

But he didn't come.

*

I didn't go. Yesterday. I didn't go to visit Kieran. It wasn't planned. I had no intention at this early stage of abandoning him. It just happened.

I had, as usual, packed my rucksack with all the provisions that I thought would please Kieran the most, including a radio, when I decided to stop off briefly at the local pub, not just for my enjoyment but to see if I could score a couple of tabs of acid from Vince. I felt no guilt at keeping Kieran waiting, having convinced myself that this slight detour was necessary for his well-being.

It was already late afternoon when I entered the pub. Colin, Jackie, Diana and Vince were sitting at our usual table. As soon as I entered the room I knew that the rest of the day would gradually slip beyond my control. Their talk and laughter could be heard even from the bar. They were an enclosed circle, wreathed in cigarette smoke and relaxed good humour. The table was already littered with empty glasses. Diana was the first to see me and smiled and waved in greeting. Even before I had joined them I was made to feel welcome. Without asking I bought them all drinks (so desperate was I to feel part of the group) and carried them across to the table.

"Excellent," said Colin, draining his glass and reaching out for its replacement. "What a good man you are."

"Absolutely," agreed Vince, with a knowing smile, "I've always said so."

Diana shuffled to one side to allow me to bring up my chair.

"Cheers," said Colin, and we all raised our glasses. Their faces were flushed with pleasure and alcohol, obviously only too aware that, for this one moment in their lives, everything in the whole world was quite simply wonderful.

"How are you?" asked Diana, quietly.

"Colin's just been fired," said Jackie, leaning across the table to come between me and Diana, "so we're celebrating."

"Cheers," Vince said, raising his glass once more.

"Fuck 'em," said Colin. "I can get a job anywhere."

"Of course you can," said Jackie, alcohol making her unexpectedly voluble, "you're a hard worker."

"Too fucking right," said Colin. "I have my pride."

"Of course you do," said Jackie, who seemed prepared to agree with anything that Colin said. "You're a proud man."

"The things we have to do just for money," said Vince, who never missed an opportunity to expand on his favourite topic of the freedom of the individual and the misuse of power. "We are given invented jobs to do to keep us in our place and to stop us from thinking; so that we can buy things that we don't need and probably don't even want. We're all exploited and we don't even know it. If we all lived our lives according to nature we wouldn't have to work at all."

"You don't," said Jackie.

"I was speaking philosophically," said Vince.

"You were speaking bollocks," said Colin.

"He's good at that," said Diana, but with good humour. "Aren't you, Vince?"

"Brilliant," said Vince, who was never too proud to laugh at his own failings. "Probably the only thing I can do well."

"I'm fine," I said to Diana. "How are you?"

"I'd like to become a hairdresser," said Jackie, "open my own shop."

"But your hair's a fucking mess," said Colin. "It always is."

"That's not true, is it Di? It's not a mess – it's the fashion. And anyway," she continued, "that's not the point. It's how I make other people look."

"Of course it's the point," Colin said. "How do you expect people to trust you when you look like that?"

"Well I like it," Jackie said. "And what do you know about fashion, anyway?"

"It's very nice," said Diana, "very – original."

"That's the trouble with this world," said Vince. "We judge too much by appearances. I mean, look at me."

Nobody turned to look at him.

"I think," said Diana, "that we all look exactly as we are. I mean, we may try to conceal our true nature, but it always shows through."

"I ask you," continued Vince, "I might have an unfulfilled desire to work in a bank, but would anyone employ me? No, and just because of the way I dress."

"But you dress like that because of what you are. You might as well carry a sign that says, not suitable for paid employment," said Diana.

"Or one that says dickhead," said Colin.

"Are you still seeing Kieran?" Diana asked me quietly.

"Yes," I said, "practically every day."

"And how is he?"

I thought for a second or two before answering. "I really don't know. The more time I spend with him the less I understand him. He seems for most of the time to exist on such a simple level, almost primitive, but just occasionally he shows ... "

"What?"

"I don't know – an intelligence – no, not intelligence, more of an awareness of himself, of the Kieran that he really is; as if he's playing at being Kieran and is just waiting to be found out. Sometimes he even smiles."

Diana too smiled. "That doesn't sound like the Kieran I know."

Without thinking I reached under the table and took hold of her hand. "I'm sorry," I said.

"What are you sorry for?" she said, her voice suddenly taking on a resilient quality. "He did what he did, whether he was playing at being Kieran or not. That violence must have always been in him, and probably still is. He didn't need anybody's permission to act on it. He didn't need you or anybody else to say, 'that's OK Kieran, now you can go ahead and rape Diana – it's allowed.'"

I squeezed her hand tighter.

"I shall never forgive him," she said, looking directly at me, "never; and not just for what he did to me, but how he has made me feel. I hate him Jonathan. Do you understand, I hate him, and I don't want to hate anyone. He has turned me into somebody else – somebody I don't know and don't like and I have no idea how I am going to live the rest of my life."

"Hey," said Jackie, who had suddenly realised that we had slipped away from the general conversation, "what are you two talking about? This is supposed to be a party."

"Then buy me another drink," said Diana, letting go of my hand. "I'm going to get very, very drunk."

"We all are," said Vince. "It's the only thing to do."

"Come on," said Colin to Jackie," I'll give you a lift."

We watched as they staggered their way to the bar.

"I don't care what anybody says," said Vince, in a rather weak attempt at humour, "I think they make a lovely couple."

I began to roll a cigarette, and waited a moment until Vince's interest had returned once more to the table before speaking. "Listen, Vince," I said quietly, leaning forward and drawing him towards me, "I don't suppose you've got any acid on you have you – or any speed?"

He feigned amazement. "Why Jonathan, how could you possibly ask me such a thing? I'm shocked. I really am."

"Don't mess me about, Vince," I said, "This is serious. Have you or haven't you?" The truth of the matter was that I suddenly felt terribly embarrassed at making such a request, as if I were a young boy ordering his first pint of bitter. Dope was one thing – everybody smoked – but acid or speed – that was something different.

Suddenly Vince became the businessman that he had always professed to hate. He reached across the table and took the cigarette from my hand. "Who's it for?" he asked, his voice cool and steady and sounding perfectly sober.

"Me, of course."

He shook his head slowly from side to side. "No it isn't. That's not your style at all."

"What do you know about my style?"

"OK then," he shrugged. "I'm sorry. I can't help you. Try somebody else."

We glared at each other for a moment, and then slowly, and in what seemed a deliberate act of confrontation he lit the cigarette – my cigarette – and let the smoke drift in between us. However frustrated I felt at being treated in such a patronising way, and by a so-called friend, I knew that it would be useless to lose my temper. He was the one in control and he knew it. However much I ranted or pleaded or begged he would never give in. My only hope lay in telling the truth. "All right," I said at last, "it's not for me. I admit it. But do you have anything or not? It's important."

"Who's it for?"

"For Christ's sake, Vince," I said, finding it more and more difficult to remain calm, "what does it matter who it's for? Just a friend OK, and I don't know why you should care anyway?"

"In case you hadn't noticed," he said, his voice now rich with pomposity, "this is my business. This is how I make my living. I need to know who I'm dealing with."

"You're dealing with me."

Again he shook his head. "Not good enough."

"It's for him, isn't it?" said Diana suddenly. She had obviously been listening to our conversation much more intently than I had realised. "It's for Kieran."

I didn't answer. Perhaps I was too ashamed.

"Is it indeed!?" exclaimed Vince. "I didn't realise you two were still involved. I thought he'd left the area ages ago."

"Why should he," said Diana, "when he has such a good friend to look after him?"

"We're not involved," I said defensively. "I'm just doing what I have to, what I'm capable of doing, and I don't have to justify my actions to anybody. Now, can you help me or not?"

"OK, take it easy, Jonathan," said Vince, sitting back in his chair and holding up his hands in an attitude of total innocence, "this has nothing to do with me. I have no opinion either way. All I care about is me, my safety. I just don't want any of this stuff traced back to me when the police finally catch him. Do you understand? You can have whatever you want, but it's your responsibility. It has nothing to do with me."

"I understand," I said. "I'll take full responsibility for everything."

"Excuse me," said Diana abruptly and with obvious disgust, "I'll just go and see if the others want a hand with the drinks."

"That's better," said Vince, as soon as Diana had left. "I don't know why but there's something about her that annoys me. She doesn't say much but it's like she's always passing judgment. I don't trust her. She's too emotional. She takes things too seriously, and that's always dangerous. If I were you I'd tell her nothing. She's unstable."

I thought of Diana's bruised and bloodied face and the words that she had said to me only a moment or two earlier while we had held hands beneath the table, but I said nothing to defend her character.

"Now," Vince continued, drawing up his chair so that our heads were nearly touching, and dropping his voice almost to a whisper, "what can I do for you?"

By the time the others had rejoined us the deal, thankfully, had been completed, and the atmosphere reverted almost immediately to its earlier mood of drunken frivolity. The conversation flowed in its usual trivial and inconclusive way, drinks were consumed with a passionate and reckless intensity and we became once more relaxed and content in our own isolation. But now, Diana no longer spoke to me directly, nor even cast a casual glance in my direction. Now it would have been impossible for me to stretch out my arm and gently take hold of her hand beneath the table.

I was aware of the passing of time, of the late afternoon light fading into dusk and the arrival of the night-time drinkers, but still I couldn't leave. What I was experiencing seemed to me to be something almost outside my life, hardly a part of me at all, as if I were taking a holiday from myself. How could I possibly leave all that simply to visit Kieran? His needs, his desires, even his very existence seemed not only an irrelevance but almost an invention, and when I eventually arrived home I fell fully dressed onto my mattress and slept a long, untroubled and dream free sleep.

*

The radio doesn't work.

I think I surprised Jonathan by just how calm I was. I didn't rave. I didn't even shout or threaten violence. I just looked at him. And he was so apologetic, so contrite, so overflowing with guilt.

"I'm so sorry," he said, as soon as he saw me; "so very, very sorry. I really meant to come yesterday but I had trouble finding the right batteries for the radio, and I wanted to score you some decent stuff, and I wasn't sure that the police weren't watching me. Anyway I'm here now, and it was only one day."

And he opened his bag and pulled out all this food and water and gas for the stove and the radio and whisky and passed it all to me as if he were doing me a favour and still I didn't get angry.

The funny thing was I really didn't feel angry. I wasn't pretending or playing a game. I really didn't care. I watched him closely while he scuttled about on the floor in front of me and felt only a mild contempt. Perhaps my day alone had affected me more than I had realised, and I now looked upon his presence not as a welcome event but as an irritation, perhaps even an intrusion; and the less I said the more agitated he seemed to become. He chatted on endlessly, filling the silence like the crackle of a tiny insect (a cockroach perhaps), until, for my own peace of mind, I felt forced to interrupt him.

"How's Diana?"

The question had not been planned. I had not thought, "What can I say to cause Jonathan the maximum distress?" It was purely instinctive. He refused to look at me, but continued to rearrange the many objects scattered about him.

"She's fine," he mumbled.

I looked down at the top of his head.

"You've seen her?"

"Yes, of course."

"Recently?"

"Yesterday."

He seemed unaware of the provocative nature of his answer.

"Yesterday," I repeated.

"Hem – yes," he hesitated. "I popped into the pub – just for a second – to score your stuff."

"And she's fine?"

"Yes, fine."

"Did she ask after me?"

Again he hesitated. "No, not really."

For a moment or two I said nothing, enjoying his discomfort. "A very attractive girl is Diana – very sexy don't you think?"

"I suppose so."

"Oh come on, Jonathan, what do you mean you suppose so? Don't tell me you don't fancy her, or have you screwed her already?"

"No, of course not!"

I found his sudden outrage at my suggestion almost laughable.

"Why not? You'd enjoy it. Firm breasts. Good arse. I'm sure she'd let you if you tried. Very accommodating is Diana. But then I'm forgetting you're in love with her, aren't you? And that makes all the difference."

It was then that he raised his head to look at me.

"And love equals respect, doesn't it, Jonathan?" I continued, really beginning to enjoy myself. "At least, that's what you tell yourself. But it's not respect, is it? It's fear. That's what it is – fear."

"You don't know anything about it," he said calmly, but I could see that he was rattled.

"I've only had her the once," I said, nonchalantly, rolling myself a joint, "but I can recommend it. It was at your flat, actually; on your mattress. She said no at first, but then they all do don't they, but I could see she wanted it; even got her to pull her own knickers down." (Now I'd started I didn't seem able to stop, as if, despite the pleasure and satisfaction I was experiencing at causing him so much pain, I was really telling the story for my benefit; to relive the pleasure I had experienced.) And the nicest little cunt you could imagine Jonathan: so warm and wet. You should have heard her moan as I stuck it in her. I tell you, Jonathan, she couldn't get enough of it."

I paused for a moment to judge his reaction. I was almost impressed. His face remained a total blank, but I could see that he wanted me to stop (his eyes were so hard and unforgiving) but he just didn't know how; he was either too afraid or too stunned to say anything. "And it wasn't just her cunt, either," I continued, meeting his gaze head on; "if you know what I mean?" I took another deep drag on the joint. "But of course you do, don't you Jonathan? You know exactly what I'm talking about. Have you ever looked at her mouth, Jonathan, I mean really looked at it: those soft, full lips and the smoothness of her skin and that beautiful, pink tongue? What else could you do with such a hole except fill it? It's what it was designed for – just like her arse-hole."

I felt rather proud of myself. I believed I had used my words and my somewhat limited powers of description to their best advantage. I still, to my surprise, felt no anger towards him, but there was no doubt that I wanted to make him suffer; to elicit some sort of response, however shallow, from that immovable lump of failed humanity.

"Oh, but I'm so sorry Jonathan," I continued, "perhaps I shouldn't be talking like this about the woman you love; perhaps you don't think it quite right. I'd hate to destroy any of your illusions."

"I don't love her," he said, "and I don't have any illusions."

"Well that's all right then," I said, "no need to worry."

"But that doesn't mean I want to hear about it."

"No, of course you don't. I keep forgetting just how sensitive you are – how vulnerable. Whatever happens Jonathan, don't get involved – it might destroy you."

Suddenly he stood up and hoisted his rucksack over his shoulder.

"I have to go."

"So soon," I said, "and just when we were getting on so well. And I have much more to tell you about Diana, but I suppose it can wait. Give her my love, won't you. In fact, why don't you bring her with you next time? It gets lonely here."

He didn't answer. He didn't even say goodbye. He just left. I listened to his footsteps echoing along the hallway and diminishing to nothing as he descended the long flight of stairs leading to the ground floor.

At another time I would have been angry at his sudden departure and the shortness of his visit but in truth, I didn't care. In fact, I was glad to see him go. He was beginning to depress me. In some strange way his presence seemed only to emphasise my loneliness as if every word I said to him was sucked into some sort of bottomless void. At least on my own I had expectations of nothing and could organise my life accordingly.

I poured myself a large whisky and reached for the radio. It doesn't work. To begin with I thought I could just discern the distant hum of voices or music, but anything recognisable was soon lost beneath a continuous crackle and hiss of shimmering white noise. I twisted the dial one way and then the other, but still nothing. The noise continued, obliterating every station and altering only in volume and intensity.

Even this set-back has failed to unleash my anger; indeed I can't help but smile at the stupidity of it all. I shall leave it on until the batteries run out. I find the noise strangely comforting, like the sound of waves falling on a distant shore.

*

I have to believe that Kieran knows exactly what he is doing. If not then he is absolved of all responsibility and incapable of being judged.

He talked of Diana. Why? Obviously he was angry that I hadn't visited him yesterday, but he failed to express his anger in the usual way. Was this a planned response simply to confuse me? I have to believe that that was the case for why else should he talk of Diana? Why pick that exact moment to mention her name? He was watching me so closely. I could feel his eyes on me, waiting to judge my reaction, but I believe I gave very little away. It wasn't easy. I longed to tell him to shut up, that I knew exactly what had happened, that I had seen the bruises, but what would have been the point? He would have loved me to respond in just that way; to give him the chance to do what he does best: to rant and to rave and to threaten and to reduce everybody around him to mere adjuncts of his own ungovernable rage.

I said nothing. I kept my head down and my eyes averted. I simply waited for him to finish. It could have been worse, I know that. He could have gone into more detail, described the removal of her clothes, the exact moment of penetration and her reaction to his assault. Everything would have been exaggerated, of course, if not actually lies, but what difference would that have made? It would have still been Diana, my Diana that he was desecrating, and could I so easily dismiss everything that he said? However much I told myself that this was not the truth there would have always been one little part of me that remained doubtful. Who am I to judge how people react in extremis? More to the point, experience has taught me that one should never put one's trust in the behaviour of other people; they continually surprise, confuse, deceive and ultimately betray, if not the trust of others then at least their own innate nature. Who is to say that at the moment of Kieran's climax Diana didn't actually moan in pleasure despite her revulsion at the consummation of the act? Would she be able, so completely, to separate herself from the pure, naked sexuality of the moment? Kieran is right about Diana's body: her breasts, her backside and her delightful little mouth. She exudes a tantalizing promise of sexual gratification that is almost impossible to ignore. I try to concentrate on other things: her generous nature; her intelligence and understanding, but while I listen to her words and look at her face I see only the perfection of her skin, the mass of pale blonde hair, her bright green eyes and the fullness of her lips. I long to lean towards her and to take her face in my hands and to kiss her half-open mouth, but perhaps Kieran is right and I really am a coward. I fear rejection or, even worse, mockery and humiliation.

Kieran, of course, suffers no such doubt; his nature will allow no thoughts of possible failure, and even if he did fail he would dismiss it out of hand as a mere irrelevance, just as he would if he were to succeed. I know that if I were to relax for just a moment I would find myself complicit in everything that he has done, not in action but in thought. That is where his true power lies: in his ability to corrupt by the simple expediency of making everything appear possible.

I shall not visit him tomorrow. I shall not pretend, even to myself, that I was waylaid or distracted or followed by the police. I shall simply not go. Perhaps not even the day after. It all depends on how I feel.

*

I shall enjoy the pain while I can. This is a rare experience for me: to suffer physically and yet not to anticipate when that suffering will cease.

Yesterday morning I put my aborted plan of a few days ago into action: I would investigate fully my surroundings.

As before I awoke early and prepared myself for the day ahead. I ate two slices of rather stale bread and butter and swallowed one of the tablets of acid, so thoughtfully supplied by Jonathan, washed down with two or three large mouthfuls of whisky. I waited patiently for the effects of the drug to kick in before I embarked on my journey. I believed that the sense of dislocation that such a drug would bring would be essential to the success of my adventure. In the background the radio still played. I would enjoy hearing the noise fade into nothing as I left my room further and further behind me, knowing that the sound would continue whether I was there or not and that it would be waiting to welcome me home. Apart from my infrequent visits to the shit-house (I had taken to peeing out of the window) this would be the first time that I had left my room since my arrival here some four, five, six (I was already unsure of the exact time span involved) or seven days ago.

This time I set off without hesitation, turning immediately left and then making my way along the darkened corridor heading towards the long flight of steps that would lead eventually to the main entrance to the mill and to the light of the outside world. Long before I reached the entrance I became aware of the change in temperature; a cold wind began to blow, channelled and exaggerated in the confines of the building. I pulled my jacket tighter about me and held my upturned collar about my face. I now no longer needed my torch and the noise from the radio had ceased altogether.

I stood at the doorway and looked out. The view was practically the same as from the window of my room, but being so close to the actual possibility of escape seemed, somehow, to infuse everything with a heightened sense of reality. This was no longer an image, a representation of something to which I could aspire (carefully hand painted and framed) but a living, breathing entity, careless and unpredictable.

For a brief moment I was shocked by my somewhat perverse reaction to what was, after all, simply a familiar and rather dull landscape. But still I could go no further. There seemed to be an invisible line over which I could not cross. Was it the drugs? I hoped so, or else my few short days of isolation had changed my character almost beyond recognition. I breathed in deeply and wiped my forehead with the back of my hand. Despite the cold I was sweating profusely.

No, this wasn't fear. This wasn't: "I have no idea what awaits me but I know it is dangerous", if anything it was completely the opposite. I knew everything; the shape, the sounds and the hidden meaning behind all that I saw and it unnerved me.

I turned my back with relief on the outside world and set my gaze on the deepest recesses of the interior of the building. I moved ahead slowly, almost as if I were a blind man sensing my surroundings only by smell and sound and touch. The broken stone floor stretched out ahead of me, narrowing to a pin-point of darkness enclosed on either side by walls of white and pale green tiles, cracked and hideously discoloured. I waited until the last possible moment before switching on my torch, reluctant to disperse and highlight the shadowy gloom that surrounded me. I stopped for a moment and took another mouthful of whisky from the bottle that I carried in my left hand. As I threw back my head to drink I felt a sudden surge of almost total dislocation as if I were on board a sailing ship, heading alone and storm-driven into uncharted waters. I think I may even have grinned to myself, resplendent in my isolation.

Where the light was at its darkest I discovered, to my left, a steep flight of wooden steps heading down into a blackness of even greater intensity. Without hesitation I began to descend. So far this was all that I had expected (perhaps only that I had underestimated the power and the effect of the drugs I had taken), but as I passed through this last ultimate darkness I was unprepared for a gentle but definite increase in light, so specific that for a moment I was almost led to believe that I had, even in so short a time, developed an ability, like a cat, to discern objects even in the gloomiest of surroundings. So positive was this influx of new light that by the time I had reached the last step I was able, without the use of my torch, to discern most of the details of the room in which I now found myself.

After my recent self-imposed incarceration the room I had now entered seemed unbelievably vast, extending, I presumed, almost the full length and width of the whole building. I looked up towards the ceiling. In the far left hand corner of the room a small section of the roof had collapsed completely, allowing me a brief glimpse of the rolling sky. This was obviously the source of this new and unexpected light. I remained perfectly still, unable at first to make sense of what I saw; not that I didn't understand what I was looking at, the interplay of wood, metal, brick and stone, but that, undoubtedly due to the effects of the drugs, wherever my gaze fell there seemed to be a new form of existence, something hidden and threatening.

Along the whole length of one wall ran a complex arrangement of metal pipes of varying design and diameter, dipping under and over and crisscrossing one another in apparent confusion. Many were discoloured with rust and, due to some chemical process of which I had no knowledge, seemed almost to be melting or rotting away and gradually disgorging the brown sticky substance that lay inside. Everything seemed to be held in stasis, like the interior of some primeval cave, and yet, the more I looked the more certain I became that I could discern movement. The whole room appeared to have a rhythm or a pulse; a gentle breathing in and out, of which I was simply one part of the whole. This was not just a room, not even a machine but a living, organic entity.

I moved forward, bottle in hand, my confidence still not totally defeated. Somewhere close to the very centre of the room I stopped and looked about me. With every step I had taken I seemed to have become less and less significant until now I hardly had any identity left at all. I became angry. Was I to be so easily intimidated, so easily reduced to nothing? I began to shout. I can't remember my exact words, if indeed there were words at all; perhaps just a noise: the cry of some lost and abandoned animal; but with each outburst my sense of isolation seemed only to increase in intensity. My voice pierced the silence for barely a second before being turned in on itself and engulfed in the vast, shadowy space that surrounded me. I attempted to fight the effects of the drugs and to tell myself that in the whole world I was still the only thing that mattered, but my desires and my imagination seemed to be beyond my control. I needed to escape and to return to what, for the past few days, I had come to think of as normality.

I moved as quickly as I could away from the light and towards the far corner of the room where I could just make out the bottom two steps of another flight of wooden stairs.

I began to climb, perhaps too quickly, my hands fumbling with the switch on my torch.

There was pain. That is beyond doubt, but for a moment or two I could hardly believe that the pain belonged to me; that its source emanated from my body. The rotting timber beneath my foot gave way and I fell forwards and down, my right leg sinking beneath the level of the wooden step. I viewed my predicament with a somewhat detached fascination, curious as to how such an incident could have occurred to me – and then, of course, there was the pain.

I am used to pain. I am used to the shock, the sudden explosion in my head and then the numbness, satisfaction and even the pleasure that it brings – but also to the knowledge that eventually the pain will cease. No such relief seemed to be forthcoming or even anticipated.

Eventually I found my torch and switched it on. I seemed to be held fast by the broken step that now encased my right leg up to the thigh. This I could understand, but the constant gnawing pain was still beyond my comprehension. The only vision I had in my head was of a swimmer caught by the jaws of a rogue shark, continually grinding away at the submerged part of his body. And yet I was calm. I still believed that this, as opposed to the mystery and the vastness of the room that I had just left, was something which made sense, something rooted in the reality of cause and effect.

I placed my bottle of whisky on the step above me (congratulating myself on not having spilt a drop) and searched my pockets for my knife. Despite the pain (at that moment I believe, like any good actor, I may even have been growling and cursing out loud) I began methodically to cut and to hack away at the splintered wood, which seemed at every second to be increasing its grip about my leg. It was a long and arduous process, but one which brought me some joy and satisfaction. I had suddenly become a craftsman: someone to be admired and congratulated upon his skill and tenacity. I even regretted the lack of an audience to appreciate and applaud my efforts. I removed all the wood from around my leg, but still the pain continued. I attempted to drag my leg free from the depths of the staircase, but the pain only intensified. I lent forward and shone my torch into the darkness, the thin beam of light tracing the outline of my leg from thigh to ankle.

The piece of wood that had embedded itself in my knee didn't at first glance appear to be particularly large or vicious, but the force of my fall must have driven it deep into my flesh. I attempted to free my leg once more, and again the pain was intense and almost instantaneous. I think it was then that I began to laugh: not the laugh of a madman, but the deep and controlled laugh of someone who has just discovered the stupidity and pointlessness of all things. I took another mouthful of whisky and lit a cigarette. Why not? The act had already been done, in the same way that I had killed the shopkeeper: a sudden surge of activity, perhaps even a brief moment's panic and then the calm of acceptance. I was under no obligation to do anything. As long as I remained still the pain was bearable; indeed, so remote that I could almost view the whole experience as dispassionately as if it were happening to somebody else.

I have no idea how long I lay there. I was far from comfortable, but even that failed to trouble me. Everything at that particular moment seemed perfect. I switched off my torch and waited once more for the darkness to engulf me. I may even have slept a little.

When eventually I did move, my actions took even me by surprise, as if my brain had made the decision to break free irrespective of my wishes or participation. Perhaps it was driven by simple boredom. I hurled myself backwards, my two hands gripping the edges of the steps above and below me. I believe I even shouted out loud: a wonderful, primeval cry of liberation. I was free, but still shrouded in darkness. I lay stunned for many minutes, listening to the harsh, rhythmic croak of my breathing breaking the heavy silence of the building.

When at last I did switch on my torch and focus the beam of light on my leg I was not disappointed. So much pain and inconvenience deserved such a wound. The piece of wood remained embedded in my knee, protruding some two or three inches from my blood soaked jeans; a sight both horrific and fascinating. At that point I had neither the desire nor the strength to deal with my damaged body. I needed to move, to make my way, if possible, back to the sanctuary of my room. Now that the excitement of the moment was over and the power of the drugs was beginning to wane I was becoming aware of the cold striking at every part of my body. Soon I would be too debilitated to decide on any course of action.

I began to crawl upwards, carrying most of the weight of my body on my arms and left leg, but even so, the sudden spasms of pain were frequent and intense. Progress was slow but constant, and how I congratulated myself on my strength and perseverance. Who else could have shown such courage, such a belief in the necessity of existence? All there was in the entire universe was my body; no brain, intelligence, reason, soul or imagination – just my body, damaged but triumphant.

I crawled on, guided by some inner instinct back to my lair. I knew that behind me I was leaving a thin trail of blood, and the thought thrilled me. My progress, my heroism would be there for all to see.

And it still is. The trail of blood remains, as does the piece of wood protruding so provocatively from my knee. It is not cowardice that has driven me to inactivity; not a fear of pain or of losing control, but a simple desire for honesty. "This," I shall say to Jonathan when he eventually reappears (for it is to him alone that my suffering is dedicated) "this is what I have undergone for your sake." He will deny it, of course, and shrink away from any such responsibility, uttering such phrases as, "but everything I have done has been for your benefit" and "I have only ever had your interests at heart" and "I can not predict the future." I shall remain unmoved; my damaged body evidence enough of his irresponsibility and lack of care.

One decision, however, has been taken out of my hands. For the time being I cannot contemplate leaving this place. If I wish to survive I am truly dependent on Jonathan's help.

*

"You're hurt."

"Thanks for telling me. I hadn't noticed."

"How long have you been like this?"

"Two or three days: the day after your last visit."

"I'm sorry, I've been busy."

"Don't worry about it," he says, his voice heavy with sarcasm. "I'd hate to be a burden."

"Let me have a look."

"Fuck off! This is my problem."

"But I might be able to help."

"I'll tell you when I need your help. Just give me something to eat."

He is sitting on his sleeping bag, his back against the wall and his right leg stretched out before him, displaying his wound to great effect. The room seems even colder than usual. I bring out a new gas canister from my bag and light the stove, holding my hands around the flame for warmth.

I had, for the last few days, done practically nothing; hardly leaving my flat. I had had no desire to see or to speak to anyone, Diana least of all. There was too much hurt in the world, too much suffering. How was I supposed to cope with it all? To see Diana's face would have broken my heart, the more so for her strength of character, for her stoicism and for her belief in some sort of justice. I had ceased to read any newspaper, to listen to the radio or even to watch any television. Even the naked antics of my neighbour in the flat opposite no longer entertained or excited me. She had become a tragic figure, somebody to be pitied. I knew that everywhere in the world people were living out their lives with joy, hope and contentment, and the thought reduced me almost to tears.

I sat before my paints and the blank sheet of hardboard and knew that I would create nothing; that even the contemplation of attempting to give some sort of expression to my thoughts would leave me feeling desolate and exhausted.

I left the curtains closed and the lights off, and moved as little as possible. I became almost an inanimate being: a mere recipient of all the emotions in the world.

But there was still Kieran. However empty or vacant my mind became Kieran still existed, growing more and more significant with every passing hour. He could not be ignored. If I were not to return to him he would haunt my imagination forever.

He is helping himself to the whisky, taking great mouthfuls straight from the bottle and allowing some of the liquid to dribble over his unshaved chin and onto the front of his t-shirt.

"You look terrible," I say.

He stops drinking for a moment and then wipes his mouth with the back of his hand. "You must be very proud?" he says.

"Of what?"

"Of your work – of all this. I don't think it could have turned out better if you'd planned it. Not that you could have planned for this, of course," he continues, reaching down and running his fingers around the broken piece of wood, "this was just a fortunate occurrence."

I pass him a cupful of soup that I have been warming on the stove and a thick slice of bread and butter.

"I don't know what you're talking about," I say.

And in truth, I don't. He seems to be making no sense at all but at least, in his damaged state, I feel fairly safe from any direct, physical assault.

He places his cup and the bread on the filthy floor by his side and turns his face towards the window. I take the opportunity to look at his injury more closely. It is truly an impressive sight: the ripped and bloody wound; the swollen and discoloured flesh; the protruding piece of wood that seems to be growing naturally out of his body. I am both fascinated and horrified.

He moves his leg slightly and grimaces in pain.

"I think you need to see somebody," I say.

He turns to look at me. "Like who?"

"Like a doctor, for instance."

"Do they do house calls this far out?"

"OK, perhaps not a doctor, but we need to do something. This is serious."

Ignoring the bread and the soup, he takes another mouthful of whisky and then very slowly and with great precision lights a cigarette, blowing out the smoke from in between his lips in one long, noisy stream. He is engaged in yet another performance: the hero and the stoic. And yet, strangely enough, at this particular moment he looks almost effete, as if he were reclining on a chaise longue in the silk-lined drawing room of some half-derelict country house.

"I've been waiting for you."

"Yes, I know," I say, "and I've said I'm sorry, but I'm here now."

"No," he continues, "you don't understand. It's you I wanted, not just your food or drink or drugs but you. Your presence is necessary to what I am about to do."

I am both alarmed and intrigued. I have never considered my presence necessary for anything. Do people actually change their behaviour when I am around? I doubt it very much.

"I'm flattered," I say, not without a certain irony. "I didn't know I was that important to you."

"Oh but you are, Jonathan," he says, curling back his lips in a half smile to reveal his yellowing teeth. "We have many things in common."

I can think of no other words guaranteed to cause me such pain. I have never desired to be associated with anyone, least of all with the type of person who I now see stretched out before me. I long to defend myself: to tell him that, unlike him, I am neither a murderer nor a rapist, that all I have wished for, all my life, was to be ineffectual, a non-entity, a body whose sudden absence would hardly be noticed at all let alone commented on – but there is something about his expression that would seem to make any such protest not only irrelevant but almost an admission of guilt. We remain locked in each other's gaze, the air around us seeming to grow dark and heavy.

"You see," he continues, "you have become a part of me. You are responsible for all this, for everything that has happened to me since you brought me here, and before. Do you now think that you can simply pretend that you are innocent, that you can become somebody else? You were with me, Jonathan, when I killed that shopkeeper. You held the knife to his stomach. You drove it in and felt the blood gush over your hand. You made your escape with me and locked us away in your flat. You defended me to the police, and lied to our friends. You brought Diana to me. You turned me into somebody to be admired, to be feared and protected. And now there is this." And again he runs his hand down his leg and takes hold of the protruding piece of wood. "I was alone. I had taken drugs and whisky, the drugs and whisky that you brought me. I couldn't go outside, you had made that impossible for me – there were police everywhere, hiding behind walls and bushes and all just waiting for me – all I had left was this mill, this coffin. I began to investigate. You didn't come, the radio played only white noise and I began to investigate. I made my way down to the cellar. There was light but not enough. I could make out certain details, certain objects but it only seemed to make things worse … I tried to escape but my leg was held fast. Eventually I cut myself free and crawled back here. And now you arrive, and you have to be made aware of what I have been through. There will be no doctor, just you and me."

And very deliberately he takes hold of the piece of wood with both hands and begins to rock it back and forth, attempting to free it from its collar of tightened flesh. He makes no sound but sweat has begun to gather on his forehead and cheeks, and his mouth is set in a concentrated grimace of pain. I can do nothing. I am both appalled and mesmerized, the more so if this performance is being enacted solely in my honour.

Eventually, and with one last effort, he pulls the chunk of wood clear of its pocket of flesh and bone, and lets out one long gasp of triumph and exhaustion. He allows his head to fall forward onto his chest, and looks up at me through half-closed and bloodshot eyes.

I creep forward and peer more closely into the open wound. There is much less blood than I would have expected, and the apparent cleanliness of the wound allows me to see only too clearly the full extent of the damage. The knee bone, cartilage and surrounding tissue and muscle are all quite plainly visible, swollen, ripped and horribly discoloured, with here and there tiny shards of wood still adhering to the torn and sticky flesh. I am so appalled that I actually shiver with horror and disgust.

"We need to get you to a hospital," I say, "and as soon as possible."

He continues to look at me but says nothing.

"Do you understand, Kieran? This is serious."

"Of course it's serious," he says eventually, his face breaking into a smug smile of self-satisfaction. "It's me, isn't it?"

There is such a casual remoteness in his voice and demeanor, such a tired amusement that I begin to wonder if I am the one who has lost touch with reality; that it is me, and me alone, who is overestimating the importance of the moment.

"Please listen to me," I try again, "you left the wood in there too long. I'm sure it's infected. If you don't get it looked at you could lose the whole leg. Do you understand?"

Perhaps I am exaggerating. After all, I know nothing of such things. Perhaps, deep down inside, I am enjoying playing my role as the concerned friend just as much as he is enjoying playing the part of the unfortunate but courageous victim.

"So, suddenly it's safe to leave this place," he says. "What happened to all the police, Jonathan? Am I no longer a dangerous criminal and the most wanted man in England? Has everybody already forgotten me?"

"That's not what I'm saying, Kieran, and you know it. But things have changed. You need help. You need looking after."

I am so caught up in the ridiculous drama of the moment (or perhaps because I have begun, inexplicably, to believe that I am truly this sympathetic person that I am pretending to be) that I am hardly aware of the inappropriateness of my words: 'you need looking after.'

"Then you'll have to do it," he says, taking another mouthful of whisky. "It's your duty."

He's mocking me, and for one brief second I begin to wonder if everything that has happened between us since he murdered the shopkeeper has, under Kieran's skillful guidance, been leading towards this one particular moment in our relationship; no, not just since the murder, but the actual murder itself. The thought is so ludicrous, so overwhelming that for an instant I am almost stunned into silence. Is Kieran really capable of creating such premeditated havoc, of causing so much pain and all for my benefit; the murder, the time spent in my flat, the rape of Diana, the flight to this place and the injury, self-inflicted or not, to his leg? It is all such impossible nonsense, and yet there is an expression on Kieran's face that leads me to doubt the motive behind everything. Once again, in Kieran's presence, I feel as if my life is running out of control, and everything that should hold has, inexplicably, dissolved into nothingness. If only I could walk away and believe that none of this ever took place. In a pathetic attempt to impress, I say, "You could die. Do you realise that, Kieran, you could die?"

His smile broadens and for possibly the first time ever he seems to be looking at me as if I were a friend, an ally and, dare I say it, a brother. "Then," he says, "we shall die. I don't think we have any other option, do you?"

I realise that I know nothing of other people: how they think; how they view the world; how they construct the personality that serves them best; how they manipulate their surroundings to give them satisfaction and hope and some glimpse, however slight, of salvation.

My parents became parents because of me. They discovered that, thrown into such a situation, they had to fulfill the role appointed to them; that my mere existence was enough to drive them into adopting certain beliefs, attitudes and modes of behaviour that were alien to them. They could only invent and pretend so much, but at least they made an effort. The women that I loved, they too took on the personae of women that I loved: they listened to my music, read the books that I read, became suddenly interested in the same things that interested me until, quite naturally, they found someone else to love them. I was not and never would be unique in my ability to live without conviction or truth. My parents were parents for a while; my lovers were lovers for a while and Diana was a rape victim – for a while.

And Kieran?

He is wearing the same clothes that I always associate with Kieran; his expression is the same, his habits and his arrogance, but I no longer know or understand him. It's not just that his use of language has changed nor his seeming ability to accept or reject another's opinion, but that he now appears only too aware of the world that exists around him and of his place in it. And if I can no longer trust Kieran to be Kieran, then how can I ever trust myself to be me?

I say:

"There are other options. It doesn't have to be like this. The police may catch us or they may not. If I take you to hospital the doctors and nurses may recognise you or they may not, but either way you will be looked after; and once free of this place who knows what may happen? But if you stay here what choices will you have? Everything will be expected."

"But I will have you," he says, and I don't know if he is being serious or not; whether he is welcoming me as a friend and ally or wishing to hold me close as a victim and an enemy.

"But there is only so much I can do," I say; "my talents are limited."

"You have no talents at all," he says, without malice. "In fact, there are times when I even doubt your existence. But, luckily for you, I expect nothing of you, simply for you to be here, to do what you do best: just to observe."

"And if I leave you? I could just walk away and not return. You're hardly in a position to stop me."

"I don't have to," he says, carelessly, "you can no more leave me than I, unaided, can leave this place. And anyway," he continues, that thin, confident smile returning to his face, "you like the excitement; it entertains you."

*

Is it possible for suicide to be a purely spontaneous event: a leap, literally, into the dark? One moment you are walking along quite happily, or sitting at home reading a book or watching television, and the next – the empty bottle of tablets lies on the floor at your feet, the smoking gun falls from your hand or the speeding truck hurtles towards your unseen and prostrate body. And your last thought, if such a thing existed, would be, 'well, that's a surprise. I never thought I'd do that.'

Of course not; such an idea is almost beyond ridicule. There must always be, however seemingly trivial, nebulous or ill-defined, a trajectory, a path leading towards the final grotesque or heroic (depending upon your beliefs or point of view) act. (Whether or not one is always aware of this path is, of course, another matter.) I killed myself through boredom, through an urge to impress, through fear, arrogance, pain (mental or physical), through a desire to be mourned, through failure or success or to be united with my god; all good reasons and all the result of continuous and self-seeking analysis. Whatever the reason there are always plans to be made.

Kieran was right: I had no option but to be with him. It was such an overwhelming desire that, like a cancer that continually gnaws away at one's guts, I was never totally free of its influence. I couldn't have been more troubled if I had been in love.

I found rest (true, refreshing and invigorating rest) almost an impossibility. I slept seldom and badly; my mind seeming to be even more preoccupied when it was in a state of repose than when it was involved in some invented activity or other. I began, over the next two days, to tidy my flat; not carelessly or through habit, but obsessively and with passion. I had few possessions, but even these (the ones that were unrelated to my immediate well-being) became an irritation to me. Soon there was little left (I had, with some relief, even thrown away my hardboard and paints) to define or reflect my character, and any stranger entering my flat for the first time would have discovered no clue as to the type of person who lived there. I inhabited my world like a dying patient in a hospital ward. Everything gleamed and shone, free from dirt or dust or any stain of human occupation. I had even cleaned and polished the windows, and thrown back the curtains to let in the light, causing the woman who lived in the flat opposite (obviously sensing in my actions a drastic change in our relationship) no longer to perform for me. Slowly I was obliterating even the most trivial aspects of my life.

I needed to see Diana again; to speak to her; to hear her voice; to immerse myself in the banality of her life.

As I approached she stood up. She hugged me. She seemed genuinely pleased to see me. "We thought you were dead." She smiled and kissed the side of my face. "Why else would you have stayed away so long?"

It had only been a few days since I had last seen her, but much seemed to have changed. I could discern no sign, mental or physical, of the beating that she had received from Kieran: her eyes were bright, her skin clear and unblemished and her whole demeanor seemed to sparkle with optimism and good health. My first reaction was one of disappointment. How could one so easily and in so short a time dismiss such a physical and mental outrage? It seemed to me that in displaying so much courage Diana was actually colluding with Kieran. Together they had conspired to belittle the whole experience and (by implication) me.

> Kieran: (Emphasizing his masculinity.) I will hurt you.
>
> Diana: (Lowering her eyes in a true gesture of feminine vulnerability.) I know.
>
> Kieran: (Encouraged by such a show of complicity.) No, I don't think you understand. I will hurt you.
>
> Diana: (Looking directly into Kieran's eyes and displaying a brief moment of bravado.) The bruises will heal. My life will go on, but I shall always have this moment.

I told her she was looking well.

"Thank you," she said, and her smile broadened and she hugged me once again. "So where have you been?"

I shrugged. "Here and there. Nowhere special."

She took hold of my arm and led me towards the others. "It's good to have you back anyway; just like it used to be."

I found this new, affectionate Diana difficult to cope with. Our relationship had always existed *in camera*, shy and distant; so reverential and vague, at least on my part, that for most of the time I could continue to live my life as if she didn't exist at all. And now she was holding my arm, and her head was almost resting against my shoulder, and I could feel the touch of her hair against my face, and I could sense the warmth and the generosity of her body, and the sudden reality of her presence made me doubt everything that I had ever believed of her.

We sat at our usual pub table, where I was welcomed with varying degrees of interest and enthusiasm by Colin, Vince and Jackie; but Diana still refused to leave my side or to let go of my arm. It seemed that in my brief absence, Diana and I had become an 'item'; a state of affairs that the others appeared to accept without question. And once again I was troubled by the thought that my life was being conspired against and that decisions and even my behaviour were being taken and enacted upon without my knowledge or consent.

Diana reached out and passed me my drink.

"She's missed you," said Jackie, leaning towards me and speaking conspiratorially. "You shouldn't leave her like that." And she put her hand over Diana's and squeezed it, and Diana looked up at me with such passionate commitment in her eyes that I felt as if I were drowning beneath her gaze.

"I'm sorry," I heard myself say. "It won't happen again."

Her love for me (either real or invented) had already forced me to lie.

"I should hope not," continued Jackie. "She needs looking after."

This was neither the Jackie nor the Diana that I thought I knew. I looked across the table towards Vince and Colin who were deep in conversation, hoping to see something recognisable in their appearance and behaviour; something that I could hold onto and in which I could believe. Aware, perhaps, of my interest in them they ceased talking for a moment and returned my gaze. Colin smiled at me. "Drink up," he said, raising his glass to his lips. "It's my round."

I obeyed, and while Colin wandered off to the bar I looked around the familiar surroundings of the pub. Nothing had changed. How could it have in so short a time? The usual drinkers were sitting in their usual places, drinking their usual drinks and talking their usual talk. Cigarette smoke curled upwards towards the brown stained ceiling, the cash register rang, music played from the never silent juke-box, and from out of one of the darker corners of the room a woman's shrill laughter pierced the murky air. Everything was so reassuringly normal, except, in a deserted and half-derelict mill less than ten miles away, Kieran, lying huddled in his sleeping bag on the dusty floor, a bottle of whisky in one hand and a cigarette in the other, was waiting for my return.

Did Diana know? Was she aware of the situation? And as if in answer to my unasked question she increased the pressure of her hand on my arm.

"Don't worry," she said. "Everything's going to be fine."

I looked down at her smiling face. For a moment I was almost tempted to put my arms around her and pull her close. It would all be so easy. In that one gesture there would be no Kieran, no murder, no rape, no involvement, nothing but my love for Diana. But it was impossible. Without Kieran and everything that had happened between us, would Diana now be sitting next to me, her hand on my arm, her head resting against my shoulder? Would I even have the opportunity to tell her of my love?

"Do you think I should thank Kieran?"

She pulled away from me a little, her forehead creased at the sudden strangeness of my question. "For what?"

"For this."

"I don't understand."

"No," I say, shaking my head, "I don't think I do either."

Colin returned from the bar and placed our drinks on the table in front of us. Diana continued to stare at me. "I don't understand," she continued, "why you had to mention his name at all and why now, just when we were getting so close?"

"Are we?"

"What?"

"Close."

"I don't know how you could even ask such a question after everything that we have been through together."

I wanted to say, "We have been through nothing together. We have lived and continue to live separate lives. We know nothing of each other. Sometimes I only recognise you by the clothes you wear."

I said: "Do you want me to tell you I love you?"

She said: "Do you want to say it?"

"I don't know," I said. "I don't see how I can – not now. And what difference would it make anyway?"

My answer, far from causing her distress seemed only to increase her obvious affection for me. She snuggled up to me even closer, resting her head on my chest and pressing her body against mine.

"You don't have to say or do anything," she whispered. "You can leave everything to me."

The offer was tempting, and even a few days ago I would have been only too ready to acquiesce, but now it seemed to me that my life was not mine to give. I felt as if I needed to seek out Kieran's permission before embarking on any such adventure.

"We're going to be so happy together," said Diana, and I couldn't tell from her tone of voice whether she was being serious or not. I tried to pull away from her to see if she was smiling but her hold on me was too strong. "To begin with we can live at your place. It's a bit small, but I don't have much stuff. And we won't need much money. I'm very cheap to run."

She was saying all the right things and making all the right gestures and there was a passion, a warmth and an almost schoolgirl delight in her voice that was hard to resist, but I was incapable of making any meaningful response. Perhaps she *was* being honest, but I couldn't relate to what she was saying to me. I looked around me for help, for some indication that it was her not me that had slipped uncharacteristically out of control. The other three were looking at us. All conversation had ceased and Diana and I seemed to have become their sole point of interest. I felt myself blush beneath the intensity of their gaze.

"Oh look," said Jackie, giggling stupidly. "He's embarrassed."

"Bollocks," said Colin, "it's the drink."

"No it's not," persisted Jackie. "He's in love."

As far as I could remember, that word had never before been uttered in our company. The stark simplicity of it was as shocking to my ears as anything I had ever heard. In such a situation the word seemed to have lost all relevance, even more so when it was used in reference to myself, and to have become merely a sound, an isolated snarl or grunt of disapproval. Or, perhaps, in my confused state the word 'love' had taken on too much meaning: to be indicative of and to encompass everything and nothing. Without a subject upon which to attach itself, love could have meant and did mean, hate, despair, rejection, hope, lust, murder or salvation. Kieran, lying alone amongst the debris of his broken life, was loved and in love.

"Leave him alone," said Diana, protectively. "He's just shy, that's all. It's all come as a bit of a shock to him, but he'll get used to it. Won't you Jonathan?"

"Sorry mate," said Colin. "It looks like you're fucked."

"Don't say that," said Jackie. "I think it's wonderful, and I'm sure they'll be very happy together. You will look after her, won't you Jonathan, she's very special?"

I couldn't answer and I couldn't have said anything that would have made any difference if I had been able to speak. My presence was required, visible but inert and nothing more.

Perhaps it was at that moment that I became truly convinced that my destiny was no longer strictly under my control. All my doubts as to the true nature of Kieran's crimes and my relationship to him and Diana seemed to be summed up in the expression on the faces of the three people sitting opposite me: Jackie's simpering and almost sycophantic smile of compassion; Vince's smug but knowing look of indifference, and Colin's grim leer of victory. All three of them seemed to be saying: "What is the use of fighting, Jonathan? You know that we have won, and all you that have to do, as you have done all your life, is to accept the inevitable."

I relaxed and smiled and even went so far as to place my arm around Diana's shoulders. I would, for the small amount of time I was with them, do as they wished. It would cost me nothing and it obviously gave them all a great deal of satisfaction to see me so compliant. Now they knew exactly who I was: I was Diana's partner; I was the man that Diana had finally chosen to spend her life with. My past, my present and my future were of no importance. I had subsumed my total existence in the life that was Diana.

What followed was, perhaps, the happiest time I had ever spent in their company. I was still largely ignored, and my opinion on any subject seldom sought, but now it was a comforting and relaxed indifference. It was as if by submitting to their wishes I had proved myself to be one of them and nothing more was expected of me. I was brought, naturally, into their confidences and treated as a trusted friend and confidante. As a form of farewell I could have wished for nothing better.

I left early the following morning; surprisingly sober considering the vast amounts of alcohol I had consumed. Diana and I had kissed once on the lips, and for the first and last time, standing in the rain outside the entrance to the pub and surrounded by Jackie, Colin and Vince. We had all parted as good friends.

There was little for me to do. My flat was practically empty of all personal possessions and my bags were already packed. I had decided to walk to the mill. It seemed a necessary and romantic gesture and I needed to feel as if I were truly embarking on a journey of some importance: an act of exploration and redemption. It continued to rain: a typical north of England drizzle that soon had me dripping wet; but even this seemed in perfect keeping with my mood of determined desperation.

I saw practically no one on my journey and arrived at the entrance to the mill just as it was getting light. I climbed the stairs towards Kieran feeling strangely optimistic. Perhaps I hoped or believed he was already dead.

He was lying in his usual position: his body stretched out on the sleeping bag, his back against the wall. His eyes were wide open and he was smiling.

"It stinks in here."

"That'll be the shit." He nods towards the far corner of the room. "I can't move very far, my leg, remember. I've been waiting for you to clear it up."

I look across at the pile of brown mess.

"You don't have to, of course, not if you don't want to. I mean it doesn't bother me, but your sense of smell is obviously a little bit more acute then mine and I'd hate for you to be offended. And I don't suppose it's very healthy either, but that doesn't seem to matter now. What do you think?"

I remain silent.

"No? Not interested?"

I turn to face him, reach into my pocket and produce a packet of tobacco. Slowly I roll a cigarette, light it and place the flattened end in between my lips. I take in a great mouthful of smoke. "I think I'll leave it."

His smile broadens into a grin.

"Well done," he says. "Let's start the way we mean to go on, shall we? No master, no slave, no 'I say this' or 'you do that'. We're all equal here. Mind you, I can't help thinking that things would be a little different if it wasn't for my leg; if I could get to you … but there's still time. I'm not totally helpless."

"I know."

"Know what?"

"Just how dangerous you can be."

This seems to please him and I watch as he visibly relaxes his body, unclenching the muscles in his face and allowing his shoulders to fall a fraction forward. It suddenly dawns on me, as if up to this moment I had come to accept his damaged body simply as a part of him, just how much pain he must be suffering, but I feel no sympathy, no sense of retribution or pleasure. I feel nothing, not even remorse.

We fall silent for a moment, smoking and drinking in unison, our two bodies echoing one another's movements. I have set up my little encampment some ten feet away and directly opposite Kieran's with the small camping stove placed in between us. To any outsider, I suspect, the scene could even appear to be hospitable: two friends pretending, for a brief moment, to be other than they are; to have succeeded in shaking off the constricting regime of their everyday lives. Soon we will grow bored and return, tired but refreshed, to the world that is our natural home.

But the space between us is too heavy with inactivity. Everything is too solid, too static. The morning light breaking in through the cracked and distorted windows brings with it some illumination but very little warmth, while around us the air continually shimmers and shivers with tiny specks of dust. It is difficult for me to associate this place with the hidden refuge of my childhood.

I roll myself another cigarette. Kieran takes a drink of whisky. I shift my position slightly on my sleeping bag and pull my rucksack towards me. Kieran heaves himself into a more upright position and straightens out his damaged leg, his face briefly shadowed in pain. I try to avoid looking directly at the wound, but my eyes are continually drawn in that direction. Soon it will be impossible for me to ignore such an appalling sight, but for the moment I will say nothing. I must give him no chance to play the role of innocent victim.

"So what shall we talk about?"

His voice sounds harsh and strangely dislocated in the almost sepulchral silence of the room.

"Do we need to talk?"

"Oh I think so. I mean, what else are we going to do? We could listen to the radio, if it worked, but let's be honest our options for entertainment are somewhat limited."

I loathe him even more when he adopts this mockery of the 'civilized human being'.

"Yes," I say, "I'm sorry. I never did bring those batteries."

He shrugs his shoulders. "It doesn't matter, Jonathan. Now we have each other for company."

The truth of his words comes as quite a shock. In my imagination, Kieran and I were together, exactly as now, but facing each other across an unbridgeable void. No form of communication was ever envisaged.

"The time will pass," he says, "one way or another. It always does. All you need is a routine; a way of doing things."

I look around the room at the chaos of Kieran's belongings. "As far as I can tell, Kieran, you have no routine at all."

"Ah," he says conspiratorially, "that's my secret. That's what I want you to believe, but don't be fooled, I'm in control of everything. You don't think that any of this is by accident, do you? It's all planned. Change one thing and everything will come crashing down." He leans forward eagerly, and lowers his voice. "Even the walls and the ceiling – the whole building – everything – even you."

I begin to wonder if I am incarcerated with a madman.

"I'd better be careful, then," I say. "I'd hate to be responsible for such a catastrophe."

"No, you don't understand," he says, emphasizing each word with a shake of his head. "It's all too late. Everything you now do is expected and beyond your comprehension. Only I have the power to change things, for good or ill."

"And your leg?"

Despite my better instincts I couldn't help but refer to his wound.

"What about it?"

"Is that part of the plan, too: that you should suffer such pain for …"(I hesitate a moment, searching for the right words) " … for the greater good?"

"Oh I should think so," he answers immediately. "Otherwise you wouldn't be here, would you? Nor me, if it comes to that. Boredom alone would have driven me from this place days ago."

I contemplate his words for a moment before speaking. "And the murder?"

He grins broadly, perhaps at just the memory of the event, showing his broken and discoloured teeth.

"I'd almost forgotten about that. You can't believe it, can you? Something so important, and probably the main reason why we're here, and I'd almost forgotten about it. It just goes to show, people think you suffer after being involved in something like that; spend your time going over and over it; reliving it every minute of the day, but it's just not true. Something happened – now it's gone – fuck it."

This is the Kieran that I understand; the type of Kieran that I need if I am to remain true to myself. The last thing I want is to be confronted by somebody made inactive by remorse and guilt; somebody desperate to confess their sins and (god help us) to apologize. If he now shows any remorse for his actions, then everything that he has done has been for nothing and every act of violence and horror that he has committed reduced to an almost insignificant level, and my being here becomes an irrelevance. I need to hate him.

I finish unpacking my rucksack and laying my provisions neatly about me. I can feel his eyes on me, watching my every move.

"I see you've come well prepared," he says, his voice heavy with amusement; "ready for all eventualities. I bet you were a boy scout, weren't you, and a good little pupil? A nice, neat little satchel and all your coloured pens and schoolbooks; how the teachers must have loved you; probably not too bright, but adequate. Work hard, Jonathan, and you'll get by. Keep your head down and don't get into trouble. Not too many friends, of course, not very popular, but that's only to be expected, given your nature. But who wants to be liked anyway? Life's too serious to worry about friends. But you've got me now, Jonathan, so everything's all right; and I promise I'll never leave you. You can trust me."

I stop what I'm doing and look him straight in the face.

"Yes, I know," I say, in all sincerity. "That's what I'm depending on."

I have brought as much food and water as I could carry, but I have absolutely no idea how long it will last, nor do I really care. This is not an experiment in survival.

"There is food and water here," I say, "and a bandage for your leg. Just help yourself."

"You're not going to pass it to me?"

"You can manage."

"If I crawl; is that what you want, Jonathan, do you want me to crawl?"

"I don't want you to do anything. I'm here and I've brought food and water, and that's all."

"I'm impressed, Jonathan. No, really, I'm very impressed. You see how I've changed you; how I've made you more like me? Just a copy, of course, and far from perfect, but still, you're not totally without promise. A few more days and you could be capable of anything."

And placing his two hands flat on his sleeping bag he hoists himself forward and, obviously with great difficulty, twists his legs sideways and under his body, so that he is perched precariously in a half-kneeling, half-sitting position. Slowly, but with no visible show of pain apart from a slight tightening of his jaw, he slides himself from the sleeping bag and onto the floor. There he pauses for a moment, allowing time for his breathing to resume its steady, natural rhythm. "What a fucking hero I am," he says. "But I will not crawl." And inch by inch and levering himself forward on his two hands he begins his slow progress towards me. There is something almost diabolical in the sight, like all the nightmares I ever experienced as a child come to life. I could move, of course, if I wished, simply stand up and cross to the window or even leave the room altogether thereby reducing this show of bravado to a mere act of self-indulgence, but I will not be thought a coward, and anyway, there is something almost hypnotic in the constant rocking of his body. I watch fascinated as he approaches; the rhythm of his forward movement; the extension of his hands, the shuffling of his body and the rasping exhalation of breath after each exhausting spasm. I gain the distinct impression that given the right circumstances and the right motivation he could travel like this forever.

I cross my legs and light a cigarette, and adopt what I hope is an attitude of contemplative indifference, but in truth however calm my outward appearance I am unable to slow the beating of my heart.

He drags himself past the primus stove and reaches, at last, my meagre stock of provisions, but he continues on his painful journey towards me. Soon I can clearly make out every line, every dirt ingrained blemish on his pale and sallow skin, and smell his breath on my face. His whole body smells, exuding a complex and pungent odour of sweat, grease, whisky, cigarettes, stale urine and blood. I am so physically repulsed that I can't help myself: "Christ, Kieran, you stink."

I wonder for a moment if I have gone too far. He neither smiles nor says anything, and being so close to him and despite his disability, I am suddenly reminded of the physical power that he still possesses. Over the past few days he has grown incredibly thin, but beneath his leather jacket, jumper and T-shirt there still exists sinew and muscle and strength and the ability to inflict pain; and as if to prove the point he suddenly thrusts out his right hand and grasps me by the throat. After the excruciating suspense of the past few minutes I find this sudden explosion of activity almost a relief. He could kill me, now, simply, almost carelessly by doing nothing more than gradually increasing the pressure of his fingers around my neck. Do I wish to die immediately and to bring this whole farce to a welcome and premature conclusion? I feel myself relax, and tilt my head backwards offering him greater access to my throat. He brings his face even closer to mine, spraying my face with tiny globules of spit as he speaks: "Don't be fooled, Jonathan, you may have changed but not that much. I am still the only one capable of committing an act of violence; the only one with experience. It's you who is the victim, Jonathan, just remember that; you always were and you always will be, and there's nothing you can do about it, however hard you try. It's only a matter of time, Jonathan, but not yet." And he lets go of my throat, rearranges the collar of my jacket and, breaking into a smile, taps me twice on my right cheek. "But don't worry, Jonathan, I'll let you know when it's time. I know how eager you are to get this over and done with, and I won't disappoint you. I promise."

And with a great effort he twists himself round on his legs and shuffles away from me.

I watch as he begins ruthlessly to go through our stock of provisions, gathering to his chest what he believes to be necessary for his well being and carelessly discarding all those things for which he has no immediate use. I am reminded of those birds, undignified and ragged, that you see on rubbish heaps, their wings folded and useless and their beaks buried deep in other people's garbage.

He will not kill me. I cannot believe that we have finally arrived at this point in our relationship for it to end in a simple and mundane act of violence. I have more faith in Kieran's desire to act creatively and to place himself above the level of the ordinary than that. If he sees himself as a wanderer, an outcast and a mercenary forced to exist in a world of obsequious mediocrity, then he will desire a death worthy of his calling; perhaps, even, a gesture of such pointless futility that only he will understand its meaning and its beauty. Except, of course, he is not alone, and I can't help but smile at the sudden realisation of just how important I am to him as a witness and a participant. I look around at the room, at the crumbling walls, the rotting floorboards and the broken windowpanes, and at the objects in it, the scattering of empty tins and bottles, the sleeping bags, the primus stove and the pile of shit in the corner, and at the two of us, thin, damaged, almost broken and totally hopeless, and I can almost cry with joy. This is not despair but perfection.

All my life I have wanted to create something worthy of myself and the world in which I found myself living; something to define myself as a separate human being, and here it is, now and forever. I am so overcome with a love for everything that I find it impossible to remain silent.

"We are artists," I say, blurting out the words almost before I know what I am saying. "Do you understand, Kieran," I continue, my voice rising with passion and excitement, "we are artists and this, all of this, is our one, great work. There is nothing left for us to achieve."

His look is neither one of disgust nor compassion, not even, as I would have expected one of incomprehension. In fact, it is almost as if he has been waiting for just such an outburst as this. He turns, he opens his eyes a little wider to look at me and he says nothing.

This is not a diary. Perhaps it should be. It would make everything so much easier: no emotion or the emotion that is expressed is twice removed; once by the experience and again by its telling, indeed, so far removed that everything that is described becomes as important or as trivial as everything else. I woke up, it is raining, I killed someone, I bought bread and milk and coffee. I have a slight head cold.

This is not a diary because:

There is no progression. Each day is not delineated by a specific time or activity. I need to accept and to hold on to every single moment to give me life; to prove that this is actually happening to me.

Since that first day when so much was achieved and so much agreed upon, not verbally, but by an unspoken understanding that this was now the only option left open to us, we have drifted into an almost meditative state of enforced inactivity. Throughout the day the light changes: slowly, almost imperceptibly. Never before have I been in such a place where one's behaviour and emotions are so dependent on the day's opening and closing hours. I awake to a cold, grey stillness, where each object, even Kieran's recumbent body laying no more than ten feet away from me, is barely discernible: a deeper shadow without definition or substance. Is he awake? Are his eyes open? Is he looking at me? There is a silence that is almost heartbreaking, as if I have been abandoned by the whole world; but slowly I become aware of Kieran's breathing: a shallow, rapid and regular exhalation of air. But this, too, signifies nothing. He is quite capable of emitting such a sound to feign the unconsciousness of sleep. Is he awake? Are his eyes open? Is he looking at me?

I am reluctant to move, to announce my presence and by so doing set the day in motion. I could light a cigarette, but the sudden burst of flame would blind my eyes. I sit upright on my sleeping bag, a blanket wrapped tightly about my shoulders, and wait.

As the light gradually increases in intensity various forms and objects take on a recognisable and comforting familiarity, and as if I am a beam of light myself my eyes travel the distance between myself and the huddled shape that is Kieran. He is already awake. His eyes are open and he is looking directly at me. Every morning I believe that it will be different and every morning it is the same. Perhaps he never sleeps or only dozes for a few minutes at a time throughout the day. I must make more of an effort to observe his every move and to pay attention to every little detail. And yet, even while I am considering such a plan of action I know that I will fail. Perhaps because of the apathy from which we both seem to be suffering (a reluctance to move or to do anything more than is absolutely necessary) or the soporific rhythm of our daily routine (the constant boredom relieved only by the necessity to feed ourselves) or the overpowering sense of stillness and dislocation engendered by the room itself (its subtle noises and ever-changing light) I seem incapable of holding my concentration on anything for longer than a few minutes at a time. Everything seems to slip from my grasp and to become either unknowable or more relevant as a key or a cipher leading to the uncovering of something else, something, perhaps, that I have only ever imagined or dreamt of, but that is still, strangely, locked away in my memory.

This room and my time with Kieran now seem to encompass the whole of my past life. Perhaps this is only normal when one finds oneself in such a situation as this. Curtailed by four walls (even, as is the case with me, voluntarily) only one's mind is allowed to roam free.

So much of my childhood was spent here, and now I seem to have returned to observe and, perhaps, even to pass judgment over my past actions. Was I ever truly innocent? I doubt it. The indifference of my parents to my well-being, either physical or mental, forced me at an early age to become aware, perhaps too aware, of myself and my behaviour. I watched myself growing up. Even as I stood at that window and looked out over the surrounding landscape it was really me that I was watching. 'This is a gesture,' I thought, 'a moment of supreme isolation,' and I struck a pose suitable to the occasion.

As the light increases I slip the blanket from my shoulders and creep forward to light the stove. Kieran is still watching me, just as I am still watching the child I used to be. I place a pan of water on the spluttering, blue/red flame and prepare to make the coffee. I have grown used to the idea of not helping Kieran, however desperate his situation seems to be, and I barely look at him as he, too, moves forward, dragging his damaged leg behind him. We each help ourselves to a spoonful of coffee and the boiling water and, cradling our cups in our hands, sit either side of the stove, leaning our bodies towards the flame for warmth. Perhaps this is the only part of the day when I feel truly comfortable. Before either of us speaks and embarks upon the futile attempt at communication, there is a stillness and a depth of understanding that is almost holy.

Once there had been a bird trapped in this room – a chaffinch, I think. I had cycled here as usual and left my bike chained up and out of sight in the downstairs corridor. At first I was aware of nothing. Every time I entered my room I would pause just inside the entrance and look eagerly around, desperate to confirm that everything was just as I had left it. I lived in horror of discovering evidence of another's presence; but I saw nothing. I crossed immediately to the window, as usual, but it was only after my senses had become accustomed to the familiar sounds of my surroundings that I became aware of something different: a vague scratching and rustling, the cause of which was beyond my comprehension, at first. Indeed, so obscure did the sound seem that for a moment I almost believed that the noise existed purely in my head. The bird was clinging desperately to a loose piece of brick and mortar, high up in the far left-hand corner of the room. For a second it ceased to struggle, and I believe for that one brief moment that we may even have looked at one another, each of us as surprised as the other to be confronted by such a spectacle. And then it took flight. The door and most of the windows were cracked and open, but it seemed incapable of differentiating one substance from another. In its panic it hurled itself repeatedly against brick, wood, plaster and glass. I crouched down as low as possible, genuinely fearful that it would fly into my face or become entangled in my clothes. How I hated it, not just for being there but for being in such distress. Was I responsible? Was something expected of me? Eventually, exhausted and driven almost to madness, it fluttered to the floor and sought sanctuary pressed tightly against the far wall, its head turned away from everything that it feared and didn't understand, and in that moment of respite I fled.

I cycled away at great speed, furious that my day had been ruined by such an insignificant event. But when could I return, and what would I find? I waited days before I even contemplated visiting my room again. I wished neither for its death nor its escape, only that no visible sign that it ever existed should remain.

When, eventually, I did return I found nothing, no fly-riddled corpse, no rotting flesh or tiny shards of bone, not even a feather – nothing – and my life returned to normal.

"The best part of the day, don't you think?" says Kieran, slurping noisily on his coffee, and eerily echoing my own sentiments; "A time full of potential." I hate him even more when he pretends to be so 'knowing'. "Here we are," he continues, "awake and alive and anything could happen. Who knows what the end of the day might bring … any ideas, Jonathan, any thoughts on the subject?"

"None."

"That's a shame. I was relying upon you. My options, as you know, are somewhat limited. Still, no doubt something will happen. It usually does."

He places his empty cup on the floor and begins to go through what's left of our provisions, picking up tins, cartons and boxes at random and scattering them about the floor. At last he comes across a stale lump of bread, which he thrusts into his mouth. "The thing is," he says, speaking with his mouth wide open and spitting crumbs over the floor and himself, "it's not as easy to die as you think. We have enough food to last a few more days, but that's not important, and we have whisky and cigarettes of course, but water – well, that's another thing. What have we got, four or five bottles, and what happens than; death, of course, but not just death, Jonathan, but the actual process of dying? Have you thought of that, Jonathan? It won't be pleasant, not what you might call artistic. Or, perhaps, you know something I don't. Is that it, Jonathan, do you have a plan?"

"I have no plan."

He swallows his last mouthful of bread and immediately lights a cigarette, "So this is it, then? Well, I can't say I'm impressed. I expected better of you. We both just sit here until we die, how dull, how unimaginative."

"It's necessary. We have no other option."

The words come easily to my lips, but even as I say them I am forced to question their authenticity. I could leave now, simply stand up and walk away, down the two flights of steps and out into the morning light. I can already feel the cold wind on my face as I lift my head towards the sky; and Kieran, of course, could do nothing. But what then: the long walk home with my heart growing less and less full and my sense of liberation diminishing with each step I took? Wherever I went Kieran would still exist, would still be a part of me; and when I finally returned to the mill (for curiosity alone would drive me back) what would I find? The bird managed, I presume, to escape, leaving no trace of its existence while Kieran is incapable of flight. His rotting corpse would destroy not only my present and my future but also my past. To leave him now would be to give him life forever.

And where would I go, back to my flat and a new life with Diana? Such a proposition is beyond my imagination. Unlike my relationship with Kieran, when I am away from Diana I can hardly convince myself that she exists at all. She grows less and less substantial with every second that we are apart. In my head there is lodged a form and a shape that I am happy to designate by the word 'Diana' but what that signifies in reality is beyond my comprehension. There is skin and hair and eyes and without too much trouble I can still feel the pressure of her body against mine. But have we ever kissed? In truth I am incapable of knowing. I close my eyes and try to remember the experience: of her face coming close to mine, of her head tilted slightly to one side, of her mouth slowly opening and the taste of her lips on mine. There is a remembrance of just such an experience, but whether or not that was Diana's mouth I was kissing I cannot say with any degree of honesty. Do I know the touch of her and her smell; the feel of her flesh under my hands; the length of her neck, the gentle swell of her breasts and the curve of her back; the roundness of her stomach and the soft, moist opening between her legs? If I try very hard I can just about envisage her naked and available, stretched out before me, but that is all. I can only look on with wonder and longing. For us to perform any act of consummation would be impossible. Perhaps this is the only way that she could ever be real to me: as a ghost, a spectre, a beautiful invention and amalgamation of every woman that I have ever known or desired. Her actual presence, the sheer physicality of her body would, strangely, make her seem less real. And I suddenly find myself thinking of the woman who lives in the flat opposite mine; of her body and her remoteness. Would she be missing me? Would she, even now, be standing at her window and looking out longingly at a world that has ceased to hold any sense of excitement and danger? Have I deserted her just as I have deserted Diana?

"She should be here."

Kieran's words take me by surprise, so engulfed have I been by my own thoughts, and I open my eyes to a world that, for a second or two, I hardly recognise.

"She should be here," he says again.

"Who?"

"Diana, of course, that's who you were thinking of."

I am both perplexed and disconcerted. This is not the first time that Kieran has seemed, apparently without effort, to be able to infiltrate and even anticipate my innermost thoughts.

"Don't look so surprised," he says, smugly, "it's not that difficult. It's not as if you've much to think of. You're no way as interesting as you think you are. In fact, you're quite superficial. Is that the right word, Jonathan, superficial? Is that how you'd describe yourself?"

"It's not up to me to say."

"Well how would Diana describe you, I mean if she had to, in one or two words: brave, courageous, sensitive, thoughtful, stupid, arrogant? Come on, you must have an opinion; just choose one, any one, it doesn't matter which. If Diana were here now and I said, after she'd sucked my dick, of course, 'Diana, how would you describe Jonathan', what would she say? For fuck's sake Jonathan you must have an idea. Just say something, anything, what the fuck does it matter if it's true or not? Just one word to describe you – what would she say?"

"I've already said, I don't know; and if it doesn't matter what's the point? This is just stupid."

"It may be stupid, but it's called making conversation. You know about conversation, don't you Jonathan? It's when two or more people make various noises with their mouths, commonly referred to as words. Sometimes it's interesting, but mainly it's just to pass the time and to fill in the fucking silences. So why don't you just humour me and answer the fucking question – how would she describe you?"

His anger is infectious, as if it's the only emotion that we can use to communicate with each other. I can feel myself losing control. "Why does it have to be like this? Tell me, Kieran, why do you always make it so difficult? You talk about making conversation, but I don't think you've ever had a proper conversation in your life. All you know how to do is to shout and to intimidate people. Why do you do it, Kieran? I mean, what's the matter with you?"

He begins to smile: that all encompassing smile of derision and victory, and the smile that I hate so much. "There you are," he says, his smile, if anything, growing even broader, "this is more like it. Now we're getting somewhere. So how do you think she would describe you?"

I suddenly realise that he is not angry in the slightest, and that were I not so totally involved in the stupidity of it all, I could almost find his persistence amusing. I take a deep breath and shake my head in despair. I am defeated. Speaking very slowly I say, "She would think me weak. OK, are you happy now? She would think me weak – now can we talk about something else?"

"That's very interesting," he says, ignoring my request, "and why do you think she would think that?"

"I don't know," I answer in exasperation. "It's just a word. You asked me, no you forced me to choose something and I have. Now can we move on?"

"No," he answers, calmly but obviously with no intention of letting me off so easily; "that's very interesting. Why should you choose that one word, I mean, above all the rest? Why do you think that is, Jonathan? What does it say about you?"

I suddenly feel very tired. So often my day begins like this, with an unexpected optimism that soon, once the reality of my situation makes itself felt or Kieran embarks upon one of his interminable tirades, degenerates into a soulless and monotonous grind. I remember overhearing my mother tell my father, when she was dying from cancer, that some mornings she would wake up feeling quite sprightly, with just, somewhere at the back of her mind, a nagging doubt that all was not as it should be, until, after a few moments, the full realisation of her own imminent death would take full control of her life and she would be swept once more into a hopeless vortex of despair. In that way, sleep can become not a blessing or a relief from pain and worry, but a cruel and heartless deception.

"You're quite right," I say, no longer interested in defending the truth. "I must have chosen the word 'weak' because deep down inside I know that that is what I am. I am weak. You know it, I know it, and I have no doubt that that is what Diana thinks. I am weak. I admit it. Now are you satisfied?"

"Certainly not," Kieran responds, obviously totally unmoved by my little outburst. "Oh it's a start, I'll give you that, but is it enough? I think not. You say you are weak, but from where does this weakness originate, what form does it take, and how can you overcome it?"

"What makes you think I want to overcome it? It's served me very well all these years. Why should I change?"

"Dignity."

"Dignity, what dignity?"

"Exactly. You haven't got any. You don't even know what it means, and that's why you're so weak."

I find his reasoning childish, superficial and absurd. "And what would I do with this 'dignity' that you seem so fond of? How would it change my life?"

"Well, for a start," he says, holding on to his words as if he is about to reveal some great undiscovered truth, "you wouldn't be here with me now. We wouldn't be having this discussion and you wouldn't be trying to outlive me. You would be home, safe and secure and fucking the arse off Diana. Now isn't that a lovely thought."

I find his vision of the life I could have had truly unsettling: a life that even I could not have imagined. Perhaps I have never realised that there are choices to be made. I try to defend myself. "I suppose that all this is just your subtle way of telling me that I should be more like you: wonderful, perfect you. Well, if this is what your 'dignity' brings you to, then no thanks, I'll stay just as I am: pathetic, weak, undignified me."

"But you are like me, Jonathan. That's the problem. You may just as well have lived my life for me. Everything I have done, you have done. You are just as guilty as me; that's why you're here now, pretending you're a hero."

"Fuck off Kieran. You're talking shit."

He remains calm, lights another cigarette and takes hold of the last bottle of whisky, unscrewing the cap with one solid, twist of his wrist. "I've changed my mind," he says, "I want you to leave."

I am so stunned that for a moment I feel as if my whole world has come to an end. I look at him in amazement, hardly believing that he could have said such a thing.

"I'm serious," he says, lifting the bottle to his lips. "I don't need you any more. I want you to leave. Now."

I long to say, "but where would I go?" or "you can't do this to me" or "you are wrong, you still need me" but I find it impossible to speak. How, after I have shuffled my way towards this, what I believed to be, my final destination, can I now contemplate continuing to live my life cut adrift, as it were, from the whole of my past existence? It's all too late. I cannot now reinvent myself. I cannot become a monk, a revolutionary, an explorer, an engineer or an assassin. I cannot build a log cabin by the side of a Norwegian fjord or rent a cottage in Norfolk or take up residence beneath a palm tree on some remote, desert island beach. There is nothing for me now except this room, where even the thought of standing alone and vulnerable beneath an open sky fills me with some sort of horror.

"You still here?" he says casually. "I thought I told you to leave."

"I can help you," I hear myself say, quietly, almost despite myself. "I can still be of some use, and don't forget that the police are still looking for you."

"The police," he sniggers; "I think they're the least of our worries, don't you?"

"But I have to stay," I say, in that same hushed tone of voice. "I have no choice."

"There you are," he says, not malevolently but carelessly as if he is just stating a well known fact, "no dignity. You even offer to help me when all you really want is to see me dead. That is what you want, isn't it Jonathan?"

"No," I say, suddenly finding strength from somewhere, "that's not enough. I want to watch you die."

He begins to laugh, uproariously and without shame, dribbling whisky from the corners of his mouth. "No you don't," he says, managing at last to regain some control. "You see, even now you are incapable of telling the truth. "It's not my death you want to watch, but your own, and the only way you can do that is through me. That's why you're here and why you can't leave. But don't worry, Jonathan, I'll do everything I can to help you; after all, what else are friends for?"

The morning moves on and we fall, thank god, into silence. Towards mid-day Kieran heaves himself free of his sleeping bag and begins to crawl across the floor, inching his way slowly towards the far corner of the room where he unfastens his jeans and assumes a squatting position, balancing precariously on the balls of his feet. The sight is both offensive and ridiculous, and I turn away in disgust. And yet, even at such a moment of almost total animal corruption, the act is not without some sense of the heroic. In being forced to adopt such a position the pain in his leg must be excruciating, but still, without a single moan or grimace of pain he perseveres. It is almost as if he is revelling in the discomfort that he is forced to endure.

I should clear up his mess. The smell, at times, is almost unbearable, but I cannot bring myself to touch it. Not only could I not stand Kieran's undoubted look of pity and condescension, but it would seem as if I were interfering unnecessarily in Kieran's life: a life that, even now, remains almost totally beyond my comprehension.

I still piss and shit in the broken and derelict urinals in the room opposite. It is the only time I leave the room. To begin with I looked forward to my little excursions, to a brief escape from the constant pressure of Kieran's overriding presence, but now I find myself more and more reluctant to leave the sanctuary of the room. Perhaps it is not the leaving that I have come to dislike so much, but the thought of the return: to find everything as it was, with Kieran as composed and immovable as ever, waiting for me.

Despite the length of time that Kieran has been here, and the deprivations that he has been forced to endure, there is very little sign of a genuine deterioration in his health. He has, of course, lost a great deal of weight, weight that he could ill afford to lose, but this seems only to have made him appear leaner, fitter and more venomous. His long, dark brown hair hangs loosely around his shoulders and frames his face perfectly, while his eyes peer out, glazed but ever watchful from above his sunken cheekbones. He has become more like an animal than ever, unfathomable and ageless. Only the wound to his leg shows any real sign of deterioration and neglect. It has begun to ooze a sickly, greenish-yellow liquid that, occasionally, Kieran attempts to wipe away with the corner of a filthy rag that he also uses as a handkerchief. I am not fooled by this rudimentary attempt at self-preservation. This is Kieran drawing attention to himself, and saying, "You see how I suffer, Jonathan, how my life is beyond my control, but I do not complain. Unlike you I am strong enough to turn everything to my advantage. That is why I will survive and you won't."

I say, "Why in your world does everything have to end up in death? Why does everything have to be a struggle for survival? There are such things as friendship, trust and love; real love; the sort of love that demands and expects nothing."

Even while I am saying such things, driven to express myself in such a forceful way by Kieran's smug cynicism, I can feel my heart sink. Do I believe any of it? Have I a genuine experience of such trust, friendship and love? I think, again, of Diana and her sudden and unexpected expression of love for me. Was it just a fear of the depth of such a love, an understanding that the pressure that such a love would bring to bear on our relationship would prove me to be a failure and eventually destroy me, or a knowledge that her protestations of love were ultimately false and manipulative that had forced me to flee her advances? I have no idea. Whatever one's character one can always find ways to justify and reinforce one's behaviour. My predictability is well known to all of my friends, even if it is interpreted as a lack of imagination or even cowardice; indeed so well known that I can hardly believe that Diana or the others would have expected me to behave in any other way. Is Diana now waiting for me? Has she called round to my flat, ringing the bell and pressing her ear to the door hoping to catch some sound of my presence? Is she, even now, seeking comfort in Jackie's arms but still, speaking in between sobs, expressing her trust in me, and her belief that I would not have deserted her so cruelly, while Jackie, as smug as ever, takes this opportunity to display her deeper knowledge of my untrustworthy character? "I always knew he would leave you. You shouldn't waste any more of your time on him."

I doubt all of it. I am not in love with Diana, nor she with me. If we are missing each other at all then it is only in our imagination where each other's presence is eternal, perfect and false. She is in the pub drinking with Jackie, Vince and Colin. They are all slightly drunk and the air is thick with cigarette smoke. Their conversation, as usual, is without direction or purpose, but just occasionally Kieran's name is mentioned, but only in the same way that one would describe a person or an event that has slipped almost into history. Invariably they smile conspiratorially when they talk of him, and each conversation begins with: "Do you remember?"

"Do you remember when he had that fight?" asks Vince, of no one in particular.

"Which one" says Colin, "there were so many?"

"That last one," says Vince. "The one before he killed that Paki."

"You mean that one here?" says Jackie. "That was horrible."

"That wasn't a fight," says Colin. "That was a massacre. He meant to get himself beaten up. That's why he did it. He needed to be hurt."

"But why?" asks Jackie. "I don't understand."

"Because he's a fucking loony, that's why," says Vince. "What's to understand?"

"He had to prove that the whole world hated him," says Colin. "That was his excuse for everything he did."

"No," says Diana, who has been listening quietly to their conversation, "it's more complicated than that. For Kieran there is no world, nothing that exists outside himself. He is incapable of understanding anything. The rain that falls or the sun that shines is as deep a mystery to him as his own existence. Everything that he tries to touch moves away from him or disintegrates or crumbles into nothing. He doesn't believe himself to be a villain, an outcast or a revolutionary, nothing so heroic, but a ghost. Everything that he says or does is a scream, a shout of agony and frustration. Only by provoking the most extreme of reactions, either in himself or in others, can he convince himself that he is living a life. He causes pain, he needs to cause pain, and especially to those that fail to acknowledge his despair and he is capable of inflicting great distress, great misery and humiliation, and of forgetting it as easily as if it never took place. "

And here, perhaps, if she were alone or with only Jackie for company she would begin to cry; for although she is strong and has done her best to distance herself from all the horrors that Kieran inflicted upon her, there are times when she remembers everything.

"There you are," says Vince, "just as I said: the man's a fucking loony."

"I raped her," says Kieran. "You know that, don't you? That time when you were out and Diana came round to the flat, I raped her. It wasn't just sex, although I have to admit that that was a great part of it. She was annoying me."

It is mid-afternoon and Kieran is leaning back on his sleeping bag and idly rolling his open knife between the fingers of his right hand.

The journey of the knife from thumb to little finger and back again is almost mesmerizing.

"She was annoying you," I say, my voice sounding cold and flat in the silence of the room; "so you raped her."

He shrugs his shoulders. "She was taking too much for granted. I don't like that."

He is waiting for a reaction. He is bored and wishes to create a little drama: something to pass the time.

"I hope you don't mind," he continues. "It was nothing personal."

I concentrate on the twisting of the knife and the rhythm of the fingers.

"She thought she could help me. Can you believe it? What fucking arrogance. So I had to teach her a lesson. I mean, who the fuck did she think she was, coming round and telling me everything would be all right? What an idiot."

"Perhaps she really cared."

"Bollocks! She just wanted a piece of the action, that's all. She wanted me to perform for her: to be the poor, misunderstood loser; the child from the broken home; the repentant criminal or the maladjusted loner; anything that she could pity or patronise. With every act of kindness that she inflicted on me I became less and less human, and less and less responsible for my own life. Everything that I have ever done, even when pissed or stoned, I have done knowingly, and I will not be reduced to a simple list of ailments. So I shut her up. It was wonderful watching her reaction when she realised just how serious I was. How her expression changed; how her smile left her face and her eyes grew wider. At first she didn't believe it, not even when I thrust my hand up her skirt. She didn't squirm much, just sort of tried to arch herself away from me. "Don't be silly," she said, and, "Stop it, Kieran, let go of me." But I continued and managed to get my hand inside her knickers, and then she became frightened and angry, and she said, "Please, Kieran, don't do this. I'm trying to help you." And she started to fight back, and I said, "If you really want to help me just open your legs." And I pushed her down onto the mattress and sat astride her chest, and now she was really frightened and trying desperately to get her hands up to my face, but I trapped her arms under my knees and unzipped my jeans. "Come on, Diana," I said. "You keep saying you want to help me, and what a good friend you are, well now's your chance to prove it." And I threatened to really hurt her if she didn't do what I wanted. She still resisted, so I hit her a couple of times and she finally got the message. And all the time I was saying, "Doesn't this make you feel good, Diana? Don't you feel proud? You see how grateful I am. I'm so grateful I could kill you."

I have ceased to listen or rather I try to disassociate myself from what he is saying. I concentrate more avidly on the rhythm of his fingers and the rotation of the knife, with his voice acting as a mere background noise to the hypnotic skill of his performance. But however hard I try certain words still break through, dragging me back to the sordid intensity of the world that Kieran inhabits. I know that he is relating his rape of Diana as much, if not more, for his pleasure as for my discomfort, and that he needs to describe everything in as much detail as possible; to relive over and over again that supreme moment of power, victory and satisfaction. But despite my best efforts and my disgust, and my undoubted sympathy for Diana's suffering and humiliation I can feel myself becoming aroused. I am experiencing vicariously the thrill of inflicting so much needless pain on Diana, and Kieran knows it.

"You should have been there."

I turn away reluctantly from the movement of his fingers and the knife.

"You should have been there," he says again. "You would have enjoyed it. I wouldn't have expected you to join in, of course, not unless you wanted to – and I really wouldn't have minded if you had. In fact, I could have helped you – lifted her head, opened her mouth, turned her over – but you would have enjoyed watching. You may even have admired me – my technique."

I am too involved, too caught up in Kieran's and my own imagination to feel anger or outrage. How, sitting here-and-now in such a place as this and surrounded by such a scattering of increasingly irrelevant artifacts can I possibly differentiate my true feelings from those concocted purely for form's sake?

Perhaps I really was there when Kieran raped Diana and when he stabbed the shopkeeper. What difference does it make whether or not it was my hand that held the knife or whether or not it was me that forced Diana to submit to such an act of intolerable barbarism? We are all free. If, now, I have one dream left it is to be somebody else.

The more Kieran describes his assault on Diana, the greater the detail and the more extreme his language, the less real it all seems. Only the actual presence of Diana herself would convince me of the truth of his words. 'I may have experienced at first hand the crucifixion but I still need to touch the wounds.'

Kieran continues to talk, but I have ceased to listen.

It is late afternoon but already it is growing dark. Soon it will be time to light the candles. This is the time of day that I find the most mysterious, when the shadows lengthen and flicker and change the shape and form of everything; the failing of light before the onset of true darkness.

Eventually, even Kieran falls silent. He begins to rearrange his sleeping bag for the night that is to come, puts on his extra clothing and gathers the blanket about him. Already the cold is beginning to strike home, creeping up from the bare floorboards and seeping in through the open and cracked windows. Outside the wind has begun to blow, rattling what remains of the roof tiles and causing the sagging beams and joists to creak and groan. This is a new music to fill the empty silences. Somewhere there is the constant drip of rain, unnoticed in the daylight hours.

I open one of the few remaining tins of soup, pour it into the filthy and badly scorched pan and place it on top of the primus stove. The flame hisses and gushes. Soon we will run out of fuel.

Kieran shuffles towards the heat. I will not offer him any food, but neither will I refuse him.

I am overcome with such a desolate longing that I could almost cry. I am walking home again, in the rain and at night, from Susan's house, only this time without hope or promise of sanctuary or relief. It is only the journey that matters, the constant going forward. Keep the soldiers moving, Jonathan: two by two; from the back to the front; across the hall carpet, up the stairs and on to the landing. Soon we will return to where we started, and be able to begin all over again.

I turn off the gas and pour half the soup into my mug. Kieran waits and watches. He must be hungry and thirsty but still he waits, smoking his cigarette and allowing the smoke to curl out from in between his half-open lips. I can't help but be impressed by this show of self-control, but I say nothing.

Only when he has finished the last of his cigarette does he reach for the soup, drinking the lukewarm liquid straight from the pan. He gurgles and snorts with every mouthful, taking in great gulps of air along with the soup. Occasionally he fills his mouth too full and thin dribbles of the brownish liquid trickle down his chin and on to the front of his blanket. He is, for once, behaving totally without concern or self-awareness. In fact, he is having fun. He withdraws his head from the inside of the pan, wipes his mouth with the back of his hand and looks up at me, his face alive with enthusiasm. Every moment seems to bring him some fresh pleasure as if he lives his life without the stultifying weight of a past or the vague promise of an uncertain future. He is marooned and isolated only in the present. I really believe that he is happy.

I light two of the candles and position them on either side of us, shrinking our world even more. Beyond our faint halo of light there exists only doubt and uncertainty.

I wish to sleep, to close my eyes for just a moment. They say that to die in the depths of winter hidden under a blanket of snow is one of the most pleasant of deaths and one much to be envied. There is no pain, not even a sense of abandonment. One simply turns in on oneself and gathers to one's exhausted mind and body all the warmth and light of the world. Imagine the dreams to be had and the visions to be seen, even while fully awake and with one's eyes wide open: nothing but a vast field of white with just the occasional cracking of ice and the steady drip of melting snow from the overhang of trees to disturb the silence.

My breathing is heavy in my ears. I can regulate it to give me the most regular and softest of rhythms. I care nothing for Kieran. I am not even sure that he exists. In my mind he disintegrates, fades, changes, evolves and expands. There is a sky without clouds; a landscape without horizon; form without substance and intelligence without reason.

My father, in his ill-fitting, shiny black suit, with his off-white shirt and his wide, multi-patterned tie is talking to my mother. She is dressed for a party: a white frock with red roses; her blonde hair piled high upon her head; her face a mask of powder and paint. I can smell her perfume even from my bedroom; except, it is not her perfume but her that I can smell. When they have left I open my mother's wardrobe and her chest of drawers just to prove to myself that she still exists. When I was younger I sat at the front room window and cried as I watched her leave me, even if she were going only to the shops. I knew she would never return, and when she did I knew that this time I was fortunate; her next departure would be forever.

My father is already drunk. I am crouched on the floor bringing to the front of my little column a regiment of grenadiers. He is drunk but he is happy, gentle and in love. My mother and father are standing opposite one another. In between them I march my troops. They are two mountains and I am the river that, eventually, will wash everything away. He is speaking of their evening out:

"I thought," he says, smoothing back his thinning hair and tightening the knot of his tie, "we would pop into the Coach and Horses. Have a drink there, see if Carol and Dennis are in, and then go on to the Cabaret Club; the Paul Scott Trio is playing tonight."

My mother feigns amazement, even though the Paul Scott Trio plays there every night:

"How wonderful," she says, "I love the Paul Scott Trio."

I march on, separating them by a whole army of well-trained and dangerous troops. My father steps over the vanguard, and he and my mother embrace. My father attempts to kiss my mother on her lips but she turns her head. "Don't smudge my lipstick," she says, smiling, "it's taken me ages. Kiss me here." And with a wonderful movement of pure sensual delight she offers him her cheek. Their kiss, although chaste, is the most obvious expression of love, fidelity, infatuation and passion that I have ever seen. I know, even at that young age, that I will never experience such a love. I look up at them. I could howl, scream, shout, beat the floor, threaten them with my instant demise, but they would still love each other and she would still, demurely, turn her cheek towards his lips for a single, solitary kiss.

When, eventually, they leave me for their evening out, offering up their routine advice as to my well-being: "be good; there's food in the fridge; don't be too late in bed, there's school in the morning," I am almost pleased and relieved to be rid of them.

The door closes and the silence is so loud it hurts my ears. My soldiers, my magnificent army has come to a full stop; they have

251

no more battles to fight. They stand to attention or hold their horses in mid gallop, resplendent but without purpose.

'With greedy ears I learned the history of that murderous monster against whom I and all the others had taken our oaths of violence and revenge.'

"'My mother," said he, "do you not acknowledge your son, since every one here has forgotten his King!" Anne of Austria started, and raised her arms towards Heaven, without being able to articulate a single word.'

"One thing was certain, that the *white* kitten had had nothing to do with it: – it was the black kitten's fault entirely. For the white kitten had been having its face washed by the old cat for the last quarter of an hour (and bearing it pretty well, considering); so you see that it *couldn't* have had any hand in the mischief."

"When he looked up again, he saw an altar and figures kneeling, and a bishop bending before the altar; the light grew ever more and more brilliant till no human eyes could endure its radiance. And he saw a white-robed figure bearing the Holy Grail. So he fell forward fainting and could no more see, for he was blinded."

"But all I could make use of was all that was valuable. I had enough to eat and to supply my wants, and what was all the rest to me? If I killed more flesh than I could eat, the dog must eat it, or the vermin. If I sowed more corn than I could eat, it must be spoiled. The trees that I cut down were lying to rot on the ground; I could make no more use of them than for fuel, and that I had no occasion for but to dress my food."

"What a joyful thing it is to awaken, on a fresh glorious morning, and find the rising sun staring into your face with dazzling brilliancy. To see the birds twittering in the bushes, and to hear the murmuring of a rill, or the soft hissing ripples as they fall upon the sea shore! At any time and in any place such sights and sounds are most charming, but more especially are they so when one awakens to them, for the first time, in a novel and romantic situation."

"I feared he would commit some act of violence, which would end in sad consequences."

Who would not wish to live in such stories?

I wait for exactly half an hour to make certain that my parents have truly left, and then I wheel my bike out from the garden shed and onto the gravel path that runs past the front of our house.

This is the most thrilling of moments and one of which I never tire. I sit for a moment, one foot raised on the pedal, the other planted firmly on the ground, and look at the dark and dead façade of my home. I can almost convince myself that this time I am leaving for good, and as I push myself away from the edge of the pavement there are even tears in my eyes.

I am eleven years of age, it is nearly ten o'clock at night, and I watch as the flickering light of my lamp bumps, bobbles and wavers on the road ahead. I leave the main roads, the side roads, the avenues and the estates behind and head off down a narrow, tree-lined lane that cuts circuitously in between fields of clover and wild flowers. I am wearing an old pair of tight, leather gloves that I have stolen from my mother. How else should a traveller dress?

Eventually, at a spot remote and almost featureless, I come to a halt. I wheel my bike into the shadows, dismount, light the remains of a cigarette that I have kept concealed in a Swan Vesta matchbox, and wait. I am cold and a little afraid, but that is all to the good. How can I possibly take such an adventure as this seriously if I am not forced to endure some hardship? Somewhere in the field opposite there is a noise: a sigh, perhaps, or a breathing out or a shifting of weight from one foot to another; while overhead something flies a regular pattern of discovery up and down the centre of the lane, its passing only occasionally glimpsed in the twilight. I finish smoking and, just like the older boys do, I make a great show of flicking the remains of my cigarette into the night where it hangs suspended for a moment before disappearing completely from view.

I retreat even more into the shadows and continue to wait.

Nothing will happen. Nothing ever does. And yet, perhaps, just this once there will be something, anything, to convince me that there exists a life outside the one I am living. I close my eyes as tightly as possible, screwing my face into a grimace, and count slowly to ten. When I open them I know things will be different.

It would serve my parents right if I were now murdered; if a local tramp, destitute and driven almost to the edge of insanity by countless years of ill-use, were to discover me standing here, alone and vulnerable, and to decide, on a whim, to take my life. He could creep up behind me and without saying a word place his hands around my throat or push a knife deep into my ribs; or, first, to prolong the pleasure, engage me in conversation. How my parents would mourn my passing and regret their past behaviour. Their lives would never be the same again.

With my eyes still closed I can hear the wind rustling amongst the grass and the leaves, and the hesitant shuffle of approaching footsteps; and feel on my cheek the fetid breath of the tramp as he pushes his face close to mine.

I open my eyes.

"You were dreaming," whispers Kieran. "I could see your eyes moving in their sockets, and your hands were twitching and you were making these little moaning sounds like some sort of trapped animal. You looked very vulnerable."

His face is very close to mine and his fetid breath is hot on my cheek. I am still dazed. The flickering candle has cast his face into an almost grotesque caricature of the Kieran that I know so well.

"I must have been more tired than I thought," I say, gently, attempting to bring some sense of normality back to the situation. "I'll be OK in a minute." And very slowly I try to raise myself into a sitting position.

"No, don't move," he says, placing the palm of his left hand flat on my chest. "I want to talk to you."

Even in my confused state I know better than to try to resist, "What about?"

His face takes on an expression of deep concentration, and in an act of pure Kieranesque drama he lifts the knife that he has been holding in his right hand up to his face and begins, rhythmically, to tap the point of the blade against his cheek. "Well," he continues, drawing out his words for maximum effect, "I've been thinking."

He falls silent, waiting for my response and forcing me to participate in his tomfoolery.

"Oh yes, and what have you been thinking about?"

"The thing is," he says, still tapping the blade against his cheek, "it's not fair."

"What isn't fair?"

Again he falls silent for a moment, before continuing: "That you can leave here any time you want and I can't."

There is a threat implicit in his words, and my eyes are drawn continually to the tapping of the knife. I am now fully awake and for a brief second I contemplate trying to free myself from his presence, but he is still strong and the weight of his hand on my chest seems more powerful than ever. 'I shouldn't have fallen asleep,' I tell myself, but I know that any such rebuke is pointless. Standing alone at night in the deserted countryside and waiting for the adventure to begin, how can I complain when I am dragged into a situation beyond my control? I decide that the quiet use of reason is my only defence, "You're saying that you don't trust me; that I'm not serious."

He smiles: a cynical and lop-sided smile that, in the flickering light, makes him seem more demonic than ever.

"You're weak," he says. "It's not your fault and I don't blame you, but sometimes people need to be protected from themselves. You'd never forgive yourself if you deserted me. How could you go on living with such guilt?"

"But I'm not going to leave you. This whole conversation is ridiculous. I'm too involved to back out now, and you know it."

"Things change, Jonathan. In a couple of days we'll run out of food and water, and what will you do then? Am I supposed to believe that you'll just sit here starving to death when it's so easy to save yourself. I'm not sure I can take that risk. Just think, Jonathan, how much simpler your last few days will be if there isn't a choice to be made; how much easier you'll feel in your mind. I'm doing this for you. Think of it as an act of kindness."

"What? What are you going to do?"

Very slowly he brings the point of his knife to my throat, and then begins to run it down the length of my body, stopping somewhere in the region of my right kneecap.

"I think they used to do this to horses or slaves to stop them running away. The only trouble is I can't quite remember which part of the leg has to be cut – which particular tendon to limit movement but not to cause too much damage. There will be pain, of course, but that will pass. I don't suppose you know, do you?"

There is a mixture of fear and panic, the like of which I have never experienced before, but I know I must remain calm. I consider, again, the possibility of escape, but I can already feel the tip of the blade pressing through the thick material of my jeans.

I should say something: berate him for his stupidity; plead for mercy; accuse him of committing a needless act of barbarity and of turning himself into nothing more than an ignorant thug, but I am incapable of speech. Everything has slowed almost to a stop. There is the flickering candle; Kieran's hunched body and bowed head, his face rapt in concentration; the glint of the knife and my own prostrate body. This is a picture, an exercise in light and shade and tension worthy of a Rembrandt or a Caravaggio. And suddenly, unexpectedly, taking even me by surprise, I begin to laugh. It is a laugh of relief and liberation.

Kieran looks up at me, his expression a mixture of anger and confusion.

"What's so funny? I can't see anything to laugh at."

"Don't you see," I say, finally regaining some control over my emotions, "this is absolutely perfect: you, me, this room, your knife, everything – absolutely perfect. And you want to destroy it all. To have us both crawling about the floor like some dumb animals, no, even worse than that, like two clowns. You would change a moment of pure, artistic beauty into one of farce. Do you really want to turn our last few days together into a comedy?"

I am speaking from the heart. This is no devious plan to avoid pain and ignominy. If Kieran now wishes to drive the knife home then let him. I care only for our dignity.

Kieran continues to stare at me, obviously weighing up my words very carefully.

"If you wish to cripple me," I continue, "then go ahead, but you are in danger of making a nonsense of everything that we have been through together. Think about it, Kieran. Don't ruin it now."

For a moment he doesn't move – not a muscle – his left hand still pinning me to the floor, his right hand holding the knife against my leg. 'Go on,' I feel like saying; 'do what you have to. Stick me with the knife and prove to the whole world just what an idiot you are.'

The muscles in his face are the first to relax; then his left hand and then his whole body. Slowly he withdraws the knife and sits back on his haunches. He is still looking at me hard, searching, perhaps, for any sign that I am not serious; that I am mocking him. And then, with a careless shrug of his shoulders he flips the knife round in his hand and closes the blade. "Perhaps you're right," he says, dismissively. "I wasn't going to do it anyway; just my little joke. Still, it passed a minute or two. What shall we play now?"

I heave myself into a sitting position and, despite myself, let out a sigh of relief.

"You didn't really think I was going to do it," he says, his voice breaking into a half laugh. "Why, Jonathan, I'm shocked. How could you think I was capable of such a thing? We're friends, aren't we, until death do us part."

And shuffling round on his knees he begins to drag himself back to his side of the room. "Mind you," he suddenly says, without stopping or turning his head to look at me, "I could always change my mind. That's always been one of my faults, you see: I'm totally unreliable; say one thing one minute and do the opposite the next. I'd be careful if I were you. Who knows what I might get up to when you're asleep? Sometimes I even surprise myself."

*

There is, now, very little sense of time passing. There is still a little food and water left, but we are both either too tired or too indifferent to care. This is not how I thought I would feel. I suppose that is the difference between a necessary and an opportunistic death. To be denied food or water by force is to suffer the anguish of persecution, either real or imaginary; to be constantly plagued by the thought: 'if only'. 'If only I had taken greater care', or, 'if only I had not embarked upon this adventure', or (perhaps the most galling of all) 'if only my captors were more humane and understood my importance and uniqueness'. But my death is of a different order altogether. I am weak, but not too weak, if I so wish, to drag myself away from this place and to return to a more civilized way of living. There is, I know, no shortage of food or water, it's just that I choose not to partake of it. Surely there is great dignity and pride in adhering to such a policy of self-denial. I am becoming a Saint, an unsung hero prepared to die for his beliefs. It matters not a jot what those beliefs are, how misguided or desperate, only that I am prepared to die for them. After all, is not this the way that the world has always worked: great courage, bravery, suffering and stupidity all rolled into one neat, little and easy to digest package. The gnawing hollowness in my stomach, my fading eyesight and my illogical ramblings all go to show just what a perfect example of a human being I am; and any discomforts that I am experiencing are dwarfed by my overwhelming sense of victory.

I now try to sleep only when Kieran sleeps. He now moves very little but, if anything, he has grown more restless. His hands, legs and head twitch continuously as if he is in the grip of some sort of hallucinatory drug, and he has developed a cough, a deep-throated and rattling cough that seems to emanate from somewhere deep in his chest. After each attack he rolls over and spits a copious amount of greenish-yellow phlegm onto the floor by his side. This seems to cause him some amusement and delight. He cleans his mouth with his handkerchief or with the back of his hand and grins over at me. "You see," he says, "how generous I am. I am prepared to spread myself over the whole world."

*

There is, now, no noticeable routine of any meaningful kind; nothing to differentiate one moment from the next; just a rhythm, a gentle breathing in and out. The clouds speed past the window, the rain is blown against the fabric of the building and Kieran coughs and mutters in his sleep.

There is music in my head, sustained and invigorated by the natural sounds of the room, and I am part of the performance. This music, I now realize, will never cease. There will be no crescendo, no sudden change of tempo or a plunge into a darker and more poignant second movement. There is no theme, no embellishments, no development or simplification – just pure sound, continuous and without form or direction. It is the music by which I have always, perhaps unknowingly, lived my life.

I now sleep almost continuously, unconcerned by Kieran's threat of violence; except it is a sleep barely skimming the depths of unconsciousness. Even with my eyes closed I can see everything just as clearly as if I were awake and fully in control of all my senses. I am slowly becoming the world that I inhabit.

*

We have ceased to speak to one another. Words no longer seem a necessity; indeed, the sound of our own voices would now shatter our world like a gunshot.

I crawl to the centre of the room and take a tiny mouthful of water. I look across at Kieran. His eyes are open but, apparently, seeing nothing. I move closer. He blinks and runs his tongue over his lips. I think he is attempting to smile. I will not help him. There is a little water left in the bottle, but I will not help him. I don't think I hate him, nor do I feel pity, perhaps only a mild curiosity. He is hardly recognisable as the Kieran I once knew. I am fascinated by the transformation: by the loss of power, of will and purpose. Perhaps somewhere deep inside there is still a personality that one could refer to as 'Kieran', but I doubt it.

*

Do I wish to be saved? Do I wish, now, for Diana to appear and for her to take me in her arms? A moment's respite – but to what end; just so that it could all begin again?

This is better, so much better: to gain comfort from a past life, either real or imaginary. The music in the room continues to play, but soon it will come to an end. Perhaps that is all I have ever wished for: just for things to stop.

*

Yesterday Kieran spoke, his voice quiet but distinct:

"What a fucking joke."

He hasn't spoken since.

*

Tomorrow I will move. I will crawl towards Kieran. Who knows, I might, if I have the strength, even do something to help him. Stranger things have happened.

Quotations taken from

Moby Dick 1851 Herman Melville

The man in the iron mask 1848 Alexandre Dumas

Alice in Wonderland 1865 Lewis Carroll

King Arthur retold by Phyllis Briggs 1965

Robinson Crusoe 1719 Daniel Defoe

Coral Island 1857 R. M. Ballantyne

Twenty thousand leagues under the sea 1870 Jules Verne